Reagan's
Ashes

by

Jim Heskett

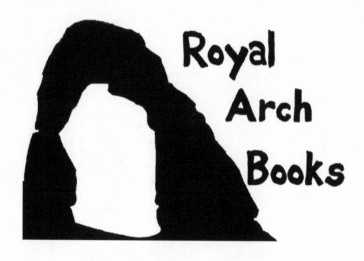

Published by Royal Arch Books
Cover Design by Kit Foster

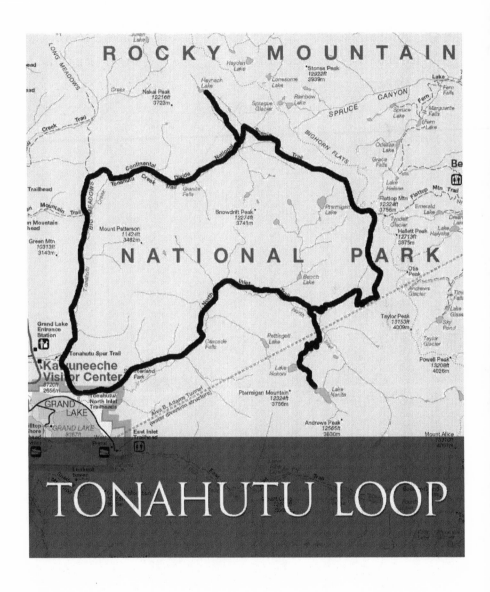

Reagan's Ashes

Jim Heskett

Monday

CHAPTER ONE

11:00 am

Reagan Darby swept a hand along the silky surface of an empty coffin. Dad's memorial service left her as hollow and pointless as the just-for-show container before her. Mitchell Darby's actual remains dwelled in a small cardboard box, his ash and bone fragments waiting to be transferred into the urn he'd owned for years.

Reagan should have been on a trip to New Orleans with her boyfriend. Instead she was in Denver at a memorial service for a man who'd been exactly twice her age when he died. He took care of his body, as far as she knew. Made no sense. Wasn't right to go out this way.

Mitchell Darby was now hidden away in a box on a shelf. Reagan Darby stood before a shell of a thing, not an actual thing. Schrödinger's coffin.

She peeked at Spoon, her fair-haired Australian boyfriend, as he sat among the onlookers in wooden pews. The pair of crutches resting next to him clashed with his charcoal-colored suit. He offered her a feeble smile, and while she appreciated the effort, she couldn't muster one in return.

Spoon's smile reminded her of Dad's smile. She could never see that again. In time, the memory of the smile would fade, and that's what twisted the vice grip of grief in her stomach.

The lid of the casket remained closed to hide the emptiness. Why was it even here? What was the point of all of this? All these people with faces pulled toward the floor, tears streaking reddened cheeks as they mourned a wooden box.

Orange began to flare as the anger built up inside her. Empty box. Just an empty box. He deserved better than an empty box.

Before rage overtook her, she fled from the raised platform, down the carpeted steps and through the aisles. Heads turned to watch her flight. She escaped out the front door, a gust of stark Colorado air stinging her nostrils. After living in Texas the last few years, she'd become ill-adjusted to both the altitude and abject dryness of her home state.

She slid onto the steps, staring at her hands. Lightheadedness spotted the world for several seconds until she reminded herself to breathe. Her face felt slick with tears.

With one hand extended, she practiced opening and closing the fingers, accepting and rejecting. Accepting and rejecting.

The door opened behind her. Spoon eased into a sit, thrusting his injured knee forward and laying it across the steps. He rested his crutches next to him, then put an arm around her shoulders. She leaned into him, feeling his solid body pressing back against her. He didn't give any ground, and she needed that right now. The comfort of stability.

"I used to get so excited about coming home," she said. "Not so much anymore. There's a reception at my dad and stepmom's house after this, then we can change our New Orleans flight to tomorrow. You can still make your interview."

"Do you reckon we should wait on that? I can call the recruiter and tell them now's not the right time."

She considered the next few days spent in Denver, visiting old friends. They would goad her into smiling, mourn with her, fill the minutes with awkward silence and offer her beer and weed to console her. "I think he would want us to go. Not wallow in it here, surrounded by all this gloom."

He sighed. "We can talk about New Orleans later. Do you want to have a chat about what happened back in there?"

"That wasn't him in that box." She adjusted her dress and pulled her hair back. "Forty-eight is too young for a heart attack, but maybe it's better this way, you know, how he went, instead of all slow and shriveled in a hospital bed or unable to move half his face from a stroke. I wouldn't want to remember him that way."

He kept silent, only leaned close and kissed her temple. Nothing he could have said would have made her feel better. Still, she felt grateful to have him sit with her, not offering advice or trying to fix her pain.

Then she considered his question. How must she have appeared to everyone else, fleeing like a woman on fire? "Okay, I shouldn't have run out. But I'm not going to have an episode, if that's what that look is for."

He averted his eyes.

"I'm just…" she almost said *sad*, but that wasn't the correct word. *Empty* would be better, but that also didn't cover it. She approximated a smile and considered trying to reassure him. But any promises about her state were only lies, and she didn't want to do that to him. "We can go back in now."

Reagan and Spoon stood together, and she helped him place the crutches under his armpits.

With each step toward the building, it seemed to move further away. She kept flashing on Dad's face and their last goodbye, six months ago at the Denver Airport. He'd smiled, but with misty eyes because she was leaving for Texas yet again.

Inside the building, two dozen people in various hues of black and gray populated the lobby. They ate finger foods and chatted in forlorn tones. Eyes trained on her, and she felt their judgment burrow into her skin.

Her cousin Dalton sauntered toward them, hands in his pockets and a smirk across his gaunt face. He looked almost grown up in his black jacket and khakis. Probably the nicest outfit in his wardrobe.

"What's up, cuz? How you holding up?"

"I'm okay," she said.

Dalton flicked a chin toward Spoon. "This the boyfriend? Didn't get a chance to say hi before."

Spoon offered his hand. "How are you going? I'm Spoon."

Dalton extended his bony arm, the cuffed sleeve of his shirt riding up to expose his tattoos. "What kind of name is Spoon?"

"It's a nickname. What kind of name is Dalton?"

Dalton chuckled and elbowed Reagan in the ribs. "Nice. I like this one. I'm guessing by the crazy accent that you're British or something?"

"I'm from Melbourne," Spoon said.

Dalton cocked his head. "Mel-bun?"

"Yeah," Spoon said. "That's in Australia."

Across the room, Reagan's stepmother Anne was leaning against a window, shards of light making her black dress sparkle. She held a flask in one hand and a stack of stapled papers in the other. She flicked through them, her mouth dropping open by increasing degrees with each page turn.

Anne slipped the flask into her purse and strode across the room, her eyes locked on Reagan. The look of disbelief morphed into anger as Anne waved the papers in front of her stepdaughter's face. "The attorney dropped this off."

"What is it?" Reagan said.

Anne sneered. "Just an official record of the nothing we have now." She snatched an envelope from her purse and pushed it into Reagan's stomach. "The attorney gave me this too. It's for you."

Reagan opened the envelope and unfolded the paper inside, and her eyes jumped to Dad's handwritten signature at the bottom of the typed note. She read from the words *Dearest Reagan* at the top. The letter requested she carry Dad's ashes into Rocky Mountain National Park and release them into Lake Nanita.

"What kind of sick person picks out his own urn?" Anne said before spinning on her heels, returning to her spot next to the window, and disappearing back into her flask.

Even in mourning, Anne could still be quite a bitch.

Reagan's eyes unfocused as the words swam on the page. Taking Dad's ashes into the park they both loved to say goodbye seemed like something she should do, but also seemed like there might not be enough tissues in the world to handle all the sobbing that would come with it. She might have to start buying Kleenex stock.

Dalton snatched the letter out of Reagan's hand and scanned it, mouthing the words as he read. "You're going camping?"

Reagan and Spoon both looked at his crutches and the brace covering his knee.

Spoon's lips parted as his eyebrows crept up his forehead.

Looking from the letter to Spoon and back, she knew what she had to do. Despite the burden, doing this would make it okay. This letter held the path to closing the empty casket. "It's okay. I can do this alone. I should do this alone."

"What about New Orleans?" Spoon said. "I thought you still wanted to go."

"If you need to go, go on without me. I have to stay and do this."

A buzzing sound. Dalton slinked away from the circle to squint at his phone, then he shot a glance at Reagan. He cupped a hand around the illuminated screen, shielding it from her. Dalton had a secret.

"Excuse me," he said. "I'll be right back."

***

11:15 am

Dalton Darby exited the stuffy funeral parlor and rounded the corner toward a blue Chevy Tahoe idling beside the curb. His pulse quickened as the passenger-side window rolled down. A mist of cigarette smoke billowed, spread, then evaporated into the air.

When Dalton looked through the open window, he didn't recognize the driver. But he knew the heavyset passenger with the banana-shaped scar under his right eye. He wore dark sunglasses, his face still and expressionless.

The large man sucked in a deep breath. "They get the will?"

Dalton fumbled in his pocket for a pack of smokes. As he lit one, the anticipation soothed his nerves before he even had a chance to inhale. "Anne just-about shit herself. I didn't get to see the will, but she made it sound like there's no inheritance."

The man grunted, which sent a shudder through Dalton.

"Your uncle always was a slippery bastard. I'm not all that surprised he'd play it this way, but I can deal with that. Anything else?"

10

"No, not really," Dalton said. Then his head twitched when he remembered the envelope. "He did leave a letter for her, though."

The man rotated toward Dalton, making the leather on the seat squeak. He took off his sunglasses. "Reagan?"

Dalton nodded.

"Did you see this letter?"

"Uncle Mitch wants her to take his ashes into Rocky Mountain and dump them in some lake."

The man sat back, leaning against the headrest and narrowing his eyes at the roof of the truck. He fingered the wiry goatee protruding from his chin. "Slippery bastard. It's on the trail somewhere and he's stashed it, thinking we won't realize he's sending her out there to get it."

Dalton stepped forward, placing his hands on the side of the car. He only half-understood what the man was talking about, but wasn't about to admit it. "Yeah, that's what I think, too. What do you want me to do?"

CHAPTER TWO

7:00 pm

Reagan arranged backpacking supplies on her old bed while Spoon rested his surgically repaired knee and flipped through her high school senior yearbook. A Tori Amos song wafted from tinny Bluetooth speakers on the nightstand.

Organize, cry, repeat. The Kleenex box followed her around the room like a puppy.

Back in Austin, she had an Arc'teryx raincoat, a Big Agnes down sleeping bag, LED Mammut headlamp and a nearly-new ultra-light GoLite tent. Here, she had her father's dilapidated camping gear and a handful of items she'd left after their last mountain excursion.

Fortunately, she had her own long underwear and non-cotton layers for the chilly high-altitude nights. What she didn't have were hiking boots that fit. Dad's size 13s were so large they might as well have been clown shoes. Just looking at them, and the possibility of slipping her feet into them brought more tears to her weary red eyes. Sleeping in his tent, not so bad. But wearing his boots… somehow, that was ground she couldn't cross.

12

She'd arranged items into categories of emergency gear, clothing, food and cooking gear, and hiking gear. Dad's hiking poles were in the worst shape, but beat-up poles were a badge of honor. Shiny new poles meant you were a noob who hadn't put in your miles on the trail.

Then there was the urn, shaped like a vase, but made from varnished wood. Slippery to the touch like porcelain and about the size of a football. She'd duct-taped it shut with multiple layers... the prospect of her father's remains spilling inside the backpack stirred the bile in her stomach.

Spoon said nothing as she took inventory of what would be her sole possessions over the next four days. He occasionally flicked his eyes toward her, over the top of her yearbook, then quickly retreated. Naturally, he acted as if he didn't want her to go, and he had good reasons.

She picked up her father's camp stove and turned it in her hands. "He was too young to have a heart attack."

Spoon took in a breath then let it eke out between his lips without saying anything. A few seconds later, he held out the yearbook toward her, his finger pointing to a grainy black and white picture of her dressed as Emily Webb in Our Town. "I didn't know you did theater."

"Just freshman and sophomore year. Too much trouble remembering all those lines. And they were going to do Greater Tuna the next year, which I've always thought was a racist play. Not for me."

She took a break from organizing and withdrew three pill bottles from her suitcase. She opened them all and took one blue pill, one pink pill, and a tiny yellow pill. He stared at her while she did this. The concern in his eyes burrowed into her as she went into the bathroom to fill a cup with water.

He propped himself up on the bed, grimacing. "Why do you reckon your mum didn't come?"

She knocked back the pills and washed them down with the sink water, then pumped a blob of lotion into her hands and slathered it on her forearms. "Why would she break her streak now?"

"I don't see how she could do that to you."

He obviously meant well, but looking for blame wasn't helping. Reagan wasn't mad at her mom for leaving, or for not reaching out when she was going through a rough time after she dropped out of college, or even for not coming to Dad's service. What was the point of being angry at someone else? All roads eventually ended.

Spoon sighed, and she saw more hiding behind his eyes; something he didn't want to say.

"Whatever you're thinking, please tell me. I know there's something wrong."

"It's just you're going through so much right now. And this trip…"

"The trip to New Orleans?"

"That's not what I meant. I'm going to call the company I was going to interview for and tell them it's going to have to wait."

"What will you do instead?"

"I'm going to stay right here in case you need anything."

She smiled. "That's sweet."

"I'm not too keen on parading my bad knee around New Orleans anyway. I was referring to the other trip. I'm trying to say… and I would never give you unsolicited advice, but… I know that, for me, when I'm in times of stress, that it becomes easy for me to think that my way of thinking is absolutely correct, when it's usually not."

She stood in the doorway of the bathroom and wiped a tear from her eye. But she was also smiling at Spoon's adorable attempt to give her non-advice advice.

She sat next to him on the bed and laced her fingers through his. He was warm, and his skin felt dry against her freshly-moisturized hands. "I know you love me."

"I do," he said.

"Baby, I need you to be supportive right now."

His mouth dropped open. "Oh, I do support you. I'm not saying you can't go, but I don't understand why you have to go out bush-walking right now. Let it sit a few months to have a good think about it, so you can go when you don't have all the rest of this hanging over you."

"It's the perfect time right now. I don't have a shift at the restaurant until next week. Besides, this is what he wanted. I owe it to him. Maybe I'm not explaining this all very well?"

He frowned at the brace imprisoning his knee.

"I understand," she said. "You're going to have to trust me that I'll be okay."

He forced a smile, and she kissed his cheek. He didn't seem to believe her, but that was okay. He was probably feeling impotent and overwhelmed. She could understand that.

"I'll be right back," she said, and walked downstairs and into the garage to search for boots. In a cardboard box marked "shoes," she unearthed a pair of Merrell boots she hadn't seen since high school. Beige and green, no tears in the fabric and laces that appeared to be sturdy. The problem was the tread on the bottom... nearly worn flat, which meant no grip on slippery surfaces. They would have to suffice. She couldn't afford to stroll into REI and drop 150 bucks on new boots.

Next, she went into the kitchen to hunt for a pocket knife. There wasn't one in the garage gear collection, so she began rifling through the drawers in hope of finding something passable.

Newly-widowed Anne faced away from her at the kitchen table, glass of wine and bottle in front of her. She didn't bother to look at Reagan.

In the back of the junk drawer, Reagan located a rusted Swiss army knife. Technically, it was hers, because Dad had given it to her when she was old enough to join him on camping trips. She must have left it here after their trip into Rocky Mountain National Park two years back. Too heavy for a backpacking knife, but so were Dad's tent, backpack, and sleeping bag. She had lost all hope of traveling light on the trail, which meant sore knees and an aching back at the end of each day. She reminded herself to hunt around for a golf ball later, one she could rub against the bottom of her feet each night to prevent foot cramps.

Sticking the knife in her pocket, she considered saying something to Anne, but all of the various comforting phrases she mulled over dried up and vanished on her lips. Anne would only snap at her, anyway. They were never more than passing acquaintances, tied together by a man who was no longer their glue. Would Anne stay? Would she go back and be with her own family? Part of Reagan wanted to ask, part of her thought Anne's future was none of her business.

On her way back up the stairs, Reagan decided that Spoon needed his own time to come to grips with the events of the last few days. She glanced at the door, which she'd once covered with posters of festivals she'd always wanted to attend but never did... Burning Man, Lollapalooza, Bonnaroo. The same doorway she used to stagger through, exhausted after staying up late into the night talking with Dad on the couch in the living room. She would beg him to tell her stories about the girls he dated when he was young, before he met her mother. She would puzzle over each story, wondering what he saw in them or how those girls saw him. She could never do that again. Never again.

She entered the room and Spoon flipped her a restrained smile, pointing at a picture of her cousin Dalton's yearbook photo. "Is he in uni somewhere around Denver?"

She shrugged. "His brother–my other cousin Charlie–goes to Regis. Dalton's not the college type."

"What does he do for work?"

"That's a good question. He used to sell weed, but now that it's legal here, I have no idea."

"I almost forgot to tell you," he said, "I changed our flight. We'll fly back to Austin on Saturday morning."

She sat next to him and put a hand on his chest. "You're a good guy to look out for me."

"My mates keep telling me I'm punching above my weight with you. I'm the lucky one."

"I need to say goodbye to my dad. Do you understand?"

He nodded.

"I appreciate that you're concerned, but I need you to believe that I'll be okay."

He ran a finger up and down her forearm, which sparked an outbreak of goosebumps along her exposed flesh. "I can try."

"I know you're going to be stuck here without me for a few days, and I feel awful about that."

"No worries. I'll find something to keep me occupied."

"Whatever happens," she said, "there's just one thing you have to keep in mind."

"And what's that?"

"Don't trust my stepmom."

Tuesday

CHAPTER THREE

6:00 am

While the day before had been blue and hollow, today felt white and numb. She wondered when Dad had written that letter asking her to take the ashes... he must have intended for her to undertake that journey many years from now, so recreating their own trip would feel nostalgic. Now, only two years removed from dropping out of college and the chaos that followed, the task before her felt like a dreamy continuation of the same backpacking trip.

But through her numbness, there was a certain amount of determination, because now she had a purpose. She would hike the thirty-mile Tonahutu loop around Flattop and onto Lake Nanita, spread his ashes and say goodbye to him in the way he would have wanted. This was better than dribbling tears onto an empty casket. This was tangible; an actual manifestation of grief instead of an intellectual exercise. Reagan understood this.

The alarm on her phone roused her at an ungodly hour. Since she'd been waiting tables at various bars and restaurants around Austin, she usually took evening shifts, and waking before sunrise seemed like a cruel punishment. Even on their regular Saturday morning bike rides, Spoon let her sleep in until 8:30 or so.

She rolled over and looked at him. He was on his back, mouth open, a tiny spot of drool shining on his lip. She brushed his hair back from his face and debated waking him.

He stirred, batting his eyes. "Morning."

"I have to go in a minute. But I was wondering if you'd tell me the story of the crabs again first. You know… the beach ones who dig. Please?"

"Of course." He propped himself on his elbows and cleared his throat. "It's the same story as last time. In Queensland, little crabs called soldier crabs–no bigger than a two-dollar piece–live buried in the sand most of the time, but when they get hungry, they emerge in these massive armies and scour the beach, eating sand. They pick out the food bits, and leave the sand in pea-sized balls everywhere. When you're walking the beach, you can see thousands of tiny holes and balls of sand everywhere."

"Why do they ball up the sand?"

"So they know what they've already looked through, I reckon. They're pretty cluey for such little beasts."

She searched his eyes for a moment and hoped that when she would see him again on Friday that she'd have some perspective on the events of the last few days. What he was going through was hard too… being unable to come with her on this trip, sitting at Dad's house, powerless and alone with her stepmom.

"Take your shirt off," she said.

He grinned and cocked his head, but did it anyway. She folded the shirt and tucked it under her arm. "Taking this with me, if that's okay."

"No worries."

She kissed his cheek and reveled in the scratchiness of his day-old facial hair. "I love you. Go back to sleep."

He nodded and closed his eyes.

With a grunt, she got up, went to the bathroom, and splashed water on her face.

She considered a shower, since she wouldn't get the chance to have another for four days, but didn't want to spend the time. No makeup, either, not that she would be much in the mood to apply any, even if she weren't hiking today.

She took her morning allotment of pills and sneaked the gear out of the bedroom, then packed all of it into Dad's car. Anne had rolled her eyes when Reagan had asked to borrow it the day before, which Reagan took to mean as consent. Anne had her own car.

Her destination was the North Inlet trailhead on the less-traveled west side of the park, most easily accessible from Denver via I-70. She navigated from her old neighborhood toward the highway. Across the street was the First Baptist church, where her mother had insisted they spend every Sunday morning until she moved out. Reagan's mother also went to that church two evenings a week, but would dodge questions about what she was doing there. A mystery Reagan never solved.

First stop would be the Kawuneeche Visitor Center on the west side of Rocky Mountain National Park to apply for a backcountry permit. Normally, to get a permit for a summertime backcountry site, she would have applied a month or two in advance, but no such luck this time. She had to hope that there would be spots available for three nights so she could hike up to granite falls then loop around to Lake Nanita and complete the circle back to the North Inlet.

I-70 took her out of Denver and to the west toward the mountains. She drove through Golden, the first city on the edge of the Front Range mountains, and home of the Coors brewery. Unlike other Colorado towns, the hills and mountains around Golden were oddly treeless.

Past Golden, the highway climbed hills and valleys. After spending several years in the flatlands of central Texas, each time she came home for a visit, she experienced at least one moment of pure awe. The polluting cars screaming along the roads stood in stark contrast to the wonder of the universe manifested in her home state. Tectonic plates colliding and thrusting upward to create these massive bumps along the surface of the earth… she could lose herself thinking about it.

In Colorado, mountain towns snaked through the valleys, nestled in the cracks like tobacco sprinkled into paper. Usually only two or three streets wide but miles long. Reagan drove through Idaho Springs and then Downieville, then turned north. To get to the west side of

Rocky Mountain National Park, the drive would take her past the southern edge of the park and then back around.

She climbed the steep and curvy road toward Winterpark, slowing occasionally behind gaping tourists leaning out of their car windows to snap pictures of the massive peaks and occasional elk or big-horned sheep that dotted the landscape. Approaching the town, houses like specks of black and brown jutted up from the hillsides.

As she rounded Lake Granby and approached the west entrance of the park, the trees grew taller and the air crisper. The altitude adjustment of changing from Austin's sea level to a mile high in Denver recurred now that she was over eight thousand feet.

She drove to the entrance booth, paid the fee, and pulled into the Kawuneeche parking lot at fifteen past eight. If she could get in and out of the backcountry office by nine, she could be on the trailhead by 9:30, then to the Tonahutu Meadows campsite by two, which would give her time to get the tent set up before the obligatory summer afternoon rainstorm assaulted the park.

The backcountry office was a small stone and wooden building to the side of the main visitor center. She pulled the door and found it locked, so she rapped the side of her fist against it, first gently, then hard enough to make the door reverberate against the frame.

A minute later, a portly man with thinning gray hair and round glasses came to the door. He was wearing the typical park ranger gray button-down shirt and green slacks, both prominently displaying the Rocky Mountain National Park arrowhead patch.

"First customer. We're not technically open yet, but you can come on inside," he said, beaming and beckoning her with a wrinkled hand.

Reagan entered the small office. On a dry-erase board hung on the wall:

Protect our bears! Never leave items unattended.
There is no such thing as bad weather - just wrong clothing choice.

The ranger stood behind her, and she pointed to the North Inlet trailhead on the park map taped to the counter. "I need backcountry camping sites for three nights, starting here."

The ranger adjusted his glasses and peered over her shoulder. "Well, let's see what we've got available." He stepped around the counter and tapped on an ancient keyboard connected to a monitor that looked like something her grade school computer lab would have used.

He spent a full minute clicking and peeking at the screen over the top of his glasses. "And where's your destination?"

The park designated specific areas sanctioned for backcountry camping, to minimize the impact on the land. Across the park, there were more than a hundred of these, and each was only big enough for a couple of tents. She'd looked up a map of the sites last night, to pick out the same ones she'd stayed at with Dad.

"I'd like sites 90, 81, and 78. 90 tonight, 81 tomorrow, and 78 on Thursday night. I'm going to cross Flattop tomorrow, then past Nanita and Nokoni, then back to North Inlet by Friday afternoon."

"How many tents?"

Empty casket.

"Just me. I mean, just one."

"Okay," he said. More clicking. "Well, I have good news and bad news."

Her heart sank and she gripped the edge of the counter.

"78 is taken for Thursday, and site 90 is taken for tonight. 81 is free for tomorrow, so there's the good news. Usually, we ask that backcountry sites are reserved in advance because we tend to fill up quickly in the summertime."

Obviously, she knew that, but family tragedy in the form of a heart attack hadn't given her advance warning. She cleared her throat. "Are there nearby sites?"

"There very well might be. Let me check." The clicking continued, but this time he threw in some small talk to offset the awkwardness. "Home from college for the summer?"

She shook her head. "Please, it's important that I get these sites."

He frowned and threw sympathetic eyes at her. "Well, I can get you in at Granite Falls Camp tonight, and Porcupine Camp on Thursday. That's 89 and 77. Pretty close, I'd say."

But Reagan and her dad hadn't pitched their tent at Granite Falls and Porcupine. They'd stayed at the sites she'd requested.

The ranger dipped his head, glancing at her over the top of his spectacles. "Would you like me to reserve these?"

Not the same trip. This wasn't right. Tears began to swell in the corners of her eyes and she tried to blink them away. "Okay," she said in a meek voice, feeling already guilty for making compromises.

The ranger typed out the itinerary while he slid a waiver form across the table for her to read. Standard warnings about setting up camp away from dying beetle-kill trees, the variable weather conditions, bears, moose, mountain lions. Reagan had read the information so many times, she could probably perform it as a one-act play.

"You have a bear box?" the ranger said.

Back in Austin, she had an ultralight clear polycarbonate bear-proof food canister. Dad's bear box was heavy and undersized, so fitting four days' worth of food inside had been a challenge. But necessary, since they'd banned tree-hanging food due to those pesky bears becoming wise to the scheme.

"I do have one. Has there been much bear activity?"

He tilted his head from side to side. "Not to speak of. Car or two been broken into, so you'll want to make sure you've got all of your trash out before you go." He repositioned his glasses and his eyebrows climbed up his forehead. "What you really have to be cautious about this time of year isn't the bears, it's the moose population. We had an injured hiker just last week because he found himself between a mama and her calf."

"I'll keep an eye out."

She filled out the backcountry form, listing Spoon as her emergency contact, and wrote a check for the backcountry fee. She slid the check and the paper into a slot at the corner of the desk.

The ranger gave her a piece of wire and a waterproof slip of paper with her trip itinerary, which she was to attach to her tent each night, in case rangers came and she wasn't nearby. They dutifully regulated the camping system ... no staying at non-site areas, and no camping at sites without a permit.

"Still some snow in parts up there," he said. "Pretty well-packed on the trail, but you'll probably want snowshoes if you go off trail at all over ten thousand feet. And watch out crossing Flattop, you don't want to get caught above treeline during the afternoon."

"Right. Got it." Getting out of this office and out into the fresh air tugged at her. Not the trip she'd expected. The more she considered that fact, the closer she came to crying, and she didn't want to let loose in front of Ranger Spectacles.

At least she would have four days to herself in the park, alone for the first time since the news about Dad.

"Great time of year to get on out there. Have a good time," the ranger said, then went back to clicking.

***

9:15 am

Outside, the scent of pine and dirt filled her nostrils and cleansed her palette. That was the last time she'd be indoors until Friday. While she didn't relish the thought of oily hair and body odor bad enough to turn heads, there was something freeing about escaping civilization for a few days.

A few more cars had joined her in the parking lot. From a car with Kansas plates emerged three kids and two butch women. All of them were in shorts, and they started shivering within seconds. Tourists always seemed to forget that summer mornings at eight thousand feet were quite chilly.

Her phone showed one flickering bar of service, so she sent a text message to Spoon:

About to enter no-service area. Going to turn phone off now. Love you, will see you on Friday.

She drove back through the tiny town of Grand Lake, since the Tonahutu/North Inlet trail began at a dirt parking lot outside the park. Grand Lake was little more than a few bait shops and restaurants filled with backpackers ripe from days out on the trail, but dying for a non-freeze-dried meal. She surveyed the town, weighing her options for where she might eat on Friday after completing the trip. While not a usual red meat eater, a steak might be in order. Dad always loved a good rare steak.

She turned onto a dirt road that would lead her to the trailhead, and the low-clearance Honda Accord bounced and rumbled across the bumpy terrain. Tires kicked up dust in clouds of brown, contrasting the massive green trees on either side of the one-lane road.

After a few twists and turns, she spied the parking lot, which was an open clearing littered with mud-caked Subarus and other four-wheel vehicles. A line of them sat next to the wooden fencing that enclosed the area.

She eased into an open spot, the last one available. Lucky there was even one left, given how late in the morning she'd arrived. The lot butted up to a thicket of trees that served as an entrance gate to the park. Above the pointy treetops, the tips of nearby mountain peaks poked out like triangular hats.

As she killed the engine, she put the park entrance receipt and parking lot permit on the dashboard, then searched the front seat of the car for stray bits of food or food packaging that might bring the woodland scavengers. Dad had always been relatively clean and organized, and she found nothing in his car that might get her into trouble.

Checked her phone, no return text from Spoon. Probably still asleep. She held the power button on her phone until it turned off. No contact with the outside world until Friday.

She kicked off her brown strappy sandals and slipped on her hiking boots, and they felt instantly familiar. Like Sunday afternoons hiking in Boulder with Dad. Eating ice cream afterward, both of them giggling while they tried to convince each other that the amount of calories in the ice cream was definitely nowhere close to the amount they'd burned on the trail.

She closed her eyes and enjoyed the warmth of the car's heater since she wouldn't feel it again for days. Cold in the morning, hot in the afternoon. Despite ranging from eight thousand to twelve thousand feet, midday in Rocky Mountain National Park could reach into the eighties.

She turned off the ignition and placed a foot on the ground, relishing the crunch of gravel under her boot. She opened the back seat and yanked the backpack free. To make room for four days of clothes and gear inside Dad's pack, she'd had to strap her sleeping bag to the bottom, which made maneuvering the beast clunky and awkward.

There was a rustling across the lot, which she ignored at first since there were other people around, stretching, applying sunblock, and locking up their vehicles for their own journeys up the Tonahutu trail.

Then the sound of shoes on gravel came closer. "There she is," said a familiar voice behind her, cutting through the quiet warble of chirping birds.

Reagan whipped around and found herself standing only twenty feet away from her cousins Dalton and Charlie.

CHAPTER FOUR

7:10 am

Liam Witherspoon—known only as "Spoon" to everyone except his parents and grandparents—woke in Reagan's old bed to the muffled sounds of an argument.

He'd been dreaming that he was with her in New Orleans, where they should have woken up this morning had it not been for the terrible news of her father's death. She skipped along Bourbon Street toward a crowd gathered around a street musician, and Spoon followed. Her long hair flowed down her back, bouncing with each step like a bedsheet in a breeze. She was barely out of reach.

He had a drink in his hand. In his dreams, he always had a drink in his hand.

She turned to him, radiance in her eyes and a lopsided grin on her face exposing straight white teeth. She was glowing and happy. Happy as he'd never seen her.

All around them, tourists drenched in beads drank from plastic cups, dancing and yelling and absorbing the decadence of Bourbon

Street. But he hardly noticed any of them; he only saw Reagan, and she was always a little out of reach.

At first, the muffled argument came into the dream disguised as the sounds of trumpet and trombone from the street musicians, then more distinctly as actual voices. Someone was arguing, but the voices appeared to come from the sky.

He stirred in bed during the split second when the dream world and the real one collided. Then he knew he was in a strange house, in a strange bed, in Colorado, not in New Orleans or at home in Austin. The skin on his hands and face felt as dry as an old well.

The muffled sounds were coming from downstairs, inside the house.

He opened his eyes to unfamiliar walls, covered with posters and magazine clippings. In a few seconds, his eyes adjusted and he remembered where he was. Details about the dream came back, and he sighed a little bit in relief that there was no drink in his hand in the real world.

"Damn it, Anne, I am not fucking around with you."

Each word came through clearly this time.

Spoon swung his legs to the side of the bed and he planted his good leg on the floor so he could reach forward and grab his crutches. He leaned until he had placed one under his armpit and pushed his weight on it to stand. He retrieved the other crutch and looked down at himself. Because he'd slept in only his grundies, he threw on a shirt, then headed for the bedroom door.

After opening the door, the conversation continued. A man and a woman were arguing, and the woman was Reagan's stepmother.

"I'm not sure what else I can tell you," she said. Her voice was tentative.

The stairs leading down into the living room were three meters to Spoon's left. He slid along the path as quietly as possible, the rubber tips of his crutches sinking into the carpet. "Alright, Spoon," he whispered. "Not a peep."

When he reached the edge of the stairs, he angled his bad leg straight, and used the crutches to lower himself to a sitting position at the top of the stairs. A partial wall running the length of the top five steps obscured his view into the living room.

"You know something," the man said. "Sounds like you don't want to tell me. This better be the only time I have to come here and ask you about this."

Spoon leaned forward far enough to bring the arguers into view. Anne stood in front of the door, clutching a stack of papers in her hand. Across from her, in the doorway, was a large man in a bright-white wifebeater t-shirt and jeans. He was balding, with a goatee and a banana-shaped scar under one eye.

"Tyson, I promise you," she said, holding out the pages. "I've told you everything it says in the will. I don't know what else you want from me."

Tyson brushed the papers aside, knocking them to the floor. "I don't care what it says there. You and I both know that everything in there is horseshit. Don't try to tell me you had no idea what he'd really been doing."

So Anne and this man Tyson were having some kind of disagreement about Reagan's father's will. That much was clear. But no clue as to who Tyson was and why he cared about it.

"Do you think if I'd known what he was doing, I would have stayed all this time?" Anne said.

"How the hell do I know why you stayed with him? That's not my problem. I think this poor little widow routine is one big fat lie. You and him worked something out so you could keep for yourself what should be mine, and now you're going to trot out the sad face to make me give up."

Spoon leaned a little toward the living room to hear better, then realized he was sitting too close to the edge of the stairs and was dangerously close to slipping. With the bad leg straight and draped over the staircase, he didn't have any leverage to stop it. His bum eked over the edge. He tried to throw his hands toward the walls to stop his forward motion, but that only threw him off balance.

He slid down four steps, in full view of Anne and Tyson. They both jerked their heads to look at him.

"Who the fuck is that?" Tyson said.

"That's... that's Reagan's boyfriend. He's staying with me for a few days."

Tyson took a step back and bared his teeth, which sent a shudder up Spoon's spine.

Tyson flashed his eyes at Anne. "Goddamn it Anne, I thought we were alone. You need to tell me these things. I'm done playing with you and doing this housecall shit. If you come to your senses, I'll be at the store."

Store? What store was he talking about?

Tyson grabbed the handle of the front door and slammed it behind him as he left.

Anne put her hands on her hips and glared at Spoon. "How long have you been sitting there?"

"Just a minute or two. I heard shouting."

"Whatever you heard, or whatever you believe you heard... it's not what you think it is."

Spoon didn't know what he thought it was. "I didn't mean to trouble you or anything like that. It's just... was that bloke bothering you?"

"There's a lot you don't know, and don't need to know." She waved a dismissive hand and tapped her foot against the floor. "Since you're up, I made some eggs. I don't have much of an appetite, so you're welcome to them."

She walked out of view, and Spoon reached behind to grab his crutches. Whatever Anne was into, he was going to find out.

***

9:35 am

Reagan blinked a few times to make sure what she was seeing was the real thing. Her cousin Dalton stood next to his brother Charlie across the dirt and gravel parking lot. One thin, wiry, and two years younger, the other pot-bellied and four years younger. Dalton was tying his shoe, but Charlie was looking straight at her.

He raised a hand and gave her a timid wave. As he did, Dalton took notice and straightened up.

"Hey there, cuz," Dalton said, yawning. "We were wondering when you were going to show up. Been here for hours."

She dropped her backpack, half in shock. "What's going on? Why are you here?"

Charlie pointed at Dalton. "He told me about your trip and said it wasn't right that you should go alone. So we packed up all our gear last night and headed out here early."

Reagan was still confused. "Packed up your gear? Why?"

"We're coming with you," Dalton said. "We're going to help you put Uncle Mitch's ashes in lake... whatever you called it. Lake Nono or whatever."

"But..."

Charlie swatted a mosquito against his neck. "You shouldn't have to do this alone, you know... not after everything you've been through. We want to help."

A million questions ran through Reagan's head, colliding and mixing. "But, do you guys even have all the right gear? Do you have sleeping bags, headlamps, your own tent, four days of food..."

Dalton trotted to her and put his hands on her shoulders, massaging them with a little too much force. She peeked at his arms, now covered in tattoos down to his wrists. He'd added a few since the last time she'd seen him.

"Hey, cuz, everything's good. We got everything we need to slog in the woods for a few days, so don't you worry about all that. We're out here because we want to help. All you gotta do is lay out the plan, and we're going to be with you, every step of the way."

A sudden change in the number of travelers on this trip from one to three jarred her. She looked at her prospective trailmates for the next four days. She'd never known Charlie to spend any time outdoors in his whole life, and Dalton had always been too stoned to participate in the family camping trips when they were teens.

She'd gone from the silver lining that she'd be able to lay Dad's ashes to rest by recreating their old trip, to having to make the trip with alternate campsites, to now not being able to make the trip alone.

Was she supposed to tell them to get lost, after they'd driven two hours from Denver to get here? Part of her wanted to say *no thank you*. This was supposed to be her time alone.

"I don't know about this," she said.

"What's not to know?" Dalton said. "Times like this, that's when you need family the most."

She watched her cousins, quietly waiting for her to accept their offer.

Maybe Dalton was right. Maybe the trip would be better if she had the support. She remembered what Spoon had said the night before, something about not always knowing what's best for ourselves.

Deep in Dalton's eyes lurked pain. He had lost his uncle and wanted to help. She could understand that. Grief needs an outlet. If this was how he intended to cope, maybe she could change her plans and it would be good for everyone.

"You're sure you want to do this?" she said.

"Absolutely," Dalton said, his face lighting up. "We're here for you."

Family time would have to take priority over her previous plans. She sighed and took out the park map, then laid it on the trunk of Dad's car. She waved for them to come closer, then took a pen from her pocket and pointed it in the bottom left quadrant of the map.

"This is us, at the Tonahutu and North Inlet trailhead." She drew a line up the map. "We're going to hike up along the Tonahutu creek until we get to the Green Mountain trail, then we turn right, which is east. There we keep on the Tonahutu trail toward Granite Falls, and camp at the site there. It's about eight miles today. Tomorrow, we hike along the trail, and we'll take a detour to Haynach lake, then get up over Flattop Mountain and south back down to July camp at the base." She curved the line of the pen to make the eastern section of the loop over Flattop mountain. "Then we turn back west to Nokoni and Nanita on day three. They're both on the same side trail."

The pen had made three-quarters of a circle to indicate the first three days of the trip. Dalton pointed in the middle of it, then drew his finger from the top to the bottom points of the circle. "Couldn't we save an assload of time if we skipped right across here before we get to Haynach? We can cut a whole day out if we go straight over this pass and right to Nanita."

"No."

"I don't get it. Seems like going all the way to Flattop is out of the way."

Reagan took a deep breath, aware that things had changed, and reminded herself that she didn't need to explain to them the importance of repeating the trail she and Dad had followed last time. "Because this is the trip we're going to take."

Dalton raised his hands in surrender. "Okay, cuz, it's totally cool if we do it your way. I shouldn't have said anything."

She realized the pen in her hand was about to snap in half from her grip. Forced herself to relax and focus on this new plan. "After Nanita, we hike back out to Porcupine camp. Thursday will be a short day, just to the lakes and back. Then on Friday, we hike back to here." She moved the pen over the last leg, and the ink pattern on the map resembled a pork chop, with two jagged lines for the side trail excursions to Haynach on Wednesday, and Nokoni and Nanita on Thursday.

The boys were both nodding their approval.

"Tomorrow's the hardest day," she said. "Most of Flattop is above treeline, so we need to be up and over by afternoon. With no trees, there's nowhere to hide. You don't want to be the tallest thing on the mountain if there's lightning."

Reagan frowned as Dalton lit a cigarette. "You're going to pack out all your garbage, right? No cigarette butts on the trail."

He took her shoulders in his hands again, and this time, something about his grip made her uncomfortable. His fingertips sunk into her flesh.

"Relax," Dalton said, cigarette dangling from his lips. "This is going to be a great trip. We're going to go out there and do what we need to do, and you'll feel a crap-ton better when it's done. Trust me. You'll be glad we came."

His look betrayed his false confidence. Reagan needed to be caring and giving at this moment, but telling herself that seemed easier than believing it.

CHAPTER FIVE

7:15 am

Spoon followed Anne into the kitchen and she set out a brekkie of scrambled eggs and American-style crispy bacon on the table, next to a glass of orange juice. She poured her own glass of juice, opened a bottle of vodka, and added a generous amount.

Spoon pointed at his orange juice. "You didn't," he said, trailing off as if it were a question.

She lifted the vodka, jiggling it at him. "No, why? Do you want some?" her voice was smoky and sultry, the way he remembered actresses speaking in the black and white movies his parents watched when he was an ankle biter.

He shook his head. "I'm alright."

She dropped her plate on the table, half a grapefruit and one piece of bacon. "Sorry, I don't have any Vegemite for you."

"No worries. This looks delicious all by itself. Maybe while we eat, you can tell me what all that was about before?"

She cleared her throat. "I love your accent. Australia seems like a lovely country, but it's so far away. I've always wanted to go, I could just never find a way to get there."

"They have airplanes and boats that go there."

She grinned. "You're feisty. I like it. My roommate in college was dating an Australian guy. You seem to have such funny words for everything. I seem to remember that he called air conditioners 'egg-nishers'. Always cracked me up."

"I had an uncle who said egg-nishers. I call them air cons, like any ordinary person. Now, about that guy…"

She gripped her spoon and thrust it into the grapefruit. A jet of juice splattered on the table. "That was nothing. Just Tyson. We were having a disagreement."

Spoon watched her as she ate a mouthful of grapefruit then gulped down half her vodka and orange juice. She grimaced, then emitted a small moan of pleasure, but there was a diffidence in her eyes. They kept flickering between him and the table.

She was hiding something. This man Tyson was clearly not nothing. "Seemed quite peeved to me. He a friend of the family or something?"

She drained the rest of her drink. "Really, don't concern yourself with him."

He studied her face: cold, impersonal, a wall of protection surrounding her features. The straight-on tactic was not working.

"I'm sorry about your husband," he said. "You and I didn't get much chance to have a chat yesterday."

She walked to the counter to refill her drink, this time forgoing the orange juice mixer. She stared over Spoon's head as if he weren't there. "Five years… Mitch treated me more like an employee than a spouse."

"How's that?"

"I don't even know why I said that. You probably wouldn't understand."

Spoon shifted in his chair. "Try me."

She chewed the inside of her mouth. "It's like… oh, I don't know. He would ask me to pick a movie to see on Saturday night, then I would have to present him with a few options and he would always have the final say. I don't know why I'm telling you any of this."

Because you're off your face and it's not even noon, he wanted to say, but held his tongue.

She closed her eyes. "But, if I'd known before…"

She stopped speaking, letting the sentence hang for a few moments while she tapped her fingernails against the side of the glass. With a sigh, she pulled a chair around the table next to him and placed a hand on his arm. "What are we going to do with you until Reagan gets back on Friday?"

He wondered if he should put his opposite hand on hers. The woman must be hurting, after all. "My Physio from Austin gave me heaps of rehab exercises to work on. Also brought my laptop, thought I might work some on a mobile app I've been developing. But, can I ask you one question about this Tyson?"

She jerked her hand back. "Jesus, let it go. I told you that was nothing to worry about."

He kept his eyes steady on her, unwilling to let her slink away or divert the topic yet again.

She pursed her lips. "Fine, what do you want to know?"

"What was the store he mentioned?"

"That would be A1 Lawnmower Repair in Broomfield. Look: I get that you're bored, searching for things to do with yourself, but there's no story here, officer."

Lawnmower shop? Why would this man go to a lawnmower shop? He said he would be waiting there for her, so maybe Tyson was the proprietor. But what did he want her to do when she got there?

Spoon took the last bite of eggs and pushed the plate away. "It's just that if you're in some kind of trouble, maybe I can help out."

"Trouble? You're adorable. I can see why Reagan seems to care so much about you."

"She does."

"And I get why you like her. She's smart, and pretty, and she can be a lot of fun when she's in a good mood. The two of us haven't always seen eye-to-eye on a lot of things, but that's probably normal. I am the stepmother, after all. She thinks I despise her."

"Do you?"

She studied him before answering. "You're young and have a long way to go to understanding women, my Australian friend. It's a lot more complicated than that. But let me tell you something about getting involved with the Darby family. I had to learn this from years of being married to her father, but maybe I can spare you some time." She paused to take a drink. "Reagan is not a well woman. I assume you know about her... issues."

He nodded, even though he wasn't sure what she was implying.

Her words were starting to slur together. "You're a handsome guy. Plus, with that accent, you could have any American woman you wanted. Trust me, that exotic stuff makes college girls swoon. You have to ask yourself if you want to get involved in an uphill battle, or if there's something better out there for you."

He resisted the urge to reply straight away. It would be easy for him to get offended, but he knew that she was likely in pain and wanting to lash out. He could forgive that.

But there was something about Anne... every word out of her mouth seemed coated in some kind of protective glaze. This Tyson character was not the harmless lamb that Anne made him out to be, and if she wasn't going to explain who this man was, then Spoon was going to have to find out for himself.

CHAPTER SIX

9:40 am

Reagan stared at her two cousins, unsure how to find the middle path between her desire to accommodate them with her desire to backpack into Rocky Mountain National Park alone. Maybe she was selfish, thinking that she should turn them away when she'd already discussed the route with them. They'd made the trip from Denver. They were ready and willing to help, and she appreciated that. Family mattered, didn't it?

She finished preparing her backpack by adjusting the hip and shoulders straps on Dad's awkwardly-shaped pack. A 70-liter Gregory pack, at least ten years old, once blue but now faded to an ashy gray. It wouldn't fit as comfortably as her pack, but she could, hopefully, lessen the shoulder and hip strain by finding the right combination of tension on the various straps. The strange placement of the internal frame pulled her shoulders backward. While comfortable enough now, experience told her that by day three, her neck would be in knots. She wished she could pop into Granby to one of the camping shops and drop three or four hundred dollars on a new pack with better airflow and variable hip and shoulder suspension. And she'd also buy a new car and maybe a speedboat while she was at it.

With her gear ready and the car emptied, she locked it and put the car keys in the top pouch of the backpack. Across the lot, Dalton and Charlie were fiddling with their own packs.

She walked to the bathrooms, which were little more than outhouses shrouded in the shade of the gigantic pine and spruce trees surrounding them. While pulling her hair back into a ponytail, she paused at a wooden sign bolted to a pole, and ran her fingers along the lettering etched into it:

ENTERING ROCKY MOUNTAIN NATIONAL PARK
BIG MEADOWS 4.4 mi
GRANITE FALLS 8.8 mi
FLATTOP MTN 15.0 mi
BEAR LAKE 19.5 mi

Behind the sign was a larger informational board, with a small shingled roof above it. A large display case housed a collection of pamphlets, describing the trail that ran alongside Tonahutu Creek, warnings of Leave No Trace, park regulations about campfires and trash, warnings about bears and moose and mountain lions.

She went into the bathroom and examined herself in the metal mirror, its surface spotted and grimy and looked as if it hadn't been cleaned all season. Her reflection came back warped and splintered. When she was little, Dad always had to convince her that the bathrooms were safe, despite the awful smell radiating from them. He would offer his handkerchief to cover her mouth when she went in to pee.

"You can still do this," she said to the warped image of her face. She ran her hand along her hairline to tame the few wisps that had strayed from the rest.

The touch made her think of Spoon, how he liked to stick his fingers into chunks of her hair and twirl them into ringlets. She missed him already.

After leaving the bathroom, she hoisted her bag over one shoulder, then the other, then buckled the hip belt in the middle. The pack's girth was overwhelming, so she immediately grabbed her hiking poles to keep from toppling over. Hiking thirty-plus miles with this monstrosity on her back was going to be like piggy-backing a child for an entire weekend.

Dalton and Charlie took their cue and started buckling their own packs.

"Dalton, don't you have hiking poles?" she said as she crossed the lot.

He shook his head. "Don't need 'em. I'll find a stick on the trail or something. Bruce Lee style." He swung an imaginary staff.

"If we cross a stream and you end up on your butt, you'll wish you had them."

Dalton sucked through his teeth. "Charlie, give me your poles."

Charlie pulled his hiking poles close to his chest. "No way. These aren't even mine. I had to borrow them."

"I'll just take them from you while you're sleeping tonight," Dalton said.

Charlie lowered his head, dropped his pack, and skulked off toward the bathroom.

Reagan took a deep breath and leaned toward her cousin. "Listen to me. It's fine if you guys want to come along, but I want you to be nice to Charlie. Understand?"

Dalton smirked. "I'm always nice to Charlie."

"If you wanted poles, you should have brought them. Leave him and his hiking poles alone."

Dalton blinked and flashed a used-car salesman smile. "Fair enough. Don't worry about it, cuz."

Charlie returned, but he didn't look at his brother.

Reagan knew full well how Dalton's offhanded comments could cut like razor blades.

Dalton patted Charlie's shoulder. "We're all going to be like The Cosby Show up in this motherfucker, right? One big happy family."

She turned from them and walked toward the trailhead, trying not to grit her teeth. Packs rustling behind her meant her two cousins were close behind.

Hiking with them could become an opportunity. Chance to heal, to be with family, to process everything. She wouldn't let Dalton's bullying get in the way.

Despite her new philosophy, as she crossed the trailhead marker and officially into the park, her day changed from white and numb to orange and irritated. If the orange became red, she would be in trouble. She recalled the breathing exercises she'd learned two years ago, and focused on the trail in front of her.

Memories flashed: bike rides from Denver to downtown Boulder with Dad, their bike shoes clicking on concrete as they perused the Saturday morning farmer's market. Also, playing with her dollhouse when she was barely out of diapers, the gigantic Victorian house she kept into her teen years until she gave it back to her grandpa.

The first few hundred feet of the trail were paved. Then it abruptly became dirt, two long ruts like tire tracks through the grass. Occasionally, planks of wood cut diagonally across the path, probably to prevent erosion. Overhead, a mass of trees shrouded the morning sun. Fluorescent pink markers nailed high on the trees every few hundred feet indicated the path for snowshoeing.

The sound of her measured breaths and the regular *click click* of each hiking pole striking the ground did have a small meditative effect. Orange mellowed.

She turned to observe her trailmates, and Dalton was close on her heels, but Charlie was already falling behind. The hip and chest straps of Charlie's pack pushed his belly into a square, drooping in front of him.

Reagan would have to slow down to accommodate them, but that also meant they might not make it to camp before the storms came in. She took deep breaths, reminding herself that she'd allowed them to come, so this was her choice. Her choice.

They approached a group of rowdy college kids, all with packs, hiking toward them. A long-haired boy in the lead winked at her, and she offered a little smile in return. Close to the trailhead would be crowded today and Friday, but deeper into the park, they should find few other people.

"Hey cuz," Dalton said after the other backpackers had gone.

She slowed her steps to allow him to pull even with her. Didn't respond, but tilted her head toward him.

"I was wondering," he said, "if you ever got a chance to catch up on *The Sopranos*?"

She didn't want to talk, she wanted to feel the ground under her feet, hear the birds, and smell the sharp fragrance of the trees. Dad had never insisted on talking while on the trail. They saved their conversation for camp, when there was nothing else to do. The trail was for focusing on the task at hand. One foot, then the next.

"No, I never watched it," she said. "An episode or two here or there, I guess. What is it with you and all those old TV shows?"

"80s and 90s stuff is way better than the shit they make now. You gotta see Sopranos, though. Tony Soprano is like the original New Jersey gangster."

"Spoon and I don't have cable."

"You're cord-cutters? That's cool. I got a torrent of every episode and I could float them to you if you got a Dropbox or G-Drive."

"I've heard of Dropbox, but I don't have an account, or whatever."

"Oh, I gotcha," he said. "Hate to drag you into the motherfucking 21st-century, like a normal twenty-five-year-old."

"I'm twenty-four." She increased her pace, hoping he would catch the subtle hint.

They hiked for several minutes through pine trees and rocks until the trail opened to a large meadow. Foothills ahead and to the right led to the towering points of Andrews Peak and Ptarmigan Mountain, but those rocky triangles seemed distant because of the expansive green plains before them. A creek snaked to their right while the trail hugged the less-dense crop of trees to the left. A thin row of trees separated them from the meadow. On the other side of the opening, green and gray trees blanketed the hillside.

Reagan checked the sky, expansive and blue save for a few clouds gathered above the mountains ahead. She powered on her phone to check the time. With no distractions, they could still make it to Granite Falls by two.

As soon as she pushed out into the meadow, Charlie started gasping for air. Deep, wheezing breaths. She stopped and saw him bent over, hands on his poles. Sweat pooled in the center of his forehead, threatening to drip onto the ground. He fumbled in the side pocket of his pack for an inhaler.

"You guys… wait… just a second. Can we take a break?"

42

She surveyed the area for larger rocks they could sit on, but there wasn't anything. She walked back into the trees and unbuckled her pack, which sent an immediate rush of cool air where the sweat along her back had collected.

The pack fell to the ground with a *thunk*, and she was grateful for the weight off her shoulders. A quick check of the ground revealed no ants, so she sat on the damp grass. Dalton and Charlie joined her, dumping their own packs and groaning with relief. If they looked this exhausted after only an hour, imagine what hiking out on Friday would look like.

"Holy Moly. You hike so fast," Charlie said, still catching his breath.

"We've got a schedule to keep."

His eyes widened. "We do?"

"Just trying to get to camp before the clouds roll in."

Charlie nodded and gave her the same sheepish grin he'd sported since he was two years old. "Oh, wow, I'm such a doofus. I forgot you mentioned that already. I'm sorry, Reagan, I wasn't even thinking about that."

Such a sweet kid. "It's okay, Charlie. No big deal."

Dalton sat up and stretched, and as he did, a creak echoed through the trees. He spun around. "What was that?"

Reagan looked at the dead pine trees. "Beetle-kill, probably," she said. "Parasites that kill the trees around here."

"Are we about to get crushed?" Charlie said, deep lines on his forehead.

Reagan stood, dusting the pine needles and dirt off her hands. "Let's not find out."

Dalton and Charlie jumped up and wriggled their packs into place.

They started back to the meadow and the trail. The wind had picked up, sending waves through the ample grass. Over the next few minutes, the trail weaved between the open meadow and back to the trees, and Reagan was grateful for the shaded tree sections as the sun had already risen high enough to bring dots of perspiration to every inch of exposed skin. Twelve hours from now, she would be huddled in her sleeping bag in 40-degree weather, but in the summertime daylight, she had nowhere to hide from the heat.

Underfoot, the trail changed from dust and grass into patches of gnarled tree roots, pebbles, shards of broken pine needles, and the occasional muddy patch created by horse hooves.

They pressed on and the meadow gradually ended as they began to gain elevation. An open space on the right moved closer to the trees on the left, the terrain became rockier, and the creek expanded into a collection of ponds. Through the rippling water, fish darted back and forth.

Up ahead, a deer drank from the creek. She came to a stop and held up a hand to get her companions to halt.

"Do you have a question?" Dalton said, laughing. "What's up with the raised hand?"

The deer looked at them, and its ear twitched before it ran into the trees and up the foothills. The sound of trots faded underneath the drilling of a nearby woodpecker.

"Was that a deer?" Charlie said.

"Yes, it *was* a deer," Reagan said, annoyed. Deep breaths. She put her poles out in front of her and continued hiking.

Soon after, they passed the turnoff for the Green Mountain trail, which would have lead them back to the Kawuneeche visitor center.

The sign read:

GREEN MTN TRLHD 1.8 MI
GRANITE FALLS 3.6 MI

They kept on their own trail, and the trail opened again to the widest section of meadow yet. The waving grass stretched for several football fields between the trees.

"Is this the big meadow thing on the trail marker?" Charlie said.

Reagan reached into the side pocket of Dad's hiking pants and took out the park map. She located the Green Mountain trail split and nodded. She checked her phone. 11:38. "You guys ready to take a break?"

They both nodded vigorously.

***

11:40 am

Dalton groaned as he let the massive backpack fall to the ground. He hadn't been this deep into the forest since Boy Scouts, and he'd quit that joke of a hobby at age fourteen. In the eight years since, never once had he felt the desire to give up all the comforts of modern society to sleep in a tent and become some bear's afternoon snack.

Every step was another annoyance: piles of dirty snow soaked his boots, downed trees required acrobatics to cross, and half the time, branch barbs scratched his exposed arms. Around every turn was some new strange sound, and the thought of these "beetle-kill" trees breaking and falling on his head put a sour taste in his mouth.

But he wasn't here to enjoy nature. Tyson wanted him here. And whatever Tyson wanted, that's what Dalton did, as long as Dalton wanted to make money to pay his rent.

But dealing with Charlie was something else entirely. Charlie didn't yet know why they were here because Dalton had fed him some bullshit. If he'd told his little brother straight out, he wouldn't have agreed to come. Charlie needed to be presented choices as if they weren't choices.

Charlie, we're going to go with Reagan tomorrow to help her spread our uncle's ashes in Rocky Mountain National Park.

Gee willikers, Dalton. That sure sounds swell.

Then the only problem was that eventually, Dalton would have to tell Charlie the real reason they came along for the trip. That would take some careful explanation since Charlie had proved plenty of times how terrible he was at extracting money or information from people who didn't want to part with it.

Reagan and Charlie took up seats on large rocks next to the trail, and Dalton stepped into the thick of the trees to find a secluded spot to take a leak. He hiked for three minutes until he was far enough away that he couldn't see them, and then found a cluster of trees to provide cover. He stood on the sloped ground, one foot rested against the trunk of a tree so moist and rotted that it barely held together when he put his weight on it.

When he'd finished, he zipped up his jeans and made the arduous trek back across the brush toward the trail. Before he was clear of the trees, he saw Reagan sitting on a rock, leaning back with her hands behind her. The way she was reclining pulled her shirt tight against her tits.

But the troubling thing was the strange guy standing over her. They were both smiling, and Dalton got the feeling this guy was a douchebag. Smarmy grin. Beady eyes.

Charlie was away from the trail, taking closeup pictures of a swarm of ants on a log. Dalton stepped out into the clearing, headed straight for his cousin.

"I came down over flattop yesterday," the strange guy said. "Saw tons of marmots up there. Seems like they're getting more fearless each year. One tried to steal my granola bar when I wasn't looking."

She laughed at this, even blushed a little. This guy looked at least ten years older than her. Just the way he loomed over her was creepy enough to say something.

"Excuse me," Dalton said. "What are you doing?"

The strange man turned and looked at Dalton for the first time. He was tall and square-jawed, wearing one of those bicycle caps with the tiny brims.

"I'm talking to my new friend here," the strange guy said.

Dalton pointed at her. "That's my cousin."

The man kept staring, a look on his mug like he couldn't care less.

"Her dad died last week," Dalton said. "I think you should move along."

Reagan and her new friend both dropped their jaws.

"Dalton, what the hell is your problem?" she said.

The stranger snatched his pack from the ground, buckled his hip strap and pulled his hiking poles from slots on either side. "I'm sorry. I didn't mean to cause any trouble or anything like that. I was just chatting with a fellow hiker."

"You're not causing any trouble," she said, raising a hand to stop him, but her words came too late. The guy was already starting down the trail.

"That's right," Dalton said. "Keep on walking, buddy."

The guy didn't turn around to respond, and Dalton kept watch as this loser slinked away. Nobody wants to mess with Dalton Darby.

Reagan leaped to her feet, her arms crossed in front of her. "Nice, Dalton. Real nice. Why did you do that?"

Dalton shrunk the space between them. "Me? I'm the dipshit here? Your dad died, you've got a boyfriend at home waiting for you, and you're flirting with some old guy out here in the middle of nowhere?"

She uncrossed her arms and put them on her hips. "Flirting with him? That's ridiculous. He was a nice guy, and we were talking about the trail up ahead. Only you would see something sinister in that."

"You were definitely flirting with him."

She huffed a sigh. "This is just like high school."

"You don't understand how guys think, Reagan," he said, pointing at his temple. "You smile at some guy, and he thinks you're inviting him into your panties. Next thing you know, that guy's following us back to our campsite tonight and stretching duct tape over your motherfucking mouth."

"You're insane."

Charlie finally took notice and wandered back to where they were standing. "Is something going on?"

"Nothing's going on," Dalton said. "She thinks she's so damn smart she can outwit some rapist."

Charlie frowned, glancing back and forth between them. Reagan's nostrils flared as she pushed air in and out. Dalton couldn't believe how unappreciative this dumb bitch was after he had just saved her life. She had no idea how the real world worked.

"You don't have to act so paranoid and be the big man out here," she said. "There are tons of nice people hiking in the park. It's not like we're on Colfax Street and someone is trying to break into your car."

"I'm just trying to keep you out of trouble."

She opened her mouth to speak, but said nothing. Tears swelled in her eyes, and Dalton felt himself getting angry. She was going to use the waterworks method of winning the argument.

"Do you think this is what my dad would have wanted? Us arguing out here when I'm... we're supposed to be taking this trip for him?"

"You have no idea what your dad would have wanted," Dalton said.

Charlie had been ping-ponging his looks back and forth between them, but he settled on Dalton. "What are you talking about?"

She glared, awaiting an answer to Charlie's question.

Frustration bubbled up and spilled over. No more of this idealized bullshit. "Fine. You think your old man was some magical, perfect, TV-dad kind of guy? He wasn't."

She seemed too shocked to speak. He knew he should stop there, but couldn't resist. "Your dad was a gambling addict and a thief who lost all your family's money, and left you all with shit. How's that for father of the year? Does that make you want to honor his memory?"

Her face transformed into horror. In a flash, she took off, rushing past them and into the cluster of trees.

Dalton watched her go, feeling the enormity of the stupid thing he'd said press against him until his head began to throb.

Charlie let out a little whimper. "What just happened?"

Dalton looked at the ground, groaned, and kicked a clump of spongy moss covering a rock. "Damn it. I fucked up; that's what happened."

CHAPTER SEVEN

11:50 am

Reagan ran. She hopped over tree branches, stumps, and crumbled bits of boulders as she dashed into the thicket and up a hill. Her ankle caught in the roots of a massive overturned tree and she tumbled.

She reached for her throbbing ankle, pushing around the bone and wriggling it. The ankle seemed to be okay, but her chest was heaving and heat flushed her face. Orange threatened to become a violent red. Panic swelled, but she forced it down.

She focused on her meditation practice. Visualize a candle. A light breeze blows it left and right, but the candle stays lit. Always lit.

Why would Dalton say those terrible things? Maybe Dad wasn't perfect, but a gambler who lost all the family's money? No way. Not possible. They never had much money to begin with. He was always away on business trips so when would he ever have had time to gamble?

Empty casket. Empty casket. Empty casket.

If Spoon were here, he would label Dalton a *bogan* or *drongo* or some other cute Australian word that would make her giggle and the whole situation seem silly. But he wasn't here, and a quick check of her cell phone showed no service, so she couldn't call him. She was on her own.

A spider the size of a quarter crawled across the ground toward her, then disappeared underneath some fallen leaves.

In a few minutes, her pulse had leveled, and she was ready to get back to the trail. Every minute spent not hiking was another minute of wasted daylight.

She resolved that not only did she have to live with her trailmates, she'd have to learn how to tune them out, which she hadn't done so far. She would survive this and honor Dad's memory, despite Dalton's jackass behavior. Time to focus again. Next step was getting to the campsite and getting some alone time. Just a few hours away.

Dalton was grieving the loss in his own way, and maybe he needed to paint Dad in a bad light to make his peace with it. Other people had lost Mitchell Darby, too. Maybe Dalton couldn't see that his chosen coping method caused Reagan pain.

She stood up, dusted the pine needles from her hands and walked back toward Dalton and Charlie. Seeing Dalton again reignited the anger, but she took a deep breath and reminded herself to stay calm. Re-frame the experience and get some time to build perspective.

"Reagan," he said as she emerged from the trees.

She held up the palm of her hand. *Don't talk to me.*

He stayed silent while she donned her pack and buckled in. As the weight settled on her shoulders, she could already feel the stiffness in her hips and neck where the pack was making contact. Another reason to hurry to the campsite.

"Alright Fatty McFatterson, get your pack on," Dalton said to Charlie.

Just like that, she lost her ability to tune them out. Red flared. She pointed a finger at Dalton's face. "And you can stop that right now. I told you already not to do that."

"I'm just playing around. He knows I'm not serious."

Charlie ducked his head, looking embarrassed.

"I don't care if you mean it or if you're joking," Reagan said. "And for the record, I was not flirting with that guy. We were talking, that's it."

"If you say so, cuz." He tilted his head at the trail. "Lead on, then."

They continued to put boot in front of boot, soon crossing a wooden bridge over the rushing Tonahutu creek. She remembered several of these stream crossings from the hike with Dad, and that she'd counted them, but now she couldn't recall how many there were. A half dozen on the first day? Maybe more.

As the trail elevated, the trashcan-sized rocks along the meadows became larger and larger, and the path soon snaked around boulders covered with some kind of orange and green algae. Charlie often paused to take closeup pictures of the rocks. The air smelled minty and the temperature difference between sun and shade became more noticeable.

The sounds of poles clicking and hip belts shifting filled her ears, and for now, her companions were at least silent.

They started up a series of switchbacks, and at each sharp turn, Reagan peeked down at her trailmates below her. Dalton had found a suitable stick somewhere to use as a pole. Earbuds dangled from his ears, and he was bobbing his head to music. Rap, probably, if he still had the same musical taste as in high school. Charlie held both of his poles in one hand, because the other hand was clutching his camera, and he was snapping pictures of the trees and mountain squirrels, barely noticing where he was going.

At the top of the switchbacks, the trail leveled and they came upon another clearing, shaped like a bowl at the foot of a steep set of foothills. Except this time, they weren't alone.

Across the clearing, maybe five hundred feet, a herd of moose hovered near the trees, munching leaves from low-hanging branches. Reagan counted a half dozen of the creatures, each of them larger than a horse. Jagged antlers like razor-sharp fingers topped their heads. Males. At least no females and therefore no calves, so less dangerous. Probably.

During mating season, however, coming in close contact with any moose could be a lethal activity. Mating season should have already ended, but she couldn't be sure. No sense being foolish. "Stop," she said to her cousins.

"Are those elk?" said Charlie.

Reagan leaned forward on her hiking poles to shift her pack and give her aching shoulders a break. "No, elk are smaller. Also usually lighter. You can tell by the big belly."

"But they're not dangerous, right?" Dalton said. "Not like bears or anything like that."

"Oh, no, they can definitely be dangerous," Reagan said. "Up close, or if you come between a cow and her calf. We'll be fine if we stay clear enough out of their way by going around the edge."

She studied the meadow. The trail twisted along the left side, near to the trees. The herd was close to where the trail disappeared back into the forest. The meadow opened to the right and ended at a scree field with a steep incline to a mountain peak. The ground between appeared wet like marshland.

Clouds rolled across the sky. They didn't look dark, but sometimes rain came from the gray ones. Detouring to the right side of the meadow would cost them twenty minutes. Or, the moose might decide to meander that way, and then they'd have to reroute again.

She pointed to the mountain peak. "We'll just hug the right side of the meadow."

"Hell no," Dalton said. "Let's keep to the trail. We can throw rocks or something to scare them off."

She stared at him, her lips pursed. "No. You listen to me. We're going to go around, and that's all there is to it." After what he'd said about Dad, she wasn't going to submit to his demands again today.

Dalton seemed to appreciate this as he lifted his hands to show her his palms. "Okay, cuz, whatever you say. It's your show."

An apology would have been better, but it would have to do.

They separated from the trail and walked as close to the edge of the meadow as possible. Reagan unbuckled her hip belt as they strode across the marshy plain. If necessary, she could drop the pack and scurry up a tree. A moose might ram the tree and knock her out of it, or it might not. They weren't like bears, which usually fled from a loud shout or a perfectly-timed rock to the nose. When moose were threatened or angry, all you could do was escape. Run like the devil and hope for the best.

She kept an eye on the herd and when they'd reached the far side of the meadow, they turned parallel to the rocky scree field, toward the trees.

"How far do we need to go this way?" Charlie said.

"Just a few minutes," Reagan said. "If they stay where they are."

Reagan looked at her youngest cousin. He was sweating, his jaw was working up and down. She stopped walking and waited for him to catch up. "It's okay, Charlie. We're going to be fine. They won't have any reason to mess with us unless we give them one."

He let out an enormous sigh. Dalton shook his head and pushed forward as if Reagan and Charlie were fools to make such a big deal out of this situation.

When they reached the trees and were the closest they'd yet come, some of the creatures finally took notice, but none of them moved. Then a black bird squawked and leaped from a perch on a branch near the moose, and it spooked the herd. Big hooves pounded the green earth as one and then all of them launched their gigantic bodies across the marsh. The ground rumbled with the thunder of their movement. Fortunately, they trotted in the direction Reagan and her trailmates had come, not where they were going.

The sound of birds returned when the meadow had cleared.

Reagan wiped her brow with the back of her hand. "Okay, we're good. Just a few minutes out of the way. No big deal."

When they returned to the trail proper, the sounds of the creek became louder, meaning Granite Falls was nearby. In another five minutes through the trees as the trail rose and a small cliff overlooked the creek, she found a wooden board atop a post. Carved into the board were five lines in the shape of a hut. Backcountry camping site. She hunted around for an arrowhead marker nailed to a tree, and there was a small footpath leading to a side trail. There was the red plastic arrowhead, ten feet off the ground.

She pointed to the marker. "Backcountry site marker. This will lead us to where we can camp."

"Fucking finally," Dalton said, wiping his sleeve across his cheek.

They crossed onto the footpath as the sounds of rushing water grew louder, drowning out the cavalcade of inner conversation galloping through Reagan's head.

"I can't wait to get this pack off," Charlie said. "My shoulders are killing me."

One red arrowhead marker, then two, then the footpath elevated over a little ridge.

"It's got to be on the other side of this ridge," Reagan said.

And it was. But not as they had hoped.

As they crossed the ridge and looked down into the open area that was Granite Falls backcountry site #89, Reagan's jaw clenched. A spiderweb of fallen trees covered the campsite, thick like off-trail brush.

Beetle kill. No one was setting up camp here.

CHAPTER EIGHT

2:10 pm

Spoon had spent the morning trying to pretend what Anne had said about the verbal altercation with Tyson was true… that the event wasn't a big deal and he should forget about it. He sat in the living room with his laptop, writing code for an app he was working on as a side project. Just a simple platformer game.

But he couldn't concentrate and instead spent most of the arvo worrying about Reagan. The text messages he sent came back as undeliverable. She'd said that mobile phone reception in the park would be dodgy, and he wondered if she might have turned hers off completely. Maybe he wouldn't get to talk to her until Friday.

In the course of his fretting, Spoon spent some time conducting internet research on all the members of Reagan's family he knew about, from her parents to her cousins, and a few Aunts and Uncles that were spread across the sprawling North American continent. California, Maine, Colorado, Washington, Manitoba. An Aunt on her mum's side had passed away quite young, but Reagan had never mentioned her.

He loaded Reagan's Facebook page to find more information on her snotty cousin Dalton. His page was sparse, mostly pictures of him at various pubs and quotes from old TV shows, but he often commented on his brother's page. Charlie's Facebook profile was private, but Spoon did find an album of pictures from a church group trip to the Grand Canyon.

Spoon even found the lawnmower shop Anne had mentioned. A1 Lawnmower Repair in Broomfield, a small suburb on the northern edge of metro Denver. The website looked like something from the ancient internet days, with odd colors and low-resolution clip art. Unfortunately, the only information about Tyson himself on the site was that he had owned the establishment for over twenty years. Not even if Tyson was the first name or surname.

The shop was a mere twenty kilometers away from Anne's house, but Spoon had no car. He wasn't even sure what a trip there would gain him. Would he just rock up and say, *Excuse me, mate, care to tell me why you're pestering my girlfriend's stepmother?*

Big beefy Tyson might not like that so much.

What the hell, though, what else did he have to occupy his time? Maybe only a look at the place.

As he had a think about his options, Anne drifted in and out of rooms in the house, mostly ignoring him. For a time, she did set out a yoga mat on the living room floor and perform a series of bendy and twisty motions, and Spoon tried his best not to pay too much attention. She seemed to be doing the sequence *at* him, which was a strangely nerve-wracking event.

After a shower, she came and sat next to him on the couch, loosely holding a glass of red wine in one hand.

"So how did you hurt your knee?"

He closed the lid of his laptop. "Footy."

"Footy? Is that football?"

"Depends on where you're from. In Melbourne, footy means AFL, which is Australian rules football. It's not much like your American gridiron football. More like soccer, actually. In Queensland, footy is rugby. In Sydney, footy means soccer, but that's just because those tossers can't put together a good AFL team to save their lives, so they pretend like they don't care about real footy."

"So which one was it? I'm confused."

"Australian Rules Football. Tore my ACL when I made a hard cut and my leg went wonky."

"And you were in Australia when this happened?"

"Oh, no," he said. "Austin has a USAFL team called the Crows. The American AFL isn't the same, but it's a bit of home."

She sipped her wine, grinning at him with her eyelids barely open. "That guy my old roommate dated was quite athletic too. You Australians are a competitive bunch."

She said this with a tone of finality, as if the small talk was over. Blank space between them grew weighty during the few seconds of silence that elapsed.

He figured he might as well come out with what he wanted. He swallowed, feeling a little tension in his jaw. "Do you think you might let me borrow your car, yeah?"

She sat back and blinked, then scrunched her face. "Do you need something? I'm going to the grocery store later. Make me a list and I can get you whatever you need."

"No... I have some errands to run and don't want to trouble you with it." Given how dismissive she'd been to his questions about Tyson, maybe this was better than telling her straight out.

"I don't know," she said with a drunken grin. "Don't you guys drive on the other side of the road? How do I know you won't crash my car?"

"I've been in America for a few years, Mrs. Darby. I can drive on the wrong side of the road just fine."

She laughed. "You have to call me Anne, darling. None of that formal stuff."

He stared at her, waiting for her to respond to his request. Only the relentless whoosh of the air con and the gentle hum of the refrigerator cut the silence in the room.

He cleared his throat. "So, do you think...?"

She huffed, stood up, and left the room. What an odd woman.

He set his laptop on the coffee table and struggled to stand up. Out of breath, he took his crutches from the other side and followed her into the kitchen. Of course, she was pouring herself another glass of wine.

"Did I say something wrong?" he said.

She was facing away from him, staring out the bay window overlooking the meager backyard with its overgrown grass. "I can't let you borrow the car. I might need to go somewhere. Reagan has the other car, so I need mine."

"I won't be gone long."

She whipped around, a splash of red wine falling from the glass onto the kitchen tile. "Fine, Spoon, or whatever your name is. I'll let you take my car and run your errands if you have a drink with me."

She motioned to the kitchen table and an empty glass sitting in front of the chair.

He shook his head. "I can't. I don't drink."

"I'm bored. Have one little drink with me. I want you to tell me all about Australia. I've always wanted to go."

"I can tell you about Australia without having a drink." He felt his temperature start to rise.

"No drink, no car."

He gripped the crutch handles, his fingers sinking into the neoprene bands. Why was she so determined? "No."

"I could even tell you stories about Reagan, all the juicy stuff she probably hasn't told you herself. Why don't you humor a poor widow?"

An incredibly callous thing to say, especially since she seemed to have no hint of mourning or sorrow on her face when she said it.

"I don't drink," he said through gritted teeth.

She pouted. "Why not?"

"Because I'm a recovering alcoholic!"

He had raised his voice accidentally. She was cowering against the sink, but with indignation on her face.

"Oh, look," he said, "I'm sorry I got loud with you. I shouldn't have done."

She strutted to her purse, took a set of keys, and hurled them at him.

"Take the damn car. Take it and do whatever. Too good to drink with me, fine. Just go."

He contemplated apologizing, but the look on her face promised a losing battle. With a half-hearted smile, he placed his crutches in front and slinked from the room as quickly as he could.

Guilt settled over him as he crossed the living room. It had been a long time since he'd lost his temper like that, or even raised his voice. He'd have to make amends for the outburst at some stage down the road.

As he walked outside, sunlight blasted his eyes. The street was empty except for a blue Chevy Tahoe parked along the curb. He approached a Subaru Outback in the driveway, then isolated the big key with the buttons on it.

As he opened the door, ready to toss his crutches in the back seat, he got a shock: a manual transmission. Three pedals requiring two feet and two healthy knees.

"Bloody hell, Spoon. You can't drive this."

He stared at it for a few seconds, considering the possibility of driving it with only one good leg. But that was crazy.

Defeated, he went back into the house and dropped the keys on the table next to the front door. He would have to find some other way to explore the city and investigate Tyson. A taxi, maybe? He was too low on funds to spend hours in a cab. And according to Reagan, Denver's public transportation system was almost non-existent.

Anne gave him a full-toothed smile as if they weren't shouting at each other two minutes ago. "That was quick."

"You have a manual. Can't drive it with my knee like this."

She took in a sharp breath and giggled. "Oh my, I didn't even think about that. You poor boy. Now you can join the rest of us who have nothing." Her laugh grew, became something dark and bitter.

"I don't understand why you keep saying that. Are you putting me on? Didn't your husband have life insurance?"

Her belly laugh turned into a cackle. "Life insurance? You must be joking. Mitchell cashed that in last year. That was another little surprise we got the day of the service. When I said he left us with nothing, I meant he left us with not a damn thing."

CHAPTER NINE

2:35 pm

Reagan stared at the mass of fallen trees obstructing the area that should have been their campsite. Logs—some of them thicker than her waist—lay crisscrossed and jutting at spiked angles. After eight miles with thirty pounds on her back, all she wanted was to set up camp, but now they had to hunt for a new clearing large enough for two tents. Her chest felt tight, like being squeezed between two massive stones.

"What are we supposed to do now?" Dalton said.

"I guess we're not camping here," she said, looking up at a sky full of charcoal-colored clouds.

Find a new spot, set up the tent, have some alone time.

She let her pack slip from her aching shoulders and began exploring the area. A skinny footpath led west from the clearing and into the trees. The walkway opened again to a privy, which was a small wooden shelter hiding a toilet positioned over a hole in the ground. Nowhere close to there was going to work, unless they wanted to sniff crap all night long.

She went back the other way to the central area and turned north into the trees. A small clearing suggested enough room for the tents, but if those other trees had fallen, there was no guarantee the trees around this clearing were safe enough to camp underneath. She listened for creaking but heard only occasional bird chirps. She moved on to find something better.

After a few minutes, a light rain started, and she gave up looking. If the tents weren't operational in ten minutes, they'd be soaking wet. "Over here," she called to Dalton and Charlie.

The best she found was a space about ten feet by ten feet. Large enough for the tents, plus a stump and a giant downed log for sitting. Technically, they were supposed to camp within fifty feet of the red backcountry site marker, but this would have to do.

The guys dumped their packs and looked at the massive trees providing shade overhead.

"Is it safe right here?" Charlie said.

The rain was already starting to plaster her hair against her neck. "Probably."

"Let's get this shit knocked out," Dalton said. He unzipped his pack and started dumping possessions onto the moist ground.

Reagan opened her pack and took out Dad's three-man tent, which was only big enough for two actual people. When she and Dad had slept in it, they wedged their packs between them, and they slept pushed up against their respective sides. This was fine most of the time, but he did have a habit of farting in his sleep, which turned her into a stink-prisoner.

Setting up the tent would be no trouble, since that was her job when they were here two years ago. Dad's was to take out the sleeping pads, unroll them, and blow them to full size. She tried not to think about how she'd feel when she had to do that by herself.

"I'll go get some firewood," Dalton said.

"Whoa, wait a second," she said. "You can't have a fire in the park. It's not allowed."

"Says who?"

"Says the park rangers. No fires inside the park."

Dalton put his hands on his hips. "That's ridiculous. I want to have a fire."

"Maybe we shouldn't," Charlie said.

Dalton groaned and sat on the log next to the stump. From a small plastic box, he took out a skinny rolled piece of paper and lit it.

"Is that a joint?" Reagan said.

"Yup."

"You can't smoke that here."

"The fuck I can't," he said. "It's legal so I don't see why not. No different than cracking open a beer."

Reagan raised her hands toward the foliage around them. "It's different because we're in a National Park on federal land. If a ranger comes by and sees you smoking that or sees us lighting a fire, they'll call the cops. You have to have *some* respect for the rules, Dalton."

He laughed and threw a glance at Charlie, probably for solidarity, but Charlie only shook his head. "Tell you what," Dalton said. "I'll smoke this here pinner real fast, and keep it in me and Charlie's tent after that. And I'll shut up about the fire."

She didn't want to spend her dwindling energy arguing with her cousin. Instead, she went back to her unpacking duties. Tent, sleeping pad, sleeping bag. Bear canister. Small dry-bags filled with first aid accessories and other things to save from water. Bag of clothes. Her possessions, packed so tightly into the backpack, exploded onto the surrounding area as if they'd come from a container twice the size.

As she hustled to get the tent poles connected, the rain let up. A nice surprise. The mostly-mesh tent rose with the poles through the slots, and then she threw the rainfly over the top and strapped it to the tent. The rainfly, packed tightly into a bag for the last couple years, came out crumpled like old paper when stretched and laid out.

Five minutes later, with the tents set up and all of the various gear in the proper places, they gathered on the stump and the log and waited for dinner time.

"What did you guys bring for dinner?" she said.

"Mostly granola bars," Dalton said. "Charlie here brought some chocolate, right?"

Charlie nodded, pleased with himself. "I thought I might save it for the last night, to give us something to look forward to."

"Fuck that," Dalton said. "I want a piece now."

Charlie grudgingly dug into his pack and gave Dalton a Hershey's bar.

Reagan sighed and pulled the freeze-dried spaghetti and meatballs she'd shoved in the pocket of Dad's cargo pants since the bear canister was overfull. On the back, the package read *serves 3*. She'd intended to eat it alone because the yawning in her stomach said she needed the calories.

"You're gonna share that with us, right? We'll share what we got with you," Dalton said.

She said nothing.

"Please?" Charlie said.

The earnestness in her youngest cousin's eyes pricked her and made her want to cry. Dalton demanded, but Charlie asked, and that was good enough.

She set up Dad's Jetboil stove and poured the last of the water from her water bottle into the pot. "In the morning, if you guys will take my water filter down to the creek and fill up all the water bottles, I'll break down the camp."

"Sure, no problem," Charlie said. "It's good we're here, right, Reagan? You know, doing all this camp stuff seems like a lot of work for one person."

"It can be," she said.

Dalton eyed her. "She wishes her hunky Australian boyfriend was here instead, I bet. I'm guessing from that knee brace and those crutches that he wasn't going to be able to hack it."

She considered it. This morning, bringing her cousins along had seemed like a good idea. Family time, healing. But now, given the choice, she would absolutely take Spoon over the two of them.

"What's it like dating a foreigner?" Dalton said.

"I don't know," Reagan said. "He's a really good guy. He's got funny words for things sometimes, like 'arvo' instead of 'afternoon,' or 'servo' instead of 'gas station.'"

Dalton cleared his throat and sat up straight. "*Moye nyme eez Spewn*," he said, slowly enunciating each word in something like an Australian accent.

Charlie cackled. "That's perfect!"

"King of comedy up in this motherfucker," Dalton said. A twig snapped behind him and he whipped around, but there was nothing there. "How can you not be paranoid about a bear walking right up into this campsite?"

"I don't think about it," she said. "A bear probably won't mess with us for no good reason."

Dalton shook his head. "I don't know if I'll sleep tonight with all this bullshit. And that is a royal pain in the ass, because I'm tired as hell."

"You'll sleep," she said.

"What time were you thinking we'd get up in the morning?" Charlie said.

Reagan screwed the stove onto the fuel canister and turned the knob to start the fuel flow. "First light. We've got a long, long day tomorrow."

"Seriously?" Dalton said. "After all that hiking, we can't sleep in a little bit?"

"It's going to be forty degrees outside at seven o'clock in the morning. You can get up and start moving, or you can sit and shiver in your tent. Besides, if you thought today was a lot of hiking, we have to go about twelve miles tomorrow."

Dalton gasped. "Jesus Christ. You trying to give us all heart attacks out here?"

Charlie's mouth dropped open. "Hey, dude, that's not cool."

Reagan pretended she hadn't heard her cousin make a heart attack joke a week after Dad had died from one. She tried to focus on the camp stove and nothing else.

Empty casket. Empty casket.

She lit a match to the fuel and tried to blink away the tears welling in her eyes.

The water took six minutes to boil, and then after pouring the water into the bag, the spaghetti took another seven minutes to cook. They hardly spoke during that time.

When the food was ready, she shared her spork with them, since neither thought to bring any utensils. She was about to dig in when Charlie held up a hand to stop her.

He closed his eyes and bowed his head. He took a deep breath, and then in one quick speech, said, "Bless us oh Lord and these thy gifts which we are about to receive through Christ our Lord amen."

Charlie nodded that they could eat now. He ate his share in silence. She assumed he was embarrassed for his brother. Dalton's silence, on the other hand, seemed more the indignant variety. Halfway through the spaghetti, she didn't care anymore. Just a stupid slip of the tongue. He couldn't possibly have made an intentional heart attack joke.

When the food was gone and the sun had escaped behind the mountains, she shivered as the cold began to descend. "Okay, guys, I'm off. I'll see you in the morning."

***

8:30 pm

Finally alone in her tent, Reagan first stretched out on top of her sleeping bag and breathed deeply for two straight minutes. She tried to empty her mind of all thoughts and instead focus on the rhythms of her body. Her shoulders and hips ached from the day's long trek, and her ankles throbbed from the boots that didn't fit quite right. Had her feet grown since high school? That was a troubling thought.

As darkness descended on the campsite, she wrapped her headlamp around a loop jutting from the roof of the tent. She sat up and removed Spoon's t-shirt and a hefty paperback from the side pocket of the pack. Spoon had given it to her a month ago, the first in a series of a dozen fantasy books about an elf searching for his sister across an unforgiving desert landscape. Not her genre, plus the female characters were either outlandishly warlike or outlandishly sexual. But Spoon loved the series and was so excited for her to read it, she couldn't say no. Before Dad died, she'd read the first two hundred pages. Since then, she'd read two hundred more, but remembered none of it. When her eyes glided over the words, she might as well have been reading a Planned Parenthood pamphlet.

Reading about elves and dragons and trolls almost felt like an escape. She wanted that.

Holding his book and smelling his scent on the t-shirt made her wish she could pull Spoon out of her bag so he could wrap his arms around her. She wanted to feel the bulge of his biceps, to smell the shampoo in his hair and to kiss the blond stubble on his scratchy cheek. She wanted to cling to him and feel his solid weight pushing back.

When she was younger, she loved packing up the family van with mom and dad, traveling to Yosemite or Yellowstone or anywhere they would take her. She became enamored with sleeping under the stars and making s'mores and listening to Dad's stories about growing up and the crazy things he and his friends had done.

Two years ago, after dropping out of college and enduring her time at that horrible place, she came home to Dad's house after to rest and regenerate. The backpacking trip around the Tonahutu loop had been Dad's idea, and she agreed to go more due to surrender than choice.

They hiked into North Inlet after dawn and watched the sun paint the mountains in front of them in yellows and greens. The sharp contrast of the craggy peaks against the green fields brought tears to her eyes. Many things brought tears to her eyes back then in her fragile state, but the pure beauty of the park became special in a way it hadn't before.

They made camp in the evening on that first day and Dad sent her out for sticks skinny enough to use as marshmallow skewers. When she came back, he was staring at the blue flame knifing the air above the camp stove.

"What's on your mind, Dad?"

He shook his head, smiling a distant and sad smile.

"Tell me, please?"

"It's just work. Someday, sweetie, when everything calms down a little bit, there's some things I'll need to tell you."

She was not used to hearing this level of melancholy in his tone. He was a man who liked to laugh and make everyone else laugh. He liked to play pranks and give funny gifts for birthdays and holidays.

"What things?"

He didn't take his eyes off the flame. "It's difficult to express. When you're young, everything feels like an opportunity. The whole world is open and it feels like everything you do is part of your grand destiny. Meant to happen, or something like that. Then, you get older, and you realize that you could have just as easily turned left when you turned right, and your life would have been different. Not everything is how people say it is, that's all."

This last sentence had stuck with her ever since that evening. She'd thought he was referring to Anne, as Reagan suspected that she'd been having an affair and they would soon divorce. Which didn't bother Reagan one bit. Anne had never gone out of her way to accommodate her husband's daughter.

Reagan turned a page in the book and felt a dryness on her lips. Couldn't remember if she'd brought any lip balm, so she started to root around the top of her pack, then dug through to the bottom. Her hands fell on the duct-taped urn, and she pulled it from the pack.

She turned it in her hands, thinking it strange that she hadn't considered the urn all day long. Nestled between her sleeping bag and tent, all that remained of Dad traveled along with her, every step. Dad was always present, not like an empty casket, but a real thing she could hold in her hands.

After unzipping the tent, she set her pack on the ground outside to free up some room inside, then zipped it back up. She held the urn up to the headlamp's light, watched the rays of the LEDs bounce off the shimmery surface, then pulled the urn to her chest.

When the urn moved, something clicked.

She held it out and paused. There was definitely some kind of click.

She moved it around again, and it wasn't a click, but more like a *clinking*, like the sound of metal on metal. As far as she could tell, the urn was solid wood. She'd heard that sometimes bone fragments remained after cremation, but the sound wasn't bone. Definitely metal. How could metal get inside there?

She peeled back the duct tape, careful not to make too much noise since her cousins were in a tent a few feet away. Her heart rate hitched a few notches. The tape came off in interrupted screeches, leaving strings of glue on the brown polished surface.

When the duct tape was gone, she placed her hand on top of the urn, and then froze. Panic welled up inside her as she realized she was about to witness the totality of the sweet man that was her dad. Ash. Bone chips. A hundred and eighty pounds reduced to ounces.

She closed her eyes and opened the urn. The clinking wasn't in the base of the urn but on the top end of it. She carefully set the lower part of the urn on the tent floor, then gingerly took her hand away once she was sure it was steady. She didn't want to look at the contents if she didn't have to.

The lid was a curved half-dome on the top and a flat circle on the bottom, two inches tall and four or five inches in circumference. She shook it, and the top clinked with every jerk of her hand. She explored the object but found no break in the wood. Then she tapped the bottom. Hollow.

She tapped harder and could hear the clinking. There was something *inside* the lid of the urn. Like a secret compartment. Her chest pounded.

She cupped the lid in her palms and placed her thumbs on the flat bottom, then pushed. There was a click, and the base depressed a fraction of an inch and then rose. She tried to push the now-detached bottom of the lid, but it wouldn't move. Then she noticed tiny grooves along the sides. She placed her fingers on the edges and twisted, and it came right off.

Squished inside the lid was a slip of paper, a key, and a piece of tape that had fallen away.

A key.

She took the key from the lid, pinched it between two fingers and held it to the light. Small, silver, with no markings. Too small to be a door or car key. Probably something like a lockbox or safe key.

Pulses of confused yellow energy shot through her. Who could have put a key in a secret compartment inside the urn that contained Dad's ashes? None of this made sense.

Shuffling came from outside the tent, and her hand flew to the headlamp dangling from the tent roof, covering the beam with the palm of her hand. Darkness. She was perfectly still, holding her breath. She waited ten seconds, fifteen seconds, but no new noises came. She relaxed.

And then she looked at the piece of paper folded into a tiny chunk and stuffed inside the lid. Written in Dad's scratchy cursive was a single, capital letter R.

Dad had somehow done this.

She removed the note from the lid and ran her fingers over the surface of the paper. When she'd read the letter he had written her at the memorial service yesterday, she'd assumed it would be the last ever communication from Mitchell Darby. Now, in her hands, she held new information, and a new way to communicate with him. Even if the conversation was only one sided. She wanted to read the note, but she also wanted to save it. If she didn't read it now, she could still savor one last exchange with him. One last way to delay the end.

A wave of sadness swept through unlike anything she'd experienced since before the dark times in Austin. Inside this note were Dad's hand-written words. She could see the shadow of ink through the folds of the paper.

Crushing, blue sadness. Sadness so stark it threatened to turn black.

She stuffed the note into her pocket and replaced the lid on the urn, trying to keep the sounds of her weeping at a volume low enough that Dalton and Charlie wouldn't hear.

When the urn was again secure, she picked up the key and curled into a ball on top of the sleeping bag.

She turned it over and over in front of her face.

"What do you unlock?" she whispered.

Wednesday

CHAPTER TEN

6:50 am

Dalton and Charlie collected the Camelbak bladders and water bottles before sunrise, and then hiked a short distance to the creek spilling out of Granite Falls to make the day's filtered water. Dalton knew from previous experience that while the mountain water might look clear and clean, it contained so many different kinds of animal shit that one gulp could leave you in the fetal position for days.

He shuddered as they hiked, and he and his brother both expelled air from their mouths in clouds of frozen vapor. Since it was July, he was completely unprepared for the frigid temperature. Perpetual cold and a lingering lightheaded feeling from the increase in altitude made him crabby.

He was also a little nervous about telling Charlie the real reason they were here. But Dalton knew if he played it right, Charlie would fall into line.

The spray from the foamy white water rushing over the falls reached them from over a hundred feet away, so they stopped when Dalton felt the mist in the air. The wooden sign next to the creek read *"LOWER GRANITE FALLS STOVES ONLY."*

"Do you want to hold the bottles, or do you want to pump?" Dalton asked his brother, emphasizing the second option.

Charlie pointed at the Katadyn water filter pump in Dalton's hand. Charlie's lips were quivering and he was shuffling from one foot to the other. "Do you know how that thing works?"

He handed the water filter to Charlie as they knelt on the grassy bank next to the creek. "Fat end goes in the water. Other tube goes in the bottle, then pump. That's it."

Charlie unspooled the tubes protruding from either end of the filter and dropped the tube with the weighted end into the water. He grasped the pump with one hand and pulled up the lever with the other. Dalton took the other tube and inserted it into a water bottle.

As Charlie started to push and pull on the lever, the weighted tube end danced as it sucked water into the filter and spat it out through the other tube, which slowly filled the water bottle.

Dalton studied his little brother. Ran a tongue around to soothe the dryness in his mouth. "You having fun out here?"

Charlie's eyes darted around the trees overhead and the water below him. "I gotta say it's beautiful. Yesterday, I saw two deers, all those moose, and so many different kinds of birds I couldn't even count all the kinds. But—holy moly—I'm seriously cold right now."

"You'll feel better once we get out on the trail."

Charlie nodded without a reply.

Dalton steeled himself and put on his Charlie-Convincing Face. "I told you that there was a special reason we needed to come out here on this trip with Reagan."

"Yeah," Charlie said, not taking his eyes off the lever as he pushed it up and down.

Dalton switched water bottles as one neared full. "That thing of Uncle Mitch's that Tyson is looking for? He told you about that, right?"

Charlie pumped faster. "Yeah."

"He thinks it may be out here. He also thinks it may be back in Denver, so he's going to look for it there, too. But we're supposed to look for it out here."

Charlie stopped pumping for a second, but still didn't look at Dalton. "I don't understand. Why would a bunch of money be in the woods?"

"He thinks her dad stashed it and Reagan knows where it is. We're supposed to watch her until she finds it, then do whatever we have to do to get it back."

Charlie's mouth dropped open and he shook his head, making his jowls bounce back and forth. "Oh, no no no. This is not okay, Dalton. This is why you made me come with you? I told you I didn't want to do that anymore."

Time to recalibrate. "Look, Chuckles, everything's cool. It's not hers, anyway. If she finds it, we're just going to take it from her and give it back to him. We're not doing anything out of bounds here."

"I don't know about this. Besides, it's crazy thinking it could be out here. Why would Uncle Mitch stash all that money in a national park?"

Dalton sighed and changed out a water bottle for a Camelbak bladder. "Because, he knew Reagan would come out here and get it. The letter for her at the funeral? The slippery motherfucking thief had it all planned out."

"Hey now, don't call Uncle Mitch names like that. Even if the money is out here, we don't even know what to look for."

"It's probably in a briefcase or a sealed package or something. Whenever we see it, it's going to be obvious. Look, we *have* to find the money. What do you think happens if we come back to Tyson and don't have the money?"

"You know he doesn't like it when you call him that," Charlie said, frowning.

"Why do you think Tyson would care what I call him?" Dalton rubbed his jaw, trying to soothe his clenched muscles. "Whatever. I don't think you understand the gravity of this situation here and how much trouble we're going to be in if we come back empty-handed."

Charlie stopped pumping and glared at his brother. "I don't care. You lied to me."

Dalton remained as still and even as possible. He could maybe handle Reagan alone, but it would be so much easier with Charlie's help. "No, I didn't lie to you. I just didn't tell you everything up front. It's not the same thing."

Jim Heskett

Charlie pushed out a few breaths like steam escaping the nose of a bull. Dalton watched as his brother's lips moved, which meant the kid was thinking.

"What would we have to do?" Charlie said, his face flat and cumbersome.

"It's easy. Just watch her. She may have even gotten it already and stashed it with her stuff. I'll find some way to go through her pack and check. But if she doesn't have it yet, we wait until she gets it."

"And then what?"

"Then we take it."

"You make it sound so simple, Dalton. What are we supposed to do if she doesn't want to give it to us?"

Dalton narrowed his eyes. "Then we convince her. This is two hundred and forty *thousand* dollars we're talking about here. We're going to do what we have to do so we can bring home what's ours. It may get messy, so you need to be prepared for that."

Charlie dropped the water filter pump and stood up. "No. No, no, no. This isn't going to be like it was with that guy in Boulder. No way am I doing that again. You promised."

Dalton rose to his feet to look Charlie in the eyes. "The Boulder guy was a mistake, you're right. I could have handled that better." He pointed at the water filter. "Pick it up, please. We're almost done here."

Charlie hesitated for a second, then did as he was told. He spent a few seconds silently mouthing some words to himself. "I don't know about this."

"You've seen the first Die Hard movie, right? Did John McClane *want* to spend his Christmas in L.A. fighting the terrorists? Hell no. But he did what he had to because it was the only thing to do."

"This isn't Die Hard."

Dalton was beginning to lose his patience. "What do I have to do to get this through your thick motherfucking skull? This has to be done."

Charlie looked at him, surprisingly stone-faced. "I need to think about it, but whatever happens, she doesn't get hurt. If you want my help, that's the deal. If anything goes beyond talking, I don't want any part of it."

75

Dalton nodded, although he had to believe that when the time came, Charlie would do what was required of him and choose to be on the right side. Disappointing Tyson was not an option.

CHAPTER ELEVEN

7:05 am

Reagan woke several times before the sun came up, and each time, the first thing that popped into her head was the key in her right pants pocket. Usually, in the backcountry, she couldn't sleep for more than an hour or so at a time. Creaking trees, the wind rustling the fabric of the tent, little animals scurrying around the campground: all of these things disturbed the quiet. But she usually got right back to sleep. Especially if she'd hiked hard enough on the trail during the day.

But last night, sleep had not come easy or often. When the sun finally started to lighten the walls of the tent, she sat up and estimated she'd slept no more than three or four hours total. The tension in her neck and hips had turned into full-blown soreness. There was an emergency kit, but given that Dad had been using the same one for a decade, she doubted that it still contained any aspirin or ibuprofen. Should have checked it before leaving Denver.

She stretched and got out of the sleeping bag, shivering. She dressed quickly, throwing on Dad's over-sized Carhartt hoodie and his thick fleece gloves. She wondered if he had ever washed these things, and doubted it. He wasn't the tidiest person. Didn't matter, she liked the idea that some of him was touching her.

She sniffed the inside of the hood, and the scent was vaguely familiar. Faded sweat, a hint of cologne.

The burning in her bladder motivated her, and she unzipped the tent. Some rain had fallen during the night and the ground was moist, but not soaked as it often was. Near the tent, piles of animal scat like over-sized M&Ms with the shells removed had blossomed. Probably deer. She snatched her boots from the tent vestibule, shook them to dump out potential spiders, and then put them on.

"Hey guys, sun's up."

No response. She walked to their tent and shook it. "Sun's up. Let's go."

Again, no response. They needed to get up and hit the trail because today was the longest of the trip. Tomorrow would be the shortest day, distance-wise, just to lakes Nokoni and Nanita then back, but tomorrow was also the day she was releasing Dad's ashes. Hard to say if she could handle a long day on the trail after all of that.

She made the short hike to the privy over tall piles of snow sprinkled with tree bark chips and pine needles like confetti, and when she returned, the brush through the trees rustled, then came the sound of voices. Dalton and Charlie emerged from the trees, holding all of their full water bottles and Camelbak bladders.

"Thought we'd get a jump on the day, and make things easier for you," Dalton said, smiling. Charlie would not look at her, his eyes on the ground and his head low.

Reagan was impressed. She had not expected this.

Dalton dumped all of the water bottles except for his and walked to his pack. They had all left their gear outside last night, resting up against the trees.

He gasped. "What the fuck is going on with this?"

She walked to where he was standing, open-mouthed, over his backpack. There was a large hole in the side, the fabric torn and frayed. "Oh my god. Why is your pack all torn up?"

Charlie held up his poles, the straps of which had been mangled as well. "Me too."

Reagan checked her pack and found that the left side of the hip-belt was missing. She dropped to one knee and felt the ruffled edge of the fabric, and it appeared to have been chewed.

"What the hell happened here?" Dalton said.

Not good. They were too deep into the park to leave and get new gear. She took a deep breath, trying to stay calm. "Some animal. Fox, or something must have chewed up the pack for some reason. Did you leave food in there?"

Dalton bristled. "Um, maybe. I don't think so."

She pursed her lips. "Dalton, you were supposed to put everything in your bear canister."

"Why did it eat my pole straps?" Charlie said. "I don't have any food on my poles."

In a few seconds, the answer came to her. "Salt. The sweat."

"That's great," Dalton said. "How am I supposed to hike with this giant hole in the side of my backpack? All my stuff will fall out. It's not like I can hike backward to make sure I'm not leaving a trail of underwear and shit behind me like motherfucking Hansel and what's-her-name."

Reagan peered at his pack's damage, and then snatched a long-sleeved shirt through the hole. She wrapped it around the pack and pulled it tight, then knotted it over the opening. She tugged on the shirt, and the cinch seemed solid.

"Look at you, cuz. Not too shabby," Dalton said, rubbing his chin.

She searched the nearby ground, hoping that whatever animal had severed the hipbelt from her pack had dropped it so she could duct-tape it back in place. But there was no sign of the thing.

Hiking three more days wearing a pack with no hipbelt was not an option. The weight needed to be distributed between her shoulders and hips evenly or she was in for a world of hurt.

She knelt by her pack and felt the torn fabric. Then inspiration struck.

She fished out the rusted Swiss army knife from the top of the pack and a length of rope Dad always insisted on carrying but neither of them had ever needed until this moment. Measuring out three arm lengths, she dragged the blade across the rope to cut it. She made a slit in the pack where the hipbelt used to connect and threaded the rope inside.

She turned on her phone to see the time. Daylight was burning. Today was going to be such a long day of tramping hard miles at high elevation.

With the rope threaded through the pack, she cut a hole above the other side and pulled the rope out. She wound it around the hipbelt so the two ends of the rope met in the middle.

She stood up, strapped on the pack and tied the rope together, cinching it against her hips. It would chafe but would be better than nothing.

"Damn, MacGuyver," Dalton said. "I didn't know you were so crafty you could make backpack belts at the drop of a hat. But what about Charlie's poles?"

"That's okay," he said. "I don't need the straps."

Reagan looked at the campsite. "Alright. If nothing else is damaged, we need to get going."

"What about breakfast?" Charlie said.

Thirty minutes cooking and eating breakfast might be too much of the day's budget. The sun had already climbed above the mountains to the east. "Going to have to be granola bars on the trail. We've wasted too much time already. Today we're going up over Flattop and back around, and we'll be above treeline, exposed the whole way. I don't need to tell you how dangerous that is."

CHAPTER TWELVE

7:40 am

Reagan's day had started and remained yellow. Yellow due to the strange key resting against her thigh. Yellow was for confusion because it easily bled into orange for irritation and red for anger.

She'd been coloring her days since her time at the hospital. Recognizing and classifying her feelings came naturally to her now, but there had been a long and challenging journey to arrive at this point. Along the trail, Reagan thought about her last semester at school in Austin and the darkest days of her life.

Memories arrived like rain droplets on a pond.

She was going to kill herself on a Tuesday evening, after going out to dinner with some friends. She called them her friends, but these were the same people who had turned their backs when her mania had reached a fever pitch. They went out to a Mexican restaurant, ate dinner, had some drinks. Her friends talked about research papers and midterms and keg parties, and this world seemed far away, in the same place where people got dressed every morning and paid bills on time and went bike riding on weekends.

When the waiter came by to explain the dessert options, a compulsion to escape overpowered her, so she ran through the kitchen and out the back door, then huddled between two dumpsters in the meat-and-bean stink, hovering among the flies. She shivered in the chilly Austin winter air.

She was sobbing and shaking, listening to her friends call her name as they searched the parking lot. She couldn't bear anyone discovering her, but had no idea why the prospect was so horrific. Going out to dinner had been a terrible idea. She'd wanted to play normal for one evening and failed miserably at it.

She slipped over the back fence and took a taxi home, turning off her phone so they couldn't contact her. It had been four months since the manic episode had ended and the descent into depression had overtaken her life.

As she walked into her apartment, her roommate Beatrice was in the kitchen, wiping the inside of the microwave.

"Hey, Rags," Beatrice said. "Do you think you could do your dishes? They've been soaking since Sunday."

In that moment, the decision to end her life solidified. Her head brimmed with lamentation about that girl, the lively and manic girl who preached the gospel of Richard Bach and Jack Kerouac in her friends' living rooms, who was sure she would go on to rewrite modern psychology, and thought that when she danced she was filled with a magic powerful enough to heal the sickness in people. How did she become the girl who was now incapable of having the simplest conversations with other people? Talking to professors. Ordering food at the drive-through. Small-talk with the landlord while paying rent. All of these seemed monumental tasks, likely to cripple her with anxiety.

"Are you going to say anything?" Beatrice said, still not looking at Reagan.

Reagan opened her mouth and nothing but air came out. She fled the living room into her bedroom, slamming the door behind her before Beatrice could launch into another lecture about *roommate responsibilities*.

She picked up her journal, and furiously scribbled.

"Depression" is a bad term for it, because it sounds like something colorless and plain. Sometimes it's like that, but more often it's a tornado or a boulder tumbling downhill that always leads to the same conclusion: I am worthless.

Self-examination turns into self-criticism and that becomes depression. I trap myself in these cyclones of thought, each one pointing back at me, arriving at the decision that everything is my fault and it's never going to get better.

The only end to the suffering of the bad thoughts is to stop myself from thinking, and the only way to get out of thinking is to sleep. Sleep rarely comes, not lately. The thoughts don't stop when I'm awake. And sleep is temporary. When I wake up, nothing has changed, so I have to find a way to sleep forever. There's only one final solution to the problem of being unable to turn off the thinking machine.

Next day, she went on campus to find the guy with the dreadlocks because she knew he always had pills. She chased him down after class, and she bought as many Valiums as she could afford. She didn't know if it would be enough, but it seemed like it.

That night, Reagan opted to give life one more go before ending things. Beatrice had gone out on a date, so Reagan had the apartment to herself. She tried to work on a term paper and spent ten minutes of actual work time. Then she got so frustrated that she was unable to focus on anything other than self-loathing, so she gave up and retreated to her bed with her laptop. She logged on to Netflix and found a show with multiple seasons available. Didn't care what show, just started with episode 1. This lasted for the next several hours, well past midnight.

The whole time she seethed, episode after episode, getting increasingly angry at herself. It became a game… how far could she push it, how late could she stay up in the glow of her laptop as time to complete her term paper evaporated. She chain-smoked cigarettes, even though she hated the way the odor infected her clothes and hair and fingers. She used to be the kind of girl who only bummed smokes at parties when she was drinking, but now she was buying packs of them.

The anger rumbled and went nowhere. By two a.m., her neighbors started coming back from the bars, stumbling and struggling to get their keys into the locks on their apartments, and she'd grown so exhausted from staring at the screen that she wore only a weary sense of failure, as the little judging demon inside her brain whispered *I told you so. I told you that you were a screw up.*

Around three a.m., she ate all the Valiums while sitting on the living room couch and chased them down with one of Beatrice's beers. She closed her eyes, and that was the last thing she knew.

She would later learn that Beatrice had come back to the apartment to get a condom before going home with the date, and found Reagan sprawled over the coffee table, pale and dribbling a trail of spit in a squiggly line.

Time shifted, and she was in a hospital, in some kind of waiting room.

A man came by and told her that her intake would begin soon, and she could hang out for a few minutes. He gave her a form to fill out. A teenager with a scar across his face sat opposite her, staring, and she nearly had a panic attack because he wouldn't look away.

"What are you here for?" he said.

"I'm not sure," she said.

He laughed and closed his eyes, then started drumming his hands on his thighs, some kind of rhythm. She wished he would stop, but felt powerless to ask him.

On a television anchored to the wall, a miniature politician was giving a speech. The volume was off, but she heard every word he said. Soon, a chant started in her mind: *they're going to assassinate him. They're going to assassinate him. They're going to assassinate him.*

She couldn't turn it off. Louder and louder, until she almost screamed.

She fantasized about what it would be like to be one of those responsible people, the kind who went to class every day and had no trouble meeting deadlines. What was so different about them? Nothing, apparently.

Those kinds of thoughts belonged to the dreaded "black and white" that her high school shrink warned her about, back when she was experiencing only the small lapses into depression and mania. That same therapist said that when people are depressed, they think irrationally and come to incorrect conclusions based on premises that are untrue, and so the goal of therapy had to be to show the patient why those basic premises arose from faulty logic. As if logic was an answer. Reagan knew this to be true, but knowing made no difference.

When the intake man called her name, she followed him to a table by the nurses' station, just to get away from the television. He was a thick man with moles all over his face, and Reagan studied the moles intently. Studying them grounded her and kept her heart rate at an even pace.

He took her blood pressure and shined a light in each of her eyes, then clicked his pen.

Reagan handed him the form, and he flipped through the pages.

"You didn't fill in the medical history." His voice was soft and had a certain music to it, like the way her mother used to read bedtime stories.

"I don't...um... I don't exactly have one."

He laid a new stack of papers on top of the clipboard. "Do you drink or use drugs?"

"A little. Not much. I mean, no drugs. Smoked pot a couple of times, I guess, but I didn't like it." Every word was a struggle.

"Do you ever hear voices or see things that aren't there?"

She could tell him about the demon in her head who judged everything she did, but then they'd label her as a paranoid schizophrenic. "There's Richard Bach, you know, he wrote *Illusions* and *Jonathan Livingston Seagull*. He didn't actually, I mean, it's all there between the lines, you know? The words aren't the words, it's what's not on the page that matters. That doesn't sound right."

"Do you believe that Richard Bach was communicating directly with you?"

She almost said *yes*, thinking someone finally understood, but she caught herself with the word on her lips. If she obliged him, he would put a little check mark next to a box that said *experiences delusions about talking with dead and/or famous people*. So she only shook her head.

"Do you have any questions for me?" he said.

"No, not really, but... I don't know what's wrong with me, I mean, they'll say it's depression, but... I mean, I don't know if I really meant to do it. You know, with the pills. I don't know what's wrong with me, I don't know..." She could see the sentences in her head as fully formed thoughts, but when they came out of her mouth, the final product sounded like gibberish.

"Why don't you take it easy for now? You've had a hard day, and we're all done with the intake. There will be plenty of time to talk in Group tomorrow."

He ushered her off to the TV room again, and after that first day alone in her bed, she was required to conform to the schedule. They arranged blocks of time with scheduled activities like Group, meals, and strictly enforced bedtimes and wake-up times.

She didn't even realize she was back in Denver until the third day. The timeline confused her, but eventually she regained some memories of having her stomach pumped, being on a plane with Dad, and checking into a mental health facility.

She spent the bulk of her days in Group. Group meant lectures about depression and schizophrenia and post-traumatic stress disorder, drawings on the dry-erase board about the medical roots of mental illness. Making healthy choices. Understanding grief and loss.

She never wanted to say anything, because there was no way to express her hopelessness and futility. The few people who did talk in Group monopolized all the time, anyway. They ranted about the various people in their lives who had wronged them, and how victimized they were by all the injustices in the world.

She wished she could join in and accuse someone, but there was no one to accuse. Dad had always given her nothing but love, and she wasn't angry with her mother for leaving them, and she wasn't angry that her stepmother Anne didn't understand her. There was no point in being mad at anyone.

If she did speak up, the counselors would tell her to take control of her life, as if it were a telescope pointed in the wrong direction.

Dad and Anne visited on the fourth day, and she stared at them as they talked about meaningless things like what colleges cousin Charlie was applying to. Reagan asked them if they had told her mother she was here, and they became silent. Mom wasn't going to visit. Reagan knew that. She wanted to ask them about her aunt Susan, the one who had killed herself when she was younger than Reagan. No one ever liked to talk about her. Maybe she'd been sick the same way Reagan was.

After their visit, she went out into the smoke hole, a fenced-in outdoor area, the only place in the compound where they allowed smoking and gave a modicum of privacy. Leaning against the building was a twenty-something with tattoos on his neck and a bandage on half his head. She'd seen him before, and he'd hardly said a word to anyone. But now, alone out there, away from the angry schizophrenics and weeping housewives, he spoke to her.

"What are you in for?" he said.

She knew the correct answer by then. "Bipolar."

He nodded. "Yeah, me too. I tried to do myself, but it didn't work." He pointed at the bandage on his head.

She wanted to ask him about it, but instead said, "I wanted to kill myself too."

"I have a son. I know now that what I did was bad. They tell me my hand slipped at the last second. I don't remember nothing."

"I tried to take some pills, but I didn't... I don't know... had no idea how many I was supposed to take."

They stared at each other for a tense second and then laughed. She liked him because he was scared, like her, and he didn't want to flirt with her and push himself on her, like some of the other guys had done in her first week.

"You're kinda new here, right?" he said.

She nodded.

"You'll get the hang of it. The staff will keep checking on you five or six times a day. They have to make sure you're all drugged up and not causing no trouble. Just make sure you take your meds, go to Group, go to your therapist, and don't start any shit with nobody. If somebody messes with you, tell your therapist. Don't react and hit the person or anything stupid like that."

"I hate it here," she said.

"This?" he said, glancing at the brick building. "This ain't shit. What's gonna keep you up at night is worrying about getting sent off to Colorado Springs, to the long-term place. You go there, and no one ever sees you again. You'll be doing the Trazodone shuffle for the rest of your days."

She flicked the ash from her cigarette and it danced in the light breeze. "I hate my shrink."

"Who you got? Ahern? Gupta?"

"It's someone named Jeanie. I don't even know what her last name is. She's the one with the curly bangs, you know, the skinny one with the blonde hair."

He snuffed his cigarette against the side of the building and lit a fresh one. "Sure, I know her. Jeanie Carmichael."

"She's like… all she does is stare at me and say 'the staff notes indicate you went to bed early last night. I think we should up your Effexor a little.' I stare at the floor for, you know, most of the time."

Reagan was pleased with herself, able to hold a regular conversation with someone. It had felt like months since she'd been able to do more than spit awkward random sentence fragments. Most people didn't even notice, so wrapped up in their own concerns.

"She tells me stuff like I need to get out of bed once a day and go for a walk, and I nod and say it sounds like a good idea."

His eyes were almost black. "You just have to play the game. Be a model patient."

She didn't tell him about the session yesterday when, after an unusually long silence, Reagan said, "Did you know I had a 4.0 in high school?" She had been trying to say that even though she seemed stupid now, she wasn't. But the shrink went on to lecture about living up to people's expectations, missing the point entirely. Reagan got mad and knocked a bowl of candy onto the floor.

When their cigarettes were finished, he gave her a wink and they both went back inside. The next day, he transferred to a different facility and she never saw him again. She didn't get to say goodbye.

During her second week, they switched her therapy to Dr. Ahern, and there Reagan experienced her first glimmer of hope.

Dr. Ahern spoke directly, and never lectured like the Group counselors or her first shrink. She would ask Reagan questions, and if Reagan didn't answer, Dr. Ahern didn't get upset and alter her medication as punishment.

By their third session, Reagan had grown comfortable enough that she had actual conversations with the therapist. Talking to the tattooed kid at the smoke hole and talking to a therapist were two different animals. But on that day, as Reagan stared out the window of

Dr. Ahern's office at a squirrel clicking, clucking, and chirping as it hopped from branch to branch of a giant oak tree, Reagan tested her.

"How do I get better?" Reagan said. She was expecting *take control of your life.*

"You just need to wait it out," Dr. Ahern said.

Reagan stopped. She hadn't expected this. "Okay. What do I do while I'm waiting it out?"

"You work on yourself."

And then Reagan sunk back into her chair, because it seemed Dr. Ahern was like everyone else, after all. But Reagan wasn't going to give up yet.

"Yes, that's what everyone says, but… how do I do that? What does that look like? It sounds like a great idea, obviously, because I realize I'm messed up, but what do I literally do about it? When we have free time, I think, *okay now I'm going to work on myself,* so I write in my journal, and that gets me more angry because I end up writing the same things over and over again. How I messed up the last two semesters, how I disappointed my family.

"And when I was in Austin, I would wake up in the morning and say 'today is the day I'm going to do something. I'm not staying in bed all day.' But there's nothing to do and I go back to bed. Do you see what I mean?"

A little glint of joy appeared at having captured her thoughts so perfectly, and then the reply changed everything.

Dr. Ahern smiled. "That's the trouble, dear. You have to wait it out. It doesn't matter what you do or what you don't do. There's only one job you have; there's only one rule: you have to stay alive, that's all. Every minute of the day that you keep on breathing is enough. You don't have to figure anything out. You don't have to finish school, or get a job, or even get happy, but you can if you want to. You can do anything you feel like. Except you have one thing you have to do: stay alive and keep on breathing."

CHAPTER THIRTEEN

7:55 am

In Spoon's dream, he had a frothing stubbie of Victoria Bitter in his hand, as he always did. This one was in a bar, maybe Australia, maybe Austin. He didn't get sober until his sophomore year of college, so he did of bit of drinking after he moved to the States.

Reagan was at the opposite end of the bar, chatting to some stranger with a thick spool of mardi gras beads around his neck. Spoon wanted to cross the room to her, but the crowd of people clogged the space between them. He couldn't find a passageway, and he tried to call to her but the collective roar of the crowd drowned out his voice.

When he woke up, the first thought that appeared in his head was whether Reagan had taken her medication. This was a strange idea, because Spoon had never considered this. Reagan always took her medication, even when she didn't want to.

When they met fifteen months ago, she explained to him about her manic and depressive episodes, her hospitalization, and her recovery. Spoon had never seen the ugly side of the illness. He might not have known otherwise.

She said that mania was like a computer program with a hundred buttons to click, and each one lights up for only a few seconds, and as she races around to click each one, the lights move faster and faster until it's all a blur. She loved it but also wanted it to stop. On the other side, depression was not usually about sleeping all day, although sometimes it was. Mostly, depression meant an endless series of rhetorical questions that resulted in a spiral of shame, judgment, and yearning to escape.

When she told him this, they were only two months into their relationship, sitting in his apartment, sharing tea. Spoon looked at her and had a hard time believing that the same charming woman sitting next to him could have acted as mad as a cut snake, as his father might say. After a few months, he did notice that she seemed to cycle through introversion and extroversion, but as long as she stayed on her meds, it never became more than that. She often wanted to chuck a sickie from work and spend evenings with him, and he would read to her when she claimed her eyes were too tired.

She dropped hints about her displeasure with the nausea and occasional dizziness some of the pills gave her, and she sometimes talked about her desire to be rid of them, to try yoga and meditation and homeopathic remedies, and Spoon never knew what to say to that. He encouraged her to do what she thought was right. But also, he would say he learned in AA that often what *he* thought was best for himself was absolutely the wrong thing, so he sometimes had to trust in others to help him make decisions about himself and his recovery.

Only two more sleeps until he could see her again.

He sat up in bed, careful not to jostle his knee, which was already throbbing. He stretched and picked up his mobile from Reagan's nightstand, checking it for messages or missed calls. There was one message, but it wasn't from Reagan.

Knee aching, he took some ibuprofen from his bag next to the bed and dry-swallowed them. He was glad not to be on painkillers any longer. Painkillers and trying to live sober never did mix well. That reminded him, he needed to get to an AA meeting, and soon.

He slipped on a pair of grundies and a t-shirt, then used his crutches to walk downstairs and into the living room. Anne was nowhere around, which was becoming a regular occurrence.

Mystery man Tyson loomed in Spoon's thoughts. Anne had lied about the fight with him, that much was certain.

He limped into the empty kitchen and set his mobile on speaker mode to listen to the message as he took a bagel from above the fridge. Americans seemed not to understand the joy of crumpets for breakfast. He'd yet to find an American grocer that sold them.

"Hey, this is Ken," the voicemail message said. "I hate to do this to you, but I was wondering if you could cut your vacation short and come back to Austin, preferably today."

Ken didn't know Spoon wasn't on holiday, but was supposed to be at a job interview in New Orleans. Spoon was waiting to hear back from their HR person to find out if he could reschedule for next week. He hadn't yet figured out how he was going to swing the extra time off.

The message continued. "We had a release last night which broke a bunch of stuff, so the team is pretty frantic. Our call volume is insane and our average hold times are around eleven minutes. As you can imagine, both Sales and Product are running around screaming about the end of the world. I wouldn't ask except that the new guy we hired no call/no showed this morning, so we're one short, no matter what. Please give me a call as soon as you can."

Spoon rested his elbows on the table, chewed on his untoasted bagel and stared at the mobile until his eyes unfocused. So typical of his boss to blindside him with such a request. Spoon was supposed to have transferred out of tech support and into project management a year ago, but the timing wasn't right, or they lost a job bid to a different department, or upper management role-reshuffling meant the Org Chart had to be remade. There was always something to keep him glued to his perch.

The mobile rang again. Spoon looked at the number, then sighed and tapped the accept button. "Hi, Ken."

"Spoon, my mate, g'day to you there."

Why did everyone think the *g'day mate* jokes were so bloody funny?

"Did you hear my message?"

"I just woke up, but yeah, I listened to it."

"Sleeping in on your vacation, are you?"

Spoon considered telling Ken something about a family emergency, but then thought about how Ken would fake sympathy for ten seconds and then get on with his point. Spoon decided to spare himself the trouble. "Yeah."

"I hate to do this to you. I really do, but these are desperate times over here. When can you get back?"

If Spoon worked for a modern company, they would have remote desktop applications and the ability to set up a virtual network. But his company was not so modern. They required you to punch in physically at your desk every day.

Spoon hated the omitted truths and promises broken. Grateful to have a job, yes, but he wanted more than tech support. He left Australia and went to college in the States to achieve more than that.

"I can't, Ken. My apologies, mate, but I'm not coming back until next week."

Silence on the other end of the line. Spoon thought he heard someone else talking in the background. With the cubicles stacked so close together like prawns in a tin, it happened all the time.

"That's not an acceptable answer, Liam."

Now Ken was using Spoon's Christian name, as his mum would, so the situation was getting serious. "It's not as if I don't give a stuff about the team. You know I wouldn't let everyone down, Ken. That's not what I'm about."

"Then why can't you come back?"

"Because I'm on my bloody PTO. You can't ask me to cut it short."

Spoon regretted letting his temper flare, even though most yanks wouldn't recognize *bloody* as being a curse word.

More silence, for almost twenty seconds. Spoon chewed quietly, waiting for Ken to say something.

Ken cleared his throat. "I didn't realize you saw it that way. We all have to make sacrifices for the team."

And so began the guilt trip.

"I have to be honest with you, Ken, I wasn't going to New Orleans for vacation. I had a job interview there."

"I see." Ken actually sounded hurt.

"It's nothing personal. It's just that I'm not so keen on tech support anymore. I want to get into project management and there's a good opportunity for me there."

"So this is how it's going to be, then? Maybe you're not a good fit for our team here," Ken said, starting to sound a little choked up.

The conversation was slipping into melodrama. "Wait, Ken, I didn't mean it like that. You know if I get the other job, I'd give a proper two-weeks' notice and work hard in the meantime."

"No, this is right. This is how it's supposed to be and this conversation is now making all of it clear to me. You can drop off your keycard next Monday, or whenever you're back from New Orleans."

Click.

Not even a chance to explain himself. Spoon dropped the mobile onto the table and put his head in his hands. Now he was unemployed, and rescheduling this other job interview may not have helped his chances at that company.

He wondered what would have happened if he'd stayed in Australia instead of coming to the States. He could have apprenticed as a tradie, out on weekdays in his high-vis gear, working on telephone lines or cable like his dad had for thirty years of his life.

"You've cocked it up now, Spoon," he said as he swallowed the last doughy bite of bagel.

What if he didn't get the other job? He and Reagan had just moved in together, and it's not as if they could pay their steep rent with her tips from waitressing.

Spoon returned upstairs. He dug into his suitcase and retrieved a small, felt-covered box. He opened it and looked at the sparkle of diamonds glaring back at him. The engagement ring he was going to give to Reagan in New Orleans, once he'd gotten the job and they had started to look for a place to live there. Now what the bloody hell was he going to do with all that?

CHAPTER FOURTEEN

8:15 am

As Reagan trudged along the Tonahutu trail between Granite Falls and Haynach Lake, she slowly settled into the blue-day realization that she was alone. Not literally. Her two cousins were huffing and puffing behind her, she had a host of friends in Austin and a boyfriend in Denver who loved her. She was alone in the sense that she was twenty-four and her parents were gone. Again, not literally. Her mother still existed, as far as she knew, but since that woman had mailed divorce papers to her father a few years ago from California, no one had seen or heard from her.

But now she supposed she was a grown-up because she had no one to fall back on. Stepmother Anne was going to fade away and disappear. Drink herself right into the arms of some other man to fulfill her needs. She had no real reason to stick around now that nothing tied her to Reagan.

Reagan and her companions crossed a tiny log bridge over a rushing creek, and the bridge was a single log laid across the water, broken and dipping into the water in the middle. They passed one at a time, not sure if it would hold all three of them. The water below was clear and bubbly, but looked the color of tea because of the rocks below.

After a few minutes of silence, they came upon a crumbling log cabin with no roof and nothing inside.

"What's that?" Charlie said.

"I'd guess it's an old ranger outpost," Reagan said. "Avalanche killed it, probably, so they abandoned the thing."

Charlie smacked his hiking pole against a decaying log, then nodded at her.

The trail became muddier, and often they had to jump across sections of miniature pools like rice patties created from the clomping of horse hooves. Then they traversed a series of dog-leg switchbacks that crested a rim and descended into a small meadow full of aspens. The change in tree types meant another shift in elevation, and the skinny aspen husks rose from the ground like a thousand bony fingers waving to her.

"What do we do if we see a bear?" Charlie said, hustling to pull even with her. He'd donned a Broncos cap, probably to cast a shadow over his sunburned cheeks. She doubted either of them had brought any sunscreen.

"Probably nothing," she said. "It won't bother us unless we get in its way. If we have to, we can throw a rock at it. But, like the moose herd, we'll avoid them if we can."

"Roger that, good buddy," Charlie said, smiling at her. He seemed to be trying to cheer her up, and she guessed that she'd been unable to hide the redness in her eyes and the weight dragging her face into a constant frown.

But the bears didn't concern her. Instead, it was the key against her thigh. With every step, it dragged on her like a dumbbell weighing pounds instead of less than an ounce. Where was the lock that fit it? Safety-deposit box? Lockbox? Safe? If the key opened a safe, then where? Dad had a safe in the house, but that opened with a combination.

"Let's stay focused on getting to Haynach by lunchtime," she said. "That'll keep us on track to getting up and over Flattop before mid-afternoon."

"Sounds like a plan," Dalton said. "If Charlie can keep his fat ass in gear."

Reagan shot Dalton daggers, and he seemed to remember he'd agreed to take it easy on Charlie. He tossed an uneasy flick of the head in her direction.

An older couple emerged from between two trees ahead. They were arguing as they hiked, in some language other than English. Reagan turned her ear toward them to focus on the words. She'd never understood why she was more likely to see European and Asian people in American National Parks than actual Americans. They didn't appreciate this immense beauty down the road from their cities.

When Reagan reached a spot in the trail under the shade of a giant boulder, they paused to check the map. Identifying the peaks to the north and south overshadowing the trail would give her a more exact location. She hunted the map and figured the jagged one to the north was Nakai peak, and Snowdrift was the one to the south. The looming specter of the steep and grassy Flattop Mountain dominated the view to the west. She studied this for a minute, and based on the distance, they should have found the turnoff for Haynach already.

"Did either of you see a wooden sign? Would have been small, like the ones that tell you to turn off for the different backcountry sites."

Dalton and Charlie glanced at each other.

"I didn't see shit," Dalton said. "Just trees and rocks and more trees and rocks."

Reagan scanned the map again as she eased the rope hipbelt away from her skin to get a little break from the burning. The blue line indicating Tonahutu creek, which led to Haynach, turned on the map just before the dotted gray line indicating the hiking trail. "Anyone remember the creek turning, at least?"

Recognition flashed in Charlie's face. "Oh, yeah. That was a little while ago. Twenty, thirty minutes. It was at a bend, going uphill."

Reagan folded the map and stuffed it in her pocket. "We have to go back."

"Why?" Dalton said. "I thought we were under this big time crunch to get up over Flathead before the storms came in."

Reagan didn't say because Haynach was where she and Dad had eaten lunch on the second day of their trip. She'd tried to explain the importance of that to Dalton yesterday, and he hadn't seemed to care.

No matter what, she was going to stick to the itinerary. They could give her that, at least.

"Because we need to go to Haynach," she said, and left it at that.

Dalton grumbled and Charlie simply turned and started hiking. Reagan followed, cursing herself for daydreaming about the key and not spending enough time focusing on the trail. Without focus, people wandered off and died. It happened all the time in the park, even though they were only a few miles in different directions from thousands of people in the little mountain towns like Estes Park and Granby.

So they hiked back through the aspens, over the crest and through the switchbacks. She kept listening for the water, watching the side of the trail for a small post with a rectangular wooden sign.

"Wait a second," Dalton said. "If the trail goes west, and the creek is back there, and Haynach is north, why don't we just turn here? It's north, right? Let's go off the trail and we'll eventually find it. I know we'll find it." ·

Reagan considered this as she squinted through the thicket of trees in the direction Dalton had pointed. "I don't think we should. If we go off trail, we could end up totally lost."

"Maybe you already know what you're looking for, but we don't," Dalton muttered, barely loud enough for Reagan to hear. He flashed a look at her, then his face fell and he diverted his eyes to the ground.

The statement came across as an accident; something he hadn't meant to say. But even more confusing was his tone and the way he seemed to catch himself after he said it.

She stared at him, and he remained frozen in place.

What the hell did he mean?

She didn't have time to puzzle it out now. They were against the clock, always against the clock. They were alone in the woods and always against the clock.

Against the empty casket.

"We're going to keep on the trail," she said. She was aware that running the show wasn't earning her too many popularity points, but this was her hike and they would have to deal with it.

The three of them pressed on, no wooden sign in sight. A collection of black birds gathered on an overhanging tree branch all launched at once, painting the sky in a dozen dots. Their caws bounced between the nearby trees like the ricochet of bullets.

Eventually, the sound of running water became clear and they glimpsed the creek.

"What the fuck?" Dalton said. "I swear, I was like a hawk looking for that sign. It's just not there."

"What do we do, Reagan?" Charlie said.

"The sign must be gone. We'll have to follow the creek."

Hip raw from the belt, shoulders aching, jaw tense, she led them along the water.

Following the stream was certainly not as desirable as following a trail, because the park rangers and volunteers regularly removed fallen branches, swept away brush and kept the path free of obstacles. Off the trail, patches of leftover spring snow still sat clumped in dirty piles sometimes four or five feet tall. Fallen trees had to be navigated, which Reagan found challenging with a bulky thirty-pound obstruction clinging to her back. Since the sleeping bag was strapped to the bottom, she kept reaching behind to feel for it.

Within minutes, Reagan and her cousins were slogging through muck created by melting snow. Boots made sucking sounds with each step. Dad had once covered his boots with trash bags and cinched them with bungee cords. At the time, Reagan thought the idea brilliant. She wished she had trash bags now.

The makeshift rope hipbelt dug into her, twisting the Indian burn deeper with every step.

Charlie and Dalton started complaining about their socks getting soaked and rubbing against their feet. She wanted to snap at them because the off trail journey was not her fault, but she'd ultimately made the decision for the group to pursue it. Their wet feet were her responsibility. Little fingers of guilt stroked her chest, and she struggled to resist the urge to ask everyone if they were okay. Not her problem.

Fifteen minutes into their creek-following excursion, no one was speaking to anyone else. And that silence allowed her to hear the grunting sounds.

Reagan halted, and Dalton and Charlie did soon after. She first thought it sounded like a moose or elk rooting through the carcass of a dead animal. Sniffing, eating, grunting.

Then Dalton exploded with laughter and pointed to a spot on the rocks uphill.

Two human faces. A topless woman leaning over a waist-high boulder and a man standing behind her, thrusting. Both of them froze in fear, wide eyed and slack-jawed.

Charlie looked mortified, but Dalton nearly fell over with glee.

"Busted," Dalton yelled through the trees. "Thought you could get in some deep-woods fucking, but there's always someone around. Don't need to stop just because we're here, though. Don't you go giving that poor dipshit blue balls!"

The couple separated and yanked up their pants, looks of indescribable embarrassment on their faces. The woman did her best to cover her face with one of her hands. Reagan cringed for her because she flashed on a memory from high school when she thought her parents had gone out to dinner, and she and a boyfriend were alone in her room. Reagan's dad threw the door open as she was climbing on top of her boyfriend, both of them naked and entirely exposed. The expression of horror on her face matched the one on Dad's face. She couldn't look him in the eyes for days afterward. Worse to walk in on your parents having sex, or worse for them to discover *you* having sex? Reagan thought she had experienced the answer to that question.

Dalton howled with delight as the lovers scurried to get dressed.

Reagan scowled at the malicious joy he seemed to take from the experience. "Come on, Dalton, they're embarrassed enough as it is. Let them have a little bit of…" The word she was looking for was *dignity*, but it caught in her throat when Dalton turned his stare onto her. His eyes bored into her as the joy melted away from his face.

With a cold, straight expression, he said, "no problem, cuz. You're the boss." And with that, he turned back toward the creek and started to walk.

The speed at which he gave up and fell into line unnerved her. He'd been nothing but a hindrance to every effort so far to keep them on track. First, the odd statement about how she knew something they didn't, and now this? Why had he so suddenly changed? What was going on with her cousin?

"My feet are killing me," Charlie said.

"We'll be at the lake soon," Reagan said. "Just swap your wet socks out for a dry pair. We'll take the trail back because it'll be easy to find once we're by the water. No muck that way."

"Oh, um… I only have one pair," Charlie said.

"One pair?" Reagan said. "You're always supposed to bring a backup."

"I thought we were supposed to pack light, and shit like that," Dalton said.

"You too? Come on, guys. You're acting like you've never been camping before."

Charlie lowered his head like a shamed dog. Dalton started whistling and hooked his thumbs into the shoulder straps of his pack.

Reagan wondered what else they hadn't brought. Emergency blankets? Water purifying tablets in case something happened to the water filter?

For fifteen more minutes, they hiked through the muck and Reagan thought about Spoon, how she wished she could call him, how she wished he could be here to nuzzle her neck and tell her that transporting Dad's ashes was *a good thing*, how it was *a necessary thing*. She would tell him the hardly-believable story of the couple in the woods and then his hot breath on her neck would wipe her memory clean.

They reached a clearing and up ahead the trees broke, just to their right. She approached it and saw the dirt line through the grass, meaning they'd found the trail again. A wave of relief lifted her.

Charlie cheered as Reagan checked the sky. The sun was not quite overhead, so they had a little time to spare. The lake was still a few more minutes along the trail, but her aching glutes told her she had to rest a minute.

She took off her pack and winced as the rope hipbelt released from her hips. If there was any ointment in the first aid kit, she was going to need it tonight.

"Why are you stopping?" Charlie said. "I thought we weren't going to break for lunch until the lake. Aren't we close?"

"Yeah," she said. "You guys go ahead. I'll catch up in a minute."

Charlie returned to the trail, but Dalton dropped his pack. "I gotta see a guy about a horse," he said, and then wandered back into the trees.

Reagan looked for a nearby fallen log to sit, and when she was off her feet, the soreness disguised by the adrenaline of constant motion caught up with her. She desperately wanted to take off her boots and rub the feet that had been terrorized by wet wool socks for the last half mile.

But when she sat, a thought struck her. The note. Too upset last night to read it, she'd pushed it from her mind and hadn't considered it yet today.

Glancing left and right, she was alone.

She reached into her cargo pocket and took it out. Ran her thumb over the handwritten R. She wanted to open and read it, but also didn't want to open and read it. Those words were the last Dad would ever speak to her. Should she save it for later? No, she needed to read it now and hear whatever he had to say to her. Maybe it explained the key. Maybe it explained a lot of things.

The note was a single piece of paper, folded into quarters. She unfolded it once. Then a rustling in the trees and the crunch of twigs filled her ears.

Dalton.

Something came over her and she shoved the note pack into her pocket. The little voice of fear told her that Dalton wasn't supposed to see it. She straightened up and put on an innocent face, as she used to do when her parents walked in while she was too close to a boy on the couch. Nothing to see here, thank you very much.

"Hey cuz, whatcha doing?" he said.

"Just resting," she said, but there was a glint in his eye that suggested he didn't believe her.

CHAPTER FIFTEEN

9:00 am

Spoon tried again to phone Reagan, but it went straight to voicemail. He wasn't sure what he would have said if she'd picked up. Tell her about losing his current job? Tell her the prospective job might not be there anymore? Tell her nothing and say he couldn't wait to see her again?

Seated on the couch in the living room of her father's house with a laptop warming his thighs, Spoon ran through the possibilities when the front door opened and Anne strode in. Seeing her spurred a resurgence of his desire to find transportation around town.

She had a yoga mat under her arm, hair pinned back, and she was wearing skin-tight clothes. For a woman who must have been on the dark side of forty, she had quite a nice figure. Flat stomach, well-shaped calves, perspiration highlighting the cleavage line in the v-neck of her shirt. Then Spoon felt guilty for noticing.

"Hello, darling," she said. "Good to see you're up and around."

"Slept in a bit. Stayed up a little too late coding."

"I can't wait to hear all about it," she said in a breezy voice, which suggested she had no desire to hear about it. She dropped the yoga mat on the floor and walked into the kitchen. When she returned two minutes later, she was dunking a celery stick into a glass of red liquid.

He'd been sober long enough that being around people who drank no longer bothered him, but Anne seemed to imbibe non-stop. He sneaked a glance at the wall clock. "Don't you reckon it's a bit early to have a drink?"

She snorted a laugh. "Reckon. You're precious. Hate to break it to you, but this isn't the first drink I've had today."

He blinked. "You go to yoga drunk."

"I don't do anything without a few drinks in me. And before you try to preach some of your recovering alcoholic nonsense to me, just know I'm a lost cause, darling." She said this last bit with a wry grin on her face, as if it were all some big joke.

He had considered trying to share some of his drinking experience with her, like the time he jumped into jellyfish infested waters in Queensland and nearly died because he was too pissed to realize what he was doing. But he knew enough to withhold the advice for drunks not yet ready to hear it. One of the cardinal rules of AA: no recruiting. "I've always been a staunch supporter of lost causes, but I wouldn't dream of it."

She sat on the couch next to him and patted the brace over his knee. "Why don't you entertain me with some stories from the red continent? Tell me about wrestling crocodiles, or riding kangaroos, or something like that."

"Afraid I can't say I've ever wrestled a crocodile."

She leaned over, closer to him, deliberately pushing her cleavage into view. "Come on now, don't hold out on me."

She extended her neck so that she was within inches of his face as beads of sweat slid from her neck to her collarbone. The mixture of sweat and alcohol and some kind of fruity fragrance wafted into his nostrils. His heart thumped against his ribcage.

"Mrs. Darby, I'm not sure what…"

"I told you to call me Anne," she said as she set her drink on the coffee table. She put her hand on his good knee and gave it a light squeeze. "That football injury didn't put all of your parts out of commission, did it?"

Elevated heartbeat turned into panic. Had he two good knees, he might have jumped up from the couch right then. But her hand pressed on his leg, effectively paralyzing him. "You seem nice, Anne, but I don't think this is a good idea."

"I've built my career on bad ideas. There's no one else here. No one else is going to be here for days. And if you and I have a little fun, there's no reason anyone has to know about it."

She caressed his leg and leaned in toward his neck, lips parting. For a split second, the warmth of her wet mouth above his collarbone shocked and thrilled him. But only a second. Like snapping awake, he became fully aware of the situation. He placed his hands on her shoulders, then pushed her back to arm's length.

"We can't do this."

Her eyes flicked open. "Are you stupid? You're not going to take what I'm offering here?"

She leaned in again, and he threw his shoulders into pushing against her this time. He used a little too much force, as she slid off the couch, yelping as her tailbone connected with the floor.

He sat upright and scooted back to the edge of the sofa. "Anne, please, I'm heaps sorry. I didn't mean to hurt you... just... please don't do that again. You have to understand that nothing like that can happen between us. I love Reagan and I can't do that to her."

She ran a hand over her brow to flatten strands of wayward hair against her scalp. Her lips jittered as tears welled in her eyes, and Spoon fought a reflex to reach out and place a soothing hand on her shoulder. Reagan's words echoed in his head from the last night they were together. *Don't trust my stepmom.*

"Damn it," she moaned as she smacked a closed fist against her thigh. "Jesus Christ. What the hell am I doing?"

He had no idea what the right move was. Comfort her, not comfort her. There seemed to be no good choice.

"No worries," he said. "It was a simple mistake, that's all." He waited, hoping she would leave, stop crying, or do something. She seemed to be stuck in place.

"It's always a mistake. You probably think I'm a terrible person." She walked to the stairs and leaned over the banister, lightly thumping her head against the wood. "You ever have pain that stays with you for a long time, then when it's gone, you've gotten so used to it, it feels wrong for it to be gone?"

Spoon stared at his knee injury, with no idea how to respond to that. He couldn't imagine the grief she was going through.

"And what does it say about me that I put up with it for so long?"

In a few seconds, she wiped her face and strode to the front door. She grabbed her keys, slid one of the keys off the ring, and stuck it in the waistband of her pants. Then she left.

Spoon readjusted himself on the couch so he was facing the door, trying to make sense of everything that had happened. The room became still, only the ticking of the wall clock to break the silence. His mind swam.

Five minutes later, Anne re-entered the house, her face now bright and lively. An entirely different woman. "You still need a car?"

"I thought I might go to a meeting," he said. He didn't say that he also intended to check out A1 Lawnmower Repair and its proprietor Tyson at some stage today.

She tossed a key in an arc toward him. "I switched cars with the neighbor for the next two days. It's an automatic, so you should be able to drive it."

Spoon gripped the key, now totally confused and unsure what to think about his host. "Ta."

"Ta?"

"That's Aussie for thanks." He considered mentioning the fumbling attempt at seduction, how it had probably been a misunderstanding, how maybe they would be able to talk about it once they'd both calmed down and gotten some perspective.

But whilst he was thinking about it, Anne left him and walked into the kitchen. "I have to run some errands in a minute," she said from the other room.

"Don't you need a car?"

"I have my bike. If you go out, you can leave the door unlocked." The sound of a blender roared from the kitchen.

Any chance to get clear about what had happened was going to have to wait. He took the opportunity to walk away from the craziness and gather his things from upstairs as quickly as his crutch-bound legs would carry him.

Stepping outside for the first time today, he breathed in a lungful of the thin Colorado air. He still hadn't adjusted to the altitude, and moving too quickly made him lightheaded. But being outside the house, he already felt the prison shackles of boredom lifting.

And that's when he saw the strangest thing.

Across the street was the same blue Chevy Tahoe from yesterday, parked along the curb. A large and ruddy-faced bloke was sitting in the driver's side of the ute. When Spoon first noticed him, the man had been staring directly at him, but he quickly sunk into the seat and lowered his eyes. The deliberate avoidance unsettled Spoon.

The man wasn't Tyson, but might as well have been. Same build, same leather jacket, same facial hair even. The only thing missing was the banana-shaped scar under his eye.

Spoon took a few steps toward the ute, and the man started it up, but didn't leave. He lifted a mobile to his ear and said a few words, then hung up the call. Spoon wondered if he took a couple more steps in that direction if the car would tear down the street.

He got the distinct impression that this man knew Tyson. Why he felt this, he could not say, but the more he stared at the bloke now looking away from him, the more he felt sure that this man was there to watch the house.

CHAPTER SIXTEEN

10:45 am

As his socks dried on the rock next to him, Dalton stared out over Haynach Lake and thought that it didn't seem much like a lake. In the shape of a swimming pool designed by one of those weird French artists he had to read about back in high school, the water stretched barely two-fifty feet by four hundred feet. Didn't look all that deep, either.

The peaks around it were impressive, though. Big, jagged rocky things with crumbles of boulder at their bases. He saw mountains all the time from Denver, but there was something different about being right up next to them, with no Starbucks or McDonalds to obscure the view. It almost made him feel peaceful, except for the birds in the trees that wouldn't shut up.

Yesterday, any time he stopped hiking, ants instantly swarmed his feet, but there were none around here. Fewer mosquitoes, too.

His little brother Charlie was sprawled next to him on the same spacious rock, eyes closed, soaking up the sun. Charlie's big fat belly rose and fell with each asthmatic breath.

Dalton pulled his pack close and readjusted the cinch Reagan had made to keep the innards from tumbling out. He had thought it impressive at the time, but it kept slipping while they hiked, and he had to check the ground behind him every few minutes to make sure his crap wasn't leaking out on the trail. At least he kept his weed in a waterproof container in his pocket. If that became ruined, he'd be in for a shitty trip.

But his backpack, his weed, or his wet socks weren't what concerned him so much as his brother napping on the broad rock hanging over Haynach Lake. He needed a commitment from Charlie that when the shit went down, he was going to man up and do what needed to be done.

And then there was that piece of paper she'd hidden from him when he came back from pissing a little while ago. Maybe directions to the money stash. Entirely possible.

Dalton scanned the shoreline for Reagan, and she was a few hundred feet away, kneeling in front of the water. She had one hand below the surface, occasionally bringing a handful of water up and then letting it slip through her fingers. As if she was going to drink it, but changing her mind each time. Also, she was crying. Dalton understood her when she was crying. Her dad just died. But when she turned into the determined, bossy, *hurry hurry hurry the storms are coming* hiker-bitch, she was like a different person. He wanted to say, *just relax, cuz. Enjoy all this nature and stop worrying so much about every little thing. And tell me where the damn money is so I don't have to go back to Tyson with nothing.*

Maybe not the last part.

Regardless, she was out of earshot, so Dalton nudged Charlie. "Hey, fatty."

Charlie murmured and turned on his side.

Dalton nudged him again, and Charlie opened his eyes. "Oh, wow," Charlie said. "My lower back hurts. Does your back hurt?"

"A lot of things hurt. If your back hurts, probably means you put too much heavy stuff at the bottom of your pack."

Charlie sat up. "How did you know that?"

"Boy scouts." Dalton took a tube of lotion from his pocket and squirted some on the days-old tattoo on his forearm, then spread the shiny substance over the inked flesh. "Look, Charlie, we need to talk about what's going to happen. What I said to you this morning, about what we have to do out here..."

Charlie turned his head and looked at Reagan. "I don't know about all that."

"What's not to know?"

"Look at her," Charlie said. "She's so sad. She's trying to keep it together, but I heard her crying in her tent last night. You know, I understand what he wants, and I understand why it has to be done, but can't it wait a few weeks? Can't we let her have this, and then let him deal with it once we're all back?"

"Because, genius, once she finds the money, she and that limey boyfriend of hers are going to up and skip town, and then Tyson doesn't get paid back for what Uncle Mitch stole, and we look like idiots for letting them get away with it. How can I make it any more clear to you?"

Reagan stood up and started walking toward them, wiping her eyes with the back of her hand. She'd be close enough to hear their conversation in thirty seconds.

Dalton grabbed his brother by the arm. "I need to know now if you're in or not. We can spend days arguing about when it would be the most convenient for everyone, but we're running out of time with this shit."

Charlie shook his head. "This isn't right. I've done a lot of things for you before, but I don't know if I can go along with you on this one. She's our cousin and that should mean something."

"Damn it, Charlie, I'm your *brother*. That means more, and you're going to do what I'm asking because of that. Don't make me give some long, drawn-out speech here."

Reagan was close enough that Dalton could see the redness of her eyes. He kept his eyes low, trying not to attract attention.

Charlie blew a sigh through his nose. "You lied to me about why we came. I'm still trying to decide if I've forgiven you for that."

Reagan cleared her throat, not looking at them. She probably hadn't heard what they were saying, or at least she didn't give any indication of anything weird.

She spoke as if she'd been gargling gravel. "We should get going."

Dalton nodded and pulled on his socks, which were still wet enough that he had to yank on them to get them past his ankle. He glared at his brother, who pretended not to notice the eyes on him.

Charlie was going to do the right thing. He had to.

CHAPTER SEVENTEEN

9:15 am

Spoon couldn't help but gawk at the heavyset bloke in the blue Chevy Tahoe parked across the street. He tried to pretend he didn't think this man was there to watch the house. Or something worse than that.

Now he had to have a think about what to do: confront him, go back inside the house and do nothing, or ignore him and investigate the lawnmower shop as planned.

Spoon walked to the car parked in the neighbor's driveway and got in. Black Lexus, late model. This year's or last year's, he wasn't sure. He ran his hands over the clean dashboard, appreciating the neighbor's excellent taste and attention to detail.

The Lexus purred like a cat as he turned the key. Spoon adjusted the rearview mirror so he could see the blue ute and the man inside, who was sneaking glances at Spoon over the top of his sunglasses.

Spoon eased the car out of the driveway, wincing at how the slight bend in his knee caused him a significant amount of pain. The ibuprofen wasn't getting the job done today.

He straightened the car on the street and readjusted the rearview so he could see behind him, then drove through the neighborhood toward the main street. He kept checking the mirror for the blue truck to start up, but it didn't.

As the Lexus glided past the rows of identical suburban American houses, he wondered what the hell he was doing. Going to the lawnmower shop, yes, but was he going to rock up to Tyson and demand answers? Probably not, but he at least had to see the place for himself. Get a better idea of whom he was dealing with.

When he reached the main street, he turned on his blinker and pulled out into traffic, barely catching the blue ute pulling away from the curb out of the edge of his vision.

"Okay. Okay. Let's just see what happens here."

Spoon tried to keep his hands loose on the steering wheel. He had no proof of anything yet, so best to wait until there was more information. He drove straight for two minutes before fumbling his mobile out of his pocket so he could open the Maps app and find out where he was going. It's not as if he knew his way around Denver and its suburbs. He looked back and forth between the road and his mobile as he tried to type "A1 Lawnmower" into the search bar with his thumb.

Then he caught the Chevy Tahoe in his rearview.

Several cars back, but the ute was there. Navy-colored, with extra-wide sideview mirrors and lots of chrome on the front grille. No mistaking it.

He dropped the mobile on the passenger seat and put two hands on the wheel.

"Alright, Spoon, no need to get nervous. Plenty of reasons why some hefty American Hell's Angel bikie behind the wheel of a gas guzzler would have been parked outside the house you're staying at and then decide to leave at exactly the same time and drive down the exact same street."

Spoon had never had a tail before. He didn't know the protocol.

He'd make a few turns and see how his tail would react. Through the first turn, he figured he'd lost the ute behind him, then it reappeared. The big blue monstrosity started to look like a shark back there, looming closer, the teeth of its grille ready to bite him once it got close enough.

Another turn, then a minute later, a flash of blue rejoined him.

Spoon needed a plan. *Why* the ute was behind him was a question he could only answer if he could ask the bloke inside it. And that wasn't likely to happen.

So how was he going to find out what was going on?

He ticked the boxes on what he knew so far: some big guy named Tyson had berated Anne yesterday morning. Anne hadn't wanted to talk about it, she'd shrugged it off as nothing, but her words were lies. Tyson thought she was hiding something. Money, most likely, or property, or something else that had belonged to Reagan's dad that Tyson was looking for. But that still didn't explain why they would bother to follow a gimp-kneed Australian around town. What could that possibly gain?

Unless, they figured Anne had told him something. Maybe they were waiting for him to leave so they could tail him and find the location of the... whatever they wanted. Too many unanswered questions.

He slowed to see how close the blue ute would get, but it maintained a distance of at least a couple cars at all times. According to the movies Spoon had seen, this meant the guy knew what he was doing.

Spoon had to get tricky. Driving up and down wide, easily-navigated main streets wasn't going to improve the distance from the car behind him. He turned onto a narrower residential street, which he assumed would give him some breathing room. If this guy was as good as Spoon thought he was, he wasn't going to tail him closely on a street with hardly any other cars. Way too obvious.

For a full thirty seconds, the truck hadn't turned. Spoon looked back and the truck had stopped in the street, blinker on, waiting to turn.

Then came his salvation.

The street was wide, with two lanes and a grassy divider separating them. Every few hundred meters, the median broke to allow cars to turn. Spoon slowed at one of these turns and yanked the wheel left to cut it as quickly as possible.

Once he'd turned, he executed the second half of his getaway. Before him was a three-story house with an open two-car garage and no cars inside. He eased into the garage and turned the key to kill the engine. The Lexus went from running to off like flicking a switch. He reclined his seat so his head was less visible, grimacing from the pain even slight movement caused his knee.

114

He waited, checked the mirror. Then it occurred to him that if the garage door was open, someone was home. He had just driven a car whose owner he didn't know into someone else's private garage. Grand theft auto as well as trespassing.

A child's bicycle hung on hooks along the back wall. On the right side of the garage was a door, presumably into the house. Spoon had a vision of some crotchety yank with a shotgun racing through that door, blasting the windshield of the Lexus into a million pieces.

He gripped the keys in the ignition and checked the rearview again. Still no Chevy Tahoe.

"Shit, Spoon, what are you doing?"

Check the door. Check the rearview. Something had to move. His pulse throbbed against his neck, making it difficult for him to swallow.

Just then, the ute drove past on the street, and Spoon knew he'd worn out his welcome in the stranger's garage. He started the car, and despite the urge to chuck it in reverse and peel out on to the street to get the hell away, he kept his movements calm and easy as he backed the car out.

The blue ute slowed at the end of the residential street, about to turn onto the next main street.

Spoon first kept the Lexus at a crawl, then a little faster as his former pursuer turned and escaped his sight. He arrived at the main street and pulled out, now several cars behind.

Spoon laughed as the tension bled out of him. Must be what James Bond felt like.

He told himself to stay two cars back and out of direct sight. Now behind the ute, with the advantage on his side, this was a much easier proposition.

Spoon followed the ute for fifteen minutes, and as far as he knew, the fat American bikie piloting the truck remained oblivious. They drove through a business district then onto a highway, finally exiting through a loop to a side street. The Maps app told him they were now in the Broomfield suburb, so Spoon had a good idea where they were going.

Then the destination came into view. A1 Lawnmower Repair, a building the size of a one-room house, with a dodgy shingled roof that looked one rainstorm away from collapsing and a chain-link fence surrounding three sides of the exterior. A graveyard of lawnmowers littered the fenced-in area. The windows of the shop were dark, and a flickering neon sign in one of them read *Open*.

He kept on driving as the Tahoe parked in one of the three available spaces in front of the shop. Spoon turned into a lot across the street, a tiny place that seemed to be a combination tattoo parlor and coffee shop named The Slinky Grape. Odd name, even odder combination of business ideas, but Spoon wasn't bothered enough to give it much more thought.

The Slinky Grape had parking on three sides of the shop, so Spoon drove behind it and then back around, parking under the shade of an awning, but with a clear view of the lawnmower shop.

The fat man stepped out of the blue ute and meandered across the lot to another man hunched over a lawnmower. That man stood up. Tyson. Their hefty bellies pointed at each other like dogs baring teeth.

The man who had been following Spoon lowered his head and spoke.

Tyson flexed a hand, then slapped the other man. He actually slapped him, hard across the jaw. The follower took a step back, put a hand to his jaw, but did nothing in retaliation.

Spoon sat shocked for a few seconds, then got his bearings. The dynamic started to make sense. Tyson was the boss. And, if Spoon had interpreted the situation correctly, he'd punished his employee for losing the guy he was supposed to tail.

Maybe this was more serious that Spoon had thought. He'd been silly not to consider the possibility of violence, especially if money was involved. If this was how Tyson treated people who seemingly worked for him, how would he treat Anne? Or anyone else?

Now, the problem was: what to do about it? He'd come here and seen what he wanted to see, but he was no better off than he was this morning. He still had more questions than answers, and confronting Tyson didn't seem like a smart move. A man who would slap another man in public may be willing to do a lot more inside the privacy of his shop. Spoon's secondary school boxing club days were long gone, and a bum knee didn't lend itself to much movement.

He waited until they had both gone and then searched the Maps app for Reagan's house. As he drove back, a million thoughts raced through his mind. What kind of trouble was Anne into? She'd shoved the will into Tyson's chest, trying to get him to look at it. She'd said the will was a record of "the nothing" Reagan's dad had left them. Tyson seemed to think that was a lie, and Anne knew something she wasn't telling. Maybe she did. Maybe Spoon needed to redouble his efforts and encourage her to have a chat to him about it.

When he got back to the house, he parked on the street and went inside. His adrenaline had subsided and his knee ached, so what he most wanted was to lie down and come up with a new plan.

Anne wasn't home, but fortunately, she'd left the front door unlocked for him.

Once inside, he lumbered upstairs and entered Reagan's room. He opened the nightstand so he could toss the car key into the drawer, but as soon as he pulled it open, three little bottles rattled around inside. Reagan's pills.

He picked up one of the bottles, turning it in his hands and reading the label. The realization dawned on him that if these pills were here, then Reagan might be without her medication.

Maybe these were spare bottles. If that was the case, no big deal. But if they weren't, and she was in the park without her meds...

He instinctively reached for his mobile, phoned Reagan, and received no answer.

CHAPTER EIGHTEEN

11:45 am

Reagan and her two companions hustled from Haynach to the main Tonahutu trail as the sun pelted them from above. The vast difference between the near-freezing temperatures of night and the sweltering heat of the summer midday sun shocked Reagan, despite having hiked and camped in Rocky Mountain National Park dozens of times over the last decade.

But, as with every day, patches of clouds threatened to gather and become vicious storms. She moved as fast as her legs would carry her, hoping her cousins would do the same. The rain was just an annoyance at lower elevations, but storms above treeline might hold real danger if they weren't down the other side in time.

Toward Flattop Mountain, the terrain changed as they broached 10,000 feet in elevation. Disintegrating logs, crumbling from years of rain, lined the sides of the trail. The taller trees of sub-alpine became alpine tundra's bushes and twisted shrubs. Thick glades of trees gave way to sparse and grassy open areas littered with fractured boulders. Packed snow on the sides of the trail that were random piles at lower elevations became patches covering dozens of square feet.

Reagan's glutes burned as the terrain became ever-steeper. Keeping a wary distance from the humans, elk grazed on the nearby slopes. A marmot chirped at Reagan as she strode past it. Its presence meant they were close to treeline.

When she and Dad had broached treeline two years ago, he flicked pebbles at marmots for fun. The bushy-tailed, obese squirrel-like creatures barked their high-pitched chirps in return. At first, she was appalled, then after the fourth or fifth marmot went scurrying, little involuntary giggles escaped her lips. He always had the ability to take something inappropriate and make it fun.

Dad. Empty casket. Note in her pocket that she couldn't get any alone time to read. Dalton saying strange things and then pretending he'd said nothing. The key. Aching to see Spoon. Her mind swirled with so many things, she couldn't concentrate on any one of them for more than a few seconds.

Reagan turned back to examine the zig-zag of the valley deepening below them as they climbed, and oddly enough, Charlie was right behind her but Dalton wasn't. She waited until Charlie hiked past her line of sight so she could see beyond him, and then she knew why. Wisps of smoke were rising from Dalton's mouth as he climbed, three switchbacks down, about five hundred feet below.

"You wouldn't have trouble with your breathing if you'd put that thing out," she called to him, thinking he was holding a cigarette.

"Fuck that. You've got it backward. This right here is my Gatorade," he yelled, holding up what she could now see was a thick joint.

She pursed her lips, not in the mood to have yet another confrontation on the trail. But they would discuss it later, for sure. Then, Reagan gasped at the sight of the green and gray outfit of a park ranger as the woman rounded a switchback ahead. She was only a few hundred feet above and could probably see exactly what Dalton was doing from that short distance.

Reagan's heart bounced into her throat. If Dalton were caught smoking pot, they could all share the blame for it. Trip over.

She tried to whip around to shout at Dalton, but the quick movement and weight of her pack knocked her off balance, and she tumbled into the grass next to the trail. The makeshift rope hipbelt dug into her side. With the wind knocked out of her, she had to gasp to catch her breath.

The park ranger raced around the trail turns to reach her. "Oh, dear, are you okay?"

Reagan looked up at the woman hovering over her. The standard-issue Stetson hat shrouded the woman's face in shadow.

"I'm fine," Reagan said. "Just turned around too fast. Thank you for stopping, though."

Charlie stopped hiking, and Reagan caught sight of Dalton approaching the nearest bend in the trail, now joint-free.

"What seems to be the trouble here, officer?" Dalton said, laughing. "I'm not sure if this young lady knows how to hike. She may need to be airlifted out of here."

The park ranger leaned closer to Reagan and revealed her face. She was older, with kind gray eyes to complement her silver hair. "These guys with you?"

Reagan nodded and accepted a hand up. "Thank you."

"You going over Flattop?" the ranger asked.

Reagan adjusted her shoulder straps. "Yes, we're staying at July camp tonight."

"Better get a move on. Weather says storms this afternoon. I'll come check on you at July later to make sure you got in safe."

"I appreciate it," Reagan said.

The ranger tipped her hat and continued down the trail. Reagan waited for her to leave earshot range, and then waved for Charlie to take the lead. Charlie's lips parted as if he had something to say, but he shut them and lumbered toward the crest of the mountain.

Reagan seethed at Dalton, red flaring her senses. How could he be so selfish? How could he behave so dangerously, so foolishly, so like a clueless stoner? Submitting to his insistence to come along on this trip began to seem more and more like a terrible idea. Healing, family time… how stupid and idealistic she'd been.

"Listen to me," she said, getting close enough to his face that she could smell the pungent aftertaste of pot on his breath. "Don't do that again. I don't know how she didn't smell it in the air just now, but I'm not kidding when I say all this immature crap ends now. I would tell you that whatever you do in your tent is fine like last night, but you heard her say she's going to come check on us later."

He smirked, pulling his face into the same sarcastic expression he'd worn since he was thirteen years old. "I don't see what the big deal—"

"Don't. Do. That. Again."

Without waiting for him to respond, she dug her poles into the dirt and pressed onward.

They crested Flattop at a little after midday as the clouds were gathering and darkening. Billowing and cottony masses of gray mixed in with charcoal patches streaking across the blue. Despite appearances, the worst rain often came from the lighter ones. The air smelled of rain. She kept waiting for the skies to open up and start pouring.

Flattop was not exactly flat, instead a broad circular shelf with no trees and clear views of most of the surrounding peaks and valleys. A field of green sprinkled with thousands of gray bumps from the rocks half-submerged in the grass. They were roughly in the center of the park, and at the geographical edge of their loop, although the return would take longer due to the side trip to Nokoni and Nanita.

Crossing Flattop and finding the trail to descend the other side would take only a half hour, but during that half hour, they would be without any kind of shelter. Not good to be the tallest thing on a mountain during a lightning storm.

The rain started as they'd hiked halfway across Flattop. At first, a few wet spots appeared on the trail in front of her, then splats connected with her hair, face, and shoulders. The drops were large and heavy, some big enough to cause a reflexive head-jerk. Larger rain was coming. There were no other hikers on the mesa, which was not unusual. The day hikers wouldn't come this deep into the park.

"Let's move it, guys. We're almost there."

"The blister on my pinky toe isn't going to be happy with me," Charlie said.

The first bolt of lightning struck the ground in the distance, briefly illuminating an area to the side of Flattop. She counted *one thousand one, one thous-*

A crack of thunder reverberated across the park. Not even two miles away. Her cousins' packs jostled as they seemed to have finally decided to take the situation seriously and add some haste to their movements.

Reagan quickened her own pace as hair started to slip from her ponytail and fall in chunks around her shoulders, and she wondered if she had wrapped her phone in a baggie or left it sitting inside her pack. Couldn't remember. It would probably not get wet unless the rain kept on for hours, but she'd check as soon as they were below treeline.

Meds.

The thought hit her like a slap across the jaw. With the chaos over the animal-chewed packs, she'd forgotten to take the lithium and Risperdal she took every morning. She hadn't taken them last night either, now that she thought about it. She was too upset about finding the strange key and the seemingly unanswerable question of what lock it might fit.

She tried to picture the pills in her pack, but she couldn't think of where they might be. In the first aid kit? In the same tiny dry-bag where she'd stored the car keys?

The realization that she likely hadn't packed her meds at all began to creep over her. Not good.

Lightning cracked the ground again, and less than a second later, thunder rolled across the surface of Flattop Mountain. That strike had been on the surface of Flattop itself. The rain was steadily growing louder and heavier, falling in sheets that turned the world blurry.

She'd taken the meds yesterday morning when she woke, before she'd packed her gear into the car. She did some quick math: if she couldn't take the pills again until Friday evening, it might be okay. Three days without her lithium sounded iffy, but she'd been stable for long enough that she figured she could handle it. Maybe. Her track record with skipping meds hadn't been the greatest, but her last episode had been a long time ago.

After the hospital and coming home to rest at Dad's house, the doctors had tried several combinations to find something that worked. And even when they found a cocktail of meds that stabilized her moods without making her constantly nauseous, or dizzy, or killing her sex drive, she still didn't like taking them. The psychiatrist switched her from lithium to Depakote, but that only made things worse. The carousel of medication-switching had begun.

Usually, she would try to think of the craziness from her last manic episode or the ruthless self-judgment she'd endured during the depression, and that was enough motivation to take the pills to feel stable, if not a little flat. Meeting Spoon had helped. She wanted to be healthy for him.

Three days without meds. She could do this.

Just as the thought occurred to her, a bolt of lightning struck a hundred feet away.

CHAPTER NINETEEN

1:30 pm

Reagan waved her arms through the dense sheets of rain to get her cousins' attention. When Dalton and Charlie looked at her, with streams of rain cascading from their foreheads, she realized this kind of downpour and lightning had become deadly. She hadn't thought about anything besides her missing meds for several seconds.

"Hunker down," she yelled, and demonstrated by crouching with her elbows resting on her knees.

They both dropped to a crouch. "Shouldn't we keep going, though?" Dalton said, his voice muffled under the splattering of rain on rock. "We're almost at the part where it goes down again and meets the trees. Let's run for it."

All the survival blogs said you were supposed to hunker in a lightning storm. Make yourself low, and if lightning struck, it might pass through without harming you. But how long were they supposed to stay like this? What if the storm didn't pass?

She didn't spend too much time debating and instead leaped to her feet. "Okay. Let's move."

They jogged, and the rope hipbelt yanked at her flesh as it slipped underneath her shirt and rubbed against bare skin. Her shirt, pants, socks, and boots were thoroughly soaked. Her feet sloshed in the boots as she jogged, and the pack bounced around on her back, nearly toppling her with every step.

Priority one was getting below treeline. Priority two had to be dry clothes. Wet clothes could kill.

A bolt struck a few hundred feet to the right.

A thousand feet ahead, two rocks on either side of the trail indicated where the descent began. She focused all her energy on that marker, throwing the left pole as right foot landed, then the right pole as left foot landed. As they ran, the lightning and thunder still flashed and bellowed behind them, but each step took them further away from the worst of it. The rain still fell in sheets and blurred the world into a dark mess, but the danger seemed to be behind them.

At least, that's what she hoped. Like a herd of moose, the storm could move at any time.

She closed the distance to the edge of the shelf, hoping her cousins were behind since she couldn't hear them and didn't want to risk another fall by turning around. When she reached the rocks signaling the beginning of the downward trail, she stopped and eased around to face them. Her cousins were only a few seconds behind her.

Charlie's eyes bulged, his chest heaved, and his face twisted into a grimace. Dalton just looked angry.

Down the trail. A hundred feet this way, sharp turn, a hundred feet that way. Repeat. The ground was already becoming slippery with patches of mud and slick rocks. She wished she had boots with good tread, but too late for that now. At each sharp angle of the switchback, she leaned both poles on the outer edge of the bend, in case the extra weight she carried tried to yank her over the edge of the trail. She wouldn't fall far, but a twisted ankle or bruised knee might strand them.

Sounds of rain and thunder drove her onward.

Within ten minutes, they had reached the trees, and Reagan let out a massive sigh. Her shoulders were so tense that an ache had spread to her neck and the pulse of a headache was forming at the back of her head. The rain still fell, but now they seemed safe.

They all sought shelter under a giant tree, huddled together.

"Whoo!" Dalton said. "Nobody told me that backpacking was like a motherfucking Bourne Identity movie, racing against the clock and all that shit. That was exciting as hell."

Reagan put a hand on Charlie's arm. "You okay?"

He was wheezing, his face red. He struggled to retrieve an inhaler from his pocket. "Just let me… catch… my breath."

"I'm fine, by the way," Dalton said. "Thanks for asking. I'm just soaked." He lowered his eyes to Reagan's shirt. "Nice nips, cuz."

She instinctively crossed her arms in front of her chest, then looked down and saw something like a Fort Lauderdale wet t-shirt contest down there. The sports bra wasn't much help when soaked.

She jabbed the tip of her hiking pole into Dalton's stomach. "I'm your cousin, you pervert," she said, but she laughed a little anyway. Maybe from embarrassment, or maybe the release of tension, but it felt good to hear that sound coming from her mouth. Had she laughed at all since getting the news about Dad? She couldn't remember.

They all turned at once to break cover of the tree, and Charlie took only one step before he stepped onto a rock and slipped.

The events passed in slow-motion: as he fell, his foot hit the ground and twisted one way as his body bent another way. A mewling grunt came from his lips as his body hit the ground.

Reagan gasped, then dropped to her knees and lunged for him. She grabbed him by the shoulders. "Charlie, are you hurt?"

"My ankle," he said, groaning.

"That's great," Dalton said. "Just great."

"It's okay, Charlie. You're going to be fine," Reagan said. "Can you stand?"

Charlie's eyes darted around. Then he nodded and she put her neck under his arm to help him up. Reagan glared at Dalton and he rolled his eyes as he took Charlie's other arm. Together, they lifted Charlie from the ground.

"Don't try to put any weight on it," she said.

"I'm fine, really," Charlie said, but his face tensed and his breaths were labored.

They helped Charlie for a few minutes along the muddy trail, then he insisted on trying it on his own. He seemed to be able to walk, but each time he placed that foot on the ground, he winced and let out a little squeak. He moved like an elderly person, gingerly and unsure.

If they were going to hike at that speed, she could forget about the timetable. Then guilt nagged at her for thinking ill of him when it wasn't his fault. At least Charlie was being cooperative, unlike Dalton, who did nothing but complain and cause problems. Charlie wasn't the villain here.

The camp was supposed to be a mile down the trail, where it flattened out and the steep switchbacks blended into grassy foothills. When they turned off at the backcountry marker after a half hour of slogging through the muck, everyone was cold and tired and grumpy. They barely spoke for twenty minutes and set up camp in silence. The rain had stopped, but the ground was slushy and covered in pine cones and needles from the trees. Boulders and razor-sharp shrub branches occupied the surrounding area.

The campsite had less tree coverage than the previous night, which would mean less chance of a tree falling, but also less shelter from wind or rain. The area was hilly and not flat enough to find level ground for the tents. Sleeping on an angle meant her sleeping bag would slip off the mattress pads all night long, making her have to continually readjust and scoot up.

They debated trying to remove the mushy pine mess versus setting up their tents on top of it, and came to a consensus that a clear campsite wasn't worth the effort to move all the junk out of the way. The ground wouldn't be comfortable, but everyone wanted to get the camp set up sooner rather than later. They put the tents near two logs that lay opposite each other. No stumps nearby big enough for sitting, but the logs would do.

As soon as she'd erected the tent, Reagan brought her pack inside it. She hated to bring something so wet and messy inside a clean tent, but she didn't want her cousins to see her hunting for her meds. They knew she was bipolar, but doing that in front of them would feel weird. None of their business.

She dumped out everything in the pack. Explored every pocket and dry bag. The three pill bottles were not inside any of the possible hiding spots.

Straining her brain, she tried to reconstruct the events of the morning she left… packing, Spoon's story about the beach crabs, kissing him goodbye, driving away. No memory of packing the meds. Could she truly go three full days without medication?

Empty pack. Empty casket.

Her heart started racing. Stay calm and breathe, focus on the task at hand, whatever it may be. She could do this.

After everyone had exchanged dry clothes for sopping wet ones, they gathered on the logs to reassess.

"Your ankle okay?" Reagan asked Charlie.

He raised that leg and rotated it. Agony on his face. "I don't know. But thank you for helping me down the mountain. I know I'm not the… you know, lightest guy."

She shrugged. "Don't worry about it."

"That was one of the scariest experiences of my life," Charlie said. "You know what I'm saying? I was just holding on and praying like crazy to get through it."

"It's been a challenging couple of days," Reagan said, casting a glance at Dalton.

"That's what I mean," Charlie said. "After all that and everything else you've been through, I think it's pretty amazing how put-together you are."

She didn't know what to say to that.

Dalton took a lighter from his pocket and flicked it several times, but no flame came out.

Charlie rested his leg on the log, elevating it as he slid onto the ground. "And at least at a time like this, you have God to turn to. He can be your comfort."

She stared at the mess of pine needles under her feet. She'd been wondering when Charlie was going to get around to this subject. "I don't believe in God."

Charlie's mouth dropped open. "You don't mean that."

"No, I do. I've been an atheist for a few years now."

"But you used to go to church with me and Dalton in high school. That wasn't so long ago. How could you lose your faith in only a few years?"

Church had always been her mom's thing. When she took off right after Reagan's high school graduation, Dad was less enthusiastic about going every Sunday. He eventually opted to stay home full time, and Reagan moved to Austin and discovered a new non-church world she'd never known existed.

"I just stopped going," she said.

"How can you believe in nothing?"

"Charlie, give it a rest," Dalton said.

"No, this is important," Charlie said, his face flushed. "How can you believe all of this came from nothing and is going nowhere? What about the Bible?"

Reagan's temper started to flare orange. "The Bible is a book, Charlie. Just because it's written down doesn't make it true. That's like saying Harry Potter proves the existence of wizards. Plus how do you know you picked the right religion? How do you know the Hindus are wrong?"

Charlie frowned. "Because I have my faith. I don't need to learn about other religions because I've found the true path."

"But that's what I'm saying. If your faith isn't strong enough to stand up to questioning, is it actually strong at all?"

"She's got you there, bro," Dalton said.

Charlie seemed stumped for a second and his face fell, which made Reagan feel guilty for attacking him. After the stress of the day, it had all slipped out, and she now regretted arguing. "Look, Charlie, forget it. I think it's great you've got faith. It's just not where I'm at right now."

"I'll pray for you," Charlie said.

"I appreciate that," she said, and she meant it.

He seemed satisfied, so Reagan stood up. "I'll be right back."

She walked away from camp toward a cluster of trees, feeling the day's miles in her legs, hips, feet, and back. She was glad the backpacking loop was half over because the trail had worn on her muscles more than she'd expected.

She entered the trees and looked back toward the camp. Suitably hidden. On the ground below her was a bed of disintegrated pine cone shards like torn bits of amber paper. Leaning against a tree, she took a moment to appreciate all that had happened that day, and hues of anxiety started to bubble up inside her. Yellow, orange, and red. She focused on slow breathing and letting the difficulties in her life pass out of her hands and into the universe, as Dr. Ahern had taught.

Some tears came, and she let them gather for a minute. Then she wiped her eyes and walked back to camp.

As she rounded the tents and her cousins came into view, she saw Dalton had taken her backpack from her tent and was rifling through it. The sheer unexpectedness of it made her take a step back. "What are you doing?"

He stood up. "Oh, uh, hey cuz. Nothing. I wasn't... I was looking for a bandage. Got a blister on my heel."

He'd removed a few things from the pack and set them on the ground, the first aid kit among them. Big white box with an unmistakable red plus sign on the top.

She grabbed the box and held it out to him. "They're right here."

He snatched it from her, opened it, and took a Band-Aid. He held it up. "Right. I should have known. Thanks for pointing that out."

He smiled, but yet again, there was something in his eyes that felt wrong. Dalton's look always betrayed his real intentions.

He wasn't looking for a bandage. He was looking for something else, and he'd lied about it.

***

8:10 pm

After dinner and a brilliant purple and orange sunset, they all retired to their tents. Reagan had been mostly quiet, rattled from Dalton's intrusion into her pack. Not so much that he'd done it, but the guilty look on his face when she caught him and the way he glared at her while lying about his purpose. She didn't like the fact that he was a few feet away from her, separated only by the thin walls of their respective tents.

The more she thought about it, the more nervous she got. Anxiety was not something she could afford right now. The park ranger hadn't stopped by, or at least she hadn't yet.

In the tent, she opened her sleeping bag, unlaced the boots and rubbed her feet. She slipped her headlamp on and took the thick fantasy paperback Spoon had given her from the pack and examined it for water damage. She'd wrapped it in his t-shirt, which no longer smelled like him, only like rain. The book's pages were wavy and crinkled, but still readable. She opened to the dog-eared page and tried to read a few lines, but the words blurred on the page. Too much was swirling around in her brain: the mystery key from the urn, her devious cousin, Spoon.

Tomorrow was the day she would open the urn and release her father's remains into Lake Nanita and he would be gone forever. Would she feel sad? Relieved? Would it feel like some kind of resolution, or would it twist the knife? Or maybe it would only send her spiraling into a depressive episode of doubt and shame and sinister self-criticism.

Without her meds to keep her stable, the last thought progressed from paranoia and into the territory of actual possibility. She would be back in Denver with Spoon and her medication in less than two days, and she could hold out until then. She could do this. She had to maintain until she returned to Spoon, and she would tell him about the key and Dalton's suspicious behavior and they could figure out what to do next.

As she pondered the key, the other thing that had come from the urn appeared in her mind: the letter.

She gasped. It had been in her pants cargo pocket all day during the rain.

She took the headlamp and hung it from the loop on the tent ceiling, then reached over to the cargo pants, which lay flat, drying next to her sleeping bag. She dug into the pocket and pulled out the piece of paper, which was soaked through.

Ruined.

She hesitated before opening it, the same fear about reading his last words reappearing. Didn't matter. She had to do it. But when she unfolded the paper, the ink inside had smeared all over the page. She read what she could still make out:

> *Dearest Reagan,*
> *I wish I had time to write everything I want to say, but...*
>
> *I had hoped that you...*
>
> *I made some mistakes. I was selfish. And I'm sorry...*

what the key in…

farmer's market. You'll understand when you get there. Your grandfather…

I hate to be so vague, but I…

to say I'm sorry, other than to tell you that I'm proud of you and I love you. I know that's not good enough.
Dad

The paper was so wet it almost tore in her hands. She read the letter several times, desperately trying to make sense of the blurred sections, but the rain had turned half of her father's looping cursive into unintelligible blurbs.

She read it again, this time focusing on the parts she could read. His tone was strange… *I made some mistakes. I was selfish. And I'm sorry.* What was he sorry about? What mistakes was he talking about?

Dalton had ranted yesterday that her dad was a compulsive gambler, but that didn't seem possible. He was a good man who always put the needs of others before his own. But then what was he talking about? Was Dad in some kind of financial trouble? That would seem to make sense since the will had indicated there was no inheritance, which had so surprised and enraged Anne.

Dad had mentioned the key, so that, at least, gave Reagan a small measure of comfort. He meant for her to find it. Dad put it there, or someone put it there for him, although *how* it had gotten in there was still a mystery. But what should she do with it? *You'll understand when you get there.* She would understand *what* when she got *where?*

The most confusing piece of information was the mention of her grandfather. He lived at an Assisted Living home in Boulder, and Reagan hadn't seen him for at least a year, maybe longer. None of these fragmented clues fit together.

The only part that made sense was the last bit, about how he was proud and loved her. She touched his words on the letter, absorbing a little of the ink into the creases of her fingertips. The last time she would ever hear that from him. The sorrow burrowed into her with such ferocity that she closed the letter and longed for her Seroquel. She wished she could take three of them and sleep away the pain.

Thursday

CHAPTER TWENTY

2:25 am

Reagan woke in total darkness, the swelling of her bladder ending a restless sleep. She fumbled for her headlamp. After slipping the elastic band over her head, she pressed the button on the side to activate the LEDs. Hundreds of tiny dust particles danced in the path of the brilliant beam of light. The crinkled rainfly covering the tent reflected some light through the black mesh of the inner tent.

She reached for the tent zipper and opened it enough to peel back the rainfly, so she could flip it back over the top of the tent. Blast of cold breeze hit her. Leaving the security of her makeshift portable home in the middle of the night to pee always unnerved her because of the possibility she might lean out of the tent and catch the eyes of some creature in her headlamp. Those surprises were not fun. Once she'd found herself face to face with a startled deer, and the way the beams of light made the animal's eyes glow an eerie green kept her up for hours that night.

She pivoted her head left and right, casting the headlamp's light on the ground close to her tent, and no surprise animals were waiting for her. Her hands found hiking boots under the tent vestibule.

She walked outside and stretched, looking up at the stars. Millions of them flooded the sky, tiny pinholes through a vast sheet of black construction paper. You couldn't get this view anywhere in the city.

She trudged a hundred feet away from the campsite, found a tree to brace herself against, and squatted.

From back at the campsite came a snuffling sound. She pointed her head toward it to focus the beam of the headlamp and saw a figure sitting outside the tent.

She pulled her long underwear up and carefully approached. Slouching on a log next to her cousins' tent, Charlie was rubbing his hands up and down his shoulders.

And crying.

She crept toward him. "Charlie? Are you okay?" She kept her voice low, since he was sitting only a few feet from where Dalton was sleeping.

Charlie didn't look at her, only shook his head.

She clicked off her headlamp, sat next to him on the log, and put an arm around him. He leaned into her and wiped a hand under his eyes.

"I'm sorry," he said.

"Whatever it is, it's okay, Charlie. There's nothing to be sorry about."

"No, it's not okay," he said, loud enough that Reagan glanced at Dalton's tent to make sure he didn't stir.

"You can tell me, if you want."

He ran a hand through his hair. "That's the thing: I can't tell you. If he finds out I said anything to you, I don't know what he would do. I don't think I can stop him."

A chill ran up Reagan's back. "You can't stop who?" But she already knew the answer.

"He tricked me, and now we're here and I can't do anything about it. I should have done something but now it's too late. I'm so sorry, Reagan."

She sneaked another look at Dalton's tent. No movement, but that didn't mean he wasn't awake. She decided to risk it. "This is about him going through my backpack, isn't it? What was he doing that for?"

Charlie lifted his face toward her, desperation coloring his red and misty eyes. His mouth hung open, air hissing out. "I can't... I shouldn't have said anything. I'm just tired. I'm going to go back to sleep."

He stood up, wiped his eyes again, and skulked back to his tent.

As she listened to him zip the tent and wrestle with his sleeping bag, she sat on the log and shivered in the stark night air, feeling more alone and unsure than she ever had in her life.

***

6:05 am

Reagan hardly slept after the cryptic conversation with Charlie. When she decided to stop trying, the sun had still not risen, but enough light from the pre-dawn lit up the inside of her tent. Her mouth felt dry so she licked her lips to produce a few seconds of relief. Thoughts snapped like firecrackers and she could barely keep up with them.

Dalton knew something. Charlie had essentially confirmed it. She was in danger, and the whole world felt like a puzzle.

The ranger hadn't come by the previous night, or if she had, she hadn't disturbed them. Reagan wished the woman had made herself known. A visit from an authority figure would have been a reassurance. Instead, Reagan had curled on her side, hoping the things she feared were only in her head as she had done so many nights after getting out of the hospital.

When Reagan checked out of the hospital in Denver two years ago, she learned that she'd failed all of her classes the previous fall, and she had missed enough of the spring semester that she was going to fail those too. A college dropout with no job, going to live at Dad and Anne's house.

Stable: the word they'd used to release her back into the world. It meant that she no longer had outbursts during Group. She no longer skipped therapy sessions to stay in bed. She no longer refused to take the medications that turned her stomach and made her eyes so blurry she could barely read more than a paragraph or two at a time without developing a splitting headache. She'd learned to play the game of the model patient.

At Dad's house in Denver, surrounded by a stepmother who seemed inconvenienced by her presence and a father who had little or no idea what to do with her, she stayed in her room for days on end. She listened to Austin college radio stations from their websites, read trashy celebrity tabloids because they required no concentration, and streamed endless hours of online video.

But she was getting better. At least that's what all the fair-weather people drifting in and out of her life told her. Friends commanded her to seize the day. They told her to be strong, to look forward, and to take control of her life. But she felt weak-willed and under the thumb of the pharmaceutical companies. How could she take charge of her life when she needed pills to wake up, to sleep, to silence the desire to slit her wrists?

Wait it out, Dr. Ahern had said. *Just keep living.*

As the weeks dragged by, particular incidents from high school resurfaced, how she displayed a tendency for mania and depression even then. She hadn't wanted to see it, but the episodes had been there. They were smaller, lasting only a few days in each direction, and never to the level she reached in Austin. Maybe that was why her mom left. Perhaps she had seen it coming and couldn't take it. Reagan suspected manic depression was the reason her mom's sister had ended her life when she was in her early twenties.

Each morning, Reagan stared at the prescription bottles lining the bathroom counter and went to war with herself. The rational mind argued she needed them to live. But they also made her a shell of what she could be. Flat, dull, unambitious. Was the mania so bad? Maybe she could manage it now, after having seen the ugliest side of it. After all, was she going to be a slave to pills for her entire life?

The lithium troubled her most of all. She had difficulty going out in public because she never knew when the violent tornado of nausea would strike. Once, halfway during a movie, she sprinted to the bathroom to retch partially-digested popcorn. She had to leave a friend's birthday party when the room spun so fiercely she couldn't do anything but cry and brace herself against the kitchen wall.

Staring at those pills one morning, she decided to stop taking them. She would practice yoga and deep meditation and free herself of this addiction. She would begin again.

Forty-eight hours later, at the beginning of a manic phase, she tried to persuade Anne to move out. When Anne refused, Reagan took it as a sign that she should move out instead. As she packed her clothes, Reagan lectured Anne about how she was too old to understand the younger generation. Confusion and disgust contorted Anne's face.

Dad found her the next day in Boulder, smoking pot under a bridge with some kids she'd met earlier in the day. She didn't even like smoking pot. They had a fierce argument about the nature of the illness, and he asked her not to talk so fast, but she kept telling him he couldn't understand what she knew now.

But she agreed to come home because, through the fog, she could see his kindness and the brilliance of his aura.

That's when he talked her into going on a backpacking trip. And as far as Reagan knew, that trip saved her life. Away from Anne, away from the city where she'd experienced sickness, away from responsibilities and pressure and tension. Reagan and Dad, alone in the wilderness, hiking and talking and not talking and doing all the things they'd loved to do when she was little.

He made sure that she took her meds at the right times, washing them down with water from Nalgene bottles and celebrating with s'mores and granola. He was her savior, and being a slave to medication was a worthwhile trade-off to have a connection with him.

Two years later, her savior had fled from this world and left her alone. In the same tent in the same national park, she had a key and a mysterious note. The last words he'd ever write to her. The empty casket.

She had a cousin who was acting strangely and had inserted himself into her backpacking trip with vague claims of support, but he hadn't been supportive at all. The only conclusion that felt right was that Dalton somehow knew about this key. That seemed impossible, because how on earth could he have known what Dad put inside his urn before he died? Unless Dalton himself had put the key in the urn, but that made no sense at all.

And how was Charlie involved in all that? Her youngest cousin seemed to have no malice in him.

Didn't matter. What mattered was the here and now, and Reagan had to prepare herself for the possibility that something bad was about to happen. Now was the time to take action.

She slid on her cargo pants, which were still a little damp, and numbingly cold. She should have stuffed them down into her sleeping bag so her body could have warmed them, but the thought hadn't occurred to her last night.

She opened her pack and found the reflective Mylar emergency blanket. If she needed to run, ditching her pack would make her more mobile, and having the crinkly heat-reflecting blanket might save her life. The package was barely bigger than a pack of cigarettes, and she stuffed that in one cargo pocket. She made sure the key was in the other pocket, and added her Swiss Army knife and car keys.

She held the urn. Too bulky to fit in a pocket. She rummaged through the pack to retrieve the last of her duct tape. After raising her shirt, she pressed the urn against her stomach and the duct tape made *skritch skritch skritch* sounds as she unspooled it and rolled it around her body. The urn created a football-sized bump in the front but wasn't too noticeable under the baggy technical t-shirt.

Her cousins stirred in their tent. Running out of time.

The food was in the bear box, nestled at a park-required two hundred feet away from camp. As soon as possible, she needed to sneak some granola bars into her pockets.

Whatever might happen today, Reagan was prepared for the worst.

CHAPTER TWENTY-ONE

8:15 am

Spoon woke to a knocking at the door. During those few seconds when reality mingled with the dream-world, he reckoned he was in Austin and Reagan was coming home from a night shift waiting tables. Then he opened his eyes and noticed what he was staring at couldn't be home. At their apartment, the ceiling was covered with a bumpy texture Reagan called "popcorn." This ceiling was smooth.

He sat up. Denver. More knocking.

"Yeah," he said.

The door opened and there stood Anne, fully dressed, with keys in hand. "I have to go see Mitchell's father. I thought you might like to come."

Spoon twisted his half-awake head toward the clock on the nightstand. Just past eight. "Who?"

"I have to go to Boulder. Thought you might like to meet your girlfriend's grandfather, if you have nothing better to do today. I'll give you a minute to get dressed."

She shut the door and Spoon threw back the covers. He must have slept too long because he felt the same lingering dehydration of a hangover. Fortunately, he hadn't experienced one of those in three years.

He readied his crutches and circled the room to pick up his clothes from yesterday. Spoon was the kind of person who usually liked to start the day with a wake-up shower and then coffee to kick the day into gear. Although he had never gotten to like weak American coffee, he at least tolerated it and found that if he drank enough, the caffeine eventually took hold.

No shower today, though. As he pulled on his shirt, he contemplated whether he actually did want to meet Reagan's grandfather. He probably should be trying to find out more about that Tyson bloke, or the man who had followed him around town yesterday, but he had no leads. He could go back to the Slinky Grape across the street from the lawnmower shop for more observation, but then he'd still have the same problem. What to do next?

Maybe sticking close to Anne was the best way to protect her and uncover more pieces of the puzzle. If she was going to Boulder, that's where he should be too.

He slipped on his trousers and shoes, and then met Anne at the foot of the stairs. She wouldn't look him in the eye, and he didn't blame her. Since she'd attempted to seduce him on the couch yesterday, she'd been distant and strange. He still didn't know what to do about all that. Pretending it hadn't happened had seemed to work okay so far.

"So, what are we doing?" he said.

"Mitchell left his father this in the will. Some old baseball cards or something," she said, holding up a rusted tin. "Since he was in surgery on the day of the service and has been bed-ridden since then, I have to drive up to Boulder and deliver them. Are you up to speed now?"

"Got it."

"I can't tell you it's going to be a pleasant experience. He's a cranky old man and he's never been shy about telling me I wasn't good enough for his son. So we're going to get in, drop this off, and get out. Do you still want to go?"

Maybe he could get Anne talking about Tyson again. "Yes."

Spoon followed her to the neighbor's car and eased into the passenger seat. As they drove the half hour to Boulder, she quizzed him about kangaroos, sharks, crocodiles, and other Australian lore. He told her the story of the drop-bear, the mythical koala-like beast with fangs that locals claimed lived in trees and dropped on unsuspecting tourists. She almost bought it, but he couldn't keep a straight face.

She didn't want to talk about Tyson, though.

There was no mention of the incident on the couch from the day before, which was fine with Spoon. As his father would say, she'd been pissed as a parrot, and Spoon had made plenty of mistakes after sucking back a few too many stubbies during his drinking days. The big question was how much to tell Reagan about it. He didn't want to lie to her, but he also didn't know what good the knowledge would do her. As soon as she came back, they would be on a plane to Texas, and they didn't ever have to see Anne again unless they wanted to.

Driving into Boulder required them to pass through the little towns of Broomfield and then Louisville, which Anne pointed out was pronounced differently than the one in Kentucky. He wasn't aware that America had so many cities they had to reuse the names in different states. To pass Louisville and get into Boulder, they climbed a steep hill, and as soon as they broached the other side, Spoon's mouth dropped open. Boulder sat in a massive valley at the foot of towering green peaks. Whilst he could see the mountains from Denver, the starkness of the difference in this closeup view blew his mind.

They parked at an Assisted Living center on the edge of town. It would have looked like a regular two-story apartment complex, were it not for the sign out front. A wrinkled old lady pushing a walker crept across the parking lot.

They entered the office in the center of the complex and Anne approached a woman wearing scrubs, seated behind a counter. Framed prints of smiling pensioners adorned the walls of the office. The room smelled of cleaning products and flowers.

When Anne asked to see Frank Darby, the woman in the scrubs placed a phone call, and then Spoon and Anne were on their way through the complex.

They stopped short of knocking on the door.

"He's still recovering from shoulder surgery and may be loopy on whatever pain meds they've got him on," she said. "Plus, he has early-stage Alzheimer's, so don't get offended if he can't remember your name,

142

or if he does something odd. Last time I was here, he threw a shoe at me. Fair warning."

Spoon pictured a barking loony on the other side of that door, frothing at the mouth and flinging his shit against the wall.

Anne knocked on the door, and a warble came from the other side. She opened it and beckoned Spoon to follow.

Looking around the apartment, Spoon thought he'd discovered the eighth wonder of the hoarder world. Stuff was packed from floor to ceiling... knick knacks, curios, antiques. He'd been to a few American theme restaurants that hung odd objects from the walls like lacrosse paddles, street signs, stuffed animals, but none of them compared to the density of junk inside this apartment. Stacks of newspapers lined the floor along the walls. Dusty art prints graced most of the available wall space, and the remaining space belonged to a collection of objects that Spoon reckoned had to do with seafaring... nautical maps, a harpoon, even a brass sextant. The sextant gleamed in the light, as if he'd taken care of it, compared to the other dusty objects on the wall.

Stacks of clothes, trinkets, piles of empty boxes of food covered every square centimeter of horizontal space. A dollhouse sat on a stand next to the TV, and that object puzzled Spoon the most. It seemed well-maintained and relatively new.

Frank Darby was sitting in a recliner in the living room of the one-bedroom apartment. He was next to the window, and the shades were slightly open, casting shards of light across his body. Thin and grizzled, a few days worth of gray stubble dotted his face. What remained of his hair looked patchy and messy, jutting out like mad scientist spikes.

Spoon checked the old man for a family resemblance. He had Reagan's nose: thin and flat at the top, then widening halfway with a slight bulb at the end.

"Who the hell are you?" Frank said.

Anne put a hand on Spoon's shoulder, then yanked it away. She spoke in loud, deliberate words. "Frank, this is Reagan's boyfriend, Spoon."

"Spoon?" He said as a snarl spread across his face.

"My name's Liam, but everyone calls me Spoon."

The snarl broke and Frank opened his mouth, clicking his dentures together. His eyes traveled up and down Spoon's face. After an endless silence, he said, "hell. A man ought to call himself whatever he wants." He waved them inside. "Come on in, you're letting all the damn air out."

Aside from Frank's recliner, one other chair sat at a tiny round dinner table. Spoon gestured Anne toward it and he sat on the bed, laying his crutches behind him.

"How are you going today, Mr. Darby?"

"You're an Aussie," Frank said.

"That's right," Spoon said. Frank had even pronounced it correctly, like *ozzie,* and not *ossie,* as most Americans did.

Frank grunted and shifted in his chair. "I spent some time in Alice Springs after Korea."

Anne lifted the rusted tin box and shook it. "Mitchell left you these in his will. We wanted to make sure you got them."

"What is it?" Frank said.

"Baseball cards or something. He told me you helped him collect them when he was a kid."

Frank recoiled. "Baseball cards? I got way more crap in here than I know what to do with already. What the hell do I want with baseball cards?"

Anne sighed and dropped the tin on the table. "I have no idea, Frank, but your son wanted you to have them, so here they are."

"You think you're Little Miss Special with your fancy teas and your hippie yoga, but you would have been nothing without Mitchell. You were a barroom floozy when he met you. He gave you a good home and all you ever did was shit on him."

"Okay," Anne said as she stood up and hitched her purse over her shoulder. "I've heard enough. Always a pleasure to see you, Frank. Glad to see living at the old folks' home at least hasn't dulled your wit. Spoon, let's go."

"No," Frank said. "He can stay. You wait outside while I chat with my granddaughter's friend."

The idea struck Spoon that maybe Frank might know what kind of trouble Reagan's dad had been in. A long shot, but with Anne out of the room, he could investigate.

Anne stared at Spoon, and he shrugged in return. Playing clueless might or might not work.

She flicked her eyes back and forth between them, checked her watch, then exited the room in a huff.

"You ever been to Alice Springs?" Frank said once they were alone.

"A long time ago, when I was a pup."

Frank smiled and cleared his throat, a strained and gurgling wet sound. "I met this young woman when I was there. Mathilda, just like the song. That was before I met Reagan's grandmother, of course. She had blonde hair, big blue eyes, and a full figure like Jayne Mansfield. You know who that is?"

"Name rings a bell."

"I wanted to marry that Mathilda, but she wouldn't move to America, and I had a job waiting for me in Alamosa for after the war, so it didn't work out."

"I'm sorry to hear that," Spoon said.

"Nothing to be sorry about, son. When you get a little bit older, you'll learn life works out the way it's supposed to. If I hadn't left, I wouldn't have met my wife, we wouldn't have had Mitchell, he wouldn't have had Reagan, and you'd be left without a girlfriend." He cackled.

"That's about the size of it, yeah," Spoon said.

"You and my granddaughter been going steady long?" Frank said as he narrowed his eyes.

"A little over a year. I'm quite keen on that girl, and she doesn't know it yet, but I plan to marry her. If she'll have me, I suppose."

This lightened Frank's hard face. "You should ask her, because my granddaughter is an exceptional girl. They don't come along like that too often. Not like her cousins, those little miscreants."

"Really? Reagan has nothing but good things to say about Charlie." He started to worry that Anne might burst in at any moment, demanding they leave. He prayed she would give him enough time to learn something useful.

"I suppose he is. Dalton's the troublemaker. His dad was worse. Always getting into trouble in high school, never even bothered to even look at going to college."

Spoon knew nothing at all about Dalton and Charlie's father. He didn't remember meeting anyone identified as Reagan's uncle at the funeral, and she'd never mentioned anything about him before. Frank's use of the past tense to describe him might have answered that question.

Frank coughed and wiped his mouth on his sleeve. "Mitchell was more of a dad to those kids than their own dad ever was."

"I'm sorry about Mitchell. Reagan loved him heaps."

Frank chewed his cheek. "What do you know about him?"

"Not much. Just what Reagan's told me."

"She was always quite attached to him. There was less to love about Mitchell than you might think, although she never wanted to see the truth about him. A daddy's girl, I heard someone say once."

Now they were getting somewhere. "What truth is that?"

Frank inhaled slowly, and let out a wheeze that turned into a cough. "Not sure if I should tell you this." He reached into his pocket and took out a lollie wrapped in foil, made a big show out of slowly unwrapping it and sticking it in his mouth. "You're going to marry her, you say?"

"I am indeed, Mr. Darby."

"Then what the hell. You should know all this, I suppose. Mitchell was a bright boy, got good grades, always popular with the girls. But then when he grew up, he got himself a taste for horses."

"Horses?"

"Gambling," Frank said. "First horses, then cards, football games, whatever."

Spoon took a deep breath. A gambling problem would explain all the lost money, the surprise about the will. Maybe even explained why this Tyson man was after Anne. Maybe he had lent Reagan's dad money and now was trying to hold her accountable for the debt.

"So Mitchell lost all the family money?"

Frank leaned forward, which made him grimace, and then launched into a coughing fit for a few seconds. When he finished, there was a dab of blood on his chin, which he wiped onto his shirt. He beckoned Spoon to lean closer. "I heard about the will. And I know it's a load of crap."

"It is?" Spoon said, checking the door to the apartment for signs of Anne.

"Mitchell's got money stashed. Safety deposit box down in Denver. He wanted to keep it out of Anne's grubby fingers."

"How do you know that?"

This seemed to incense Frank. "Because he told me, that's how." His eyes dimmed and then darted around Spoon's face. "Mitchell wanted to get that money to Reagan, then he was going to skip town the way he always did."

Frank's harsh words didn't match up to how Reagan talked about her father. This all sounded like a bit of a yarn. "But how would he get her the money if it wasn't in the will?"

"Safety deposit box got to have a key, don't it? He would have sent her the key somehow. Where is she, anyway? Why didn't she come today?"

"She's backpacking in Rocky Mountain National Park."

"Strange time to go camping, if you ask me."

Spoon smiled. "True enough, mate."

Frank cleared his throat again, then scowled. "That money will be in cash, and there's a lot of it. No idea how much. Enough that if he had to pay taxes, the lawyers and money-lenders would end up getting most of it. They get their grubby little fingers around it and you're none the wiser."

Spoon sat back as a frown darkened his face. Until now, he'd been surprised how lucid Frank had been, given Anne's description.

"You think I'm joking," Frank said, spittle flying from his lips. "First they come around, telling you how they can just *hold* the money for you in escrow, and they won't let the government get it, and then they're all there stealing it out from under you and you can't do a damn thing about it."

"Mr. Darby, I don't understand what this has to do with—"

"And don't even get me started about those crooks at the bank. Liars, all of them. Listening in to my phone calls like that goddamned bleeding heart liberal Governor. You know they can smoke marijuana legally in this state now like it's all one big flower-power rally? What the hell has Colorado come to? You ask my son Mitchell, he lives down in Denver. He knows all about it."

Spoon's shoulders slumped. Maybe what Frank said about the key and the safety deposit box was true. Maybe not. Maybe the ravings of an imaginative oldie with Alzheimers.

A knock at the door. Spoon turned around as Anne leaned in.

"I have to go to work," she said.

"Okay," Spoon said. He stood up and shook Frank's hand. "Cheers, mate. Thanks for talking to me."

Frank said his goodbyes, and Spoon walked toward the door. He paused as an urge to ask Frank about the clean dollhouse or the shiny sextant struck him, but Anne was already jingling the car keys.

Outside, Anne took his crutches after he'd gotten in the car, then placed them in the backseat. "What did he want?" she said as she started the car.

"I chatted to him about Reagan for a minute. He's a bit of an odd fellow."

"That's an understatement. He's turning into one of those paranoid old men. I can barely stand it anymore, it's all about the government coming to steal our guns and tap our phones."

Spoon didn't know what to believe.

Anne reversed in the parking lot, headed for the street. As she did, a familiar blue Chevy Tahoe parked a few spots down from where they had parked. Spoon braced himself against the car window as he gulped an involuntary breath. Anne hadn't seemed to have noticed.

Out of the truck emerged two men. One of them was Tyson, walking toward Frank's apartment.

CHAPTER TWENTY-TWO

8:10 am

Reagan managed to sneak a few granola bars from the bear box and stash them in her cargo pants. The pockets bulged, but her cousins hadn't noticed. The idea of abandoning her stuff and making a hasty escape seemed crazy, but she had to prepare for the worst.

While Charlie packed up the campsite, Dalton was busy getting stoned. Reagan didn't say a word about it. She didn't want to look him in the eye or have any kind of exchange with him.

They ate a breakfast of oatmeal bars in silence and started along the trail for lakes Nokoni and Nanita. Their destination was on a side trail that branched from the main Tonahutu loop, about six miles roundtrip. She would release Dad's ashes and they would hike back out and stay at Porcupine Campsite, then hike back to their cars at North Inlet by tomorrow afternoon.

At least, that was how the day was supposed to go. But with each passing minute, the suspicion grew inside her that Dalton was planning something, and the plan had to do with either the key or the note.

The area after July camp toward the North Inlet trailhead was the most beautiful scenery yet. Massive round trees slicing the sky with their pointy tops, clear water coursing through deep streams and over dozens of little waterfalls, the clash of summer birds chirping different songs. The smell of pine reminded her of Christmas. The trail itself was free of obstructions, a tamped-down path of pine needles and moist dirt twisting through the trees.

If only she could appreciate it for more than a second or two at a time. Her mind buzzed like an air conditioner.

Charlie lagged behind them, farther than usual. He tried his best to present the appearance that his ankle wasn't hurting, but Dalton's repetitive mocking of Charlie's speed didn't help.

"Damn it, bro, if you don't pick up the pace, I'm going to drag you along," he said as they stopped for their first break, at the turnoff for the lakes.

"I'm doing the best I can," he said, wheezing and grinding his teeth.

Reagan hadn't wanted to speak to him, but she wasn't going to let Dalton bully Charlie. "That's enough, Dalton. He should probably be in a hospital getting that thing looked at."

Dalton glared at her and she couldn't hold his gaze. The look was like ice picks penetrating her eyeballs.

She wanted to distract herself from his cold stare, so she ran her hands over the trail sign, feeling the indentations of the carved words. *Nokoni 2.1 MI Nanita 3 MI.*

With a grunt, she lifted her pack and started toward the lakes. She briefly entertained the fantasy that they might not come with her; that they might allow her this one last day in peace to accomplish what she'd initially set out to do. She considered saying something about how important today would be, but Dalton would only fake sympathy and spit some crap about coming along to support her and she shouldn't be alone at a time like this and that it's important to be with family during the hard times in life. Lying, manipulative bullshit.

They followed as she'd expected. She cursed herself for not standing up for what she wanted and letting fear rule her.

Nokoni and Nanita both emerged every year from the snowpack runoff of the surrounding mountains. The trails to each required tough hiking to the crest of a bowl, and then steep descents to the lakes themselves at the bottom of those bowls. Dad had wailed and moaned with each step, pretending that he was close to passing out. Reagan had giggled like a schoolgirl.

She tried to focus on that memory, laughing at Dad's silliness as they hiked a section of trail made from manually-carved steps on boulders, her knees and hamstrings screaming with exhaustion.

After more than twenty miles on the trail with a too-heavy backpack and a chafing rope hipbelt that didn't properly distribute the weight, she was ready for all this to be over.

Fill the empty casket. Close the empty casket.

If she could just release the ashes, then she could worry about Dalton. Maybe he would let her have this moment.

Halfway up the trail, a massive downed tree lay across the path. It sat three feet off the ground, at least two feet in diameter and covered with spiky branches like the sharpened pins on a music box. Passing it would not be easy.

"We should take off our packs," she said. "And watch out for the branches."

They all took off their packs, and the thought struck her that the urn taped to her belly might scrape on the tree. Her shirt was baggy enough to hide it, but not if it caught on a spike.

Dalton went over the tree first, and a branch snagged his pant leg, tearing it a little. He grunted and ripped it free. "Motherfucking tree. Ruined my pants, you little dipshit."

Charlie lifted Dalton's pack and hoisted it over the tree to his brother, then he threw each leg over the obstruction. He had less trouble than Dalton. "Hand me your pack," he said to Reagan once he was on the other side.

She held it out to him and put one foot on the log. She could try to stand on it and jump over, but she might slip. She slid down until she was straddling it, barely avoiding a wooden spike right in front of her crotch. The temptation to place a hand on the urn grew strong, but she resisted. Flipping her other leg high and then down, she found herself on the other side, staring at her cousins.

"Way to make a big show of it," Dalton said, snorting.

She said nothing, only tied herself into her pack, and continued along the steepening trail.

When they broached the crest of Lake Nokoni, Reagan paused to take in Ptarmigan Mountain, a collection of flat-topped spires jutting above treeline. The lake below seemed small, with piles of scree resting at the base of the surrounding sheer cliff. Trees dotted the sides of those angled cliffs.

She had to pee, and the thought occurred to her that if she left her pack on the ground, Dalton might search it again. Taking it with her was out of the question, because she'd have to climb over several downed logs to find a secluded spot.

The key and the note were in her pockets, so she dropped her pack to see what would happen. "I'll be right back."

She walked along the crest and found a spot downhill and between two trees to go to the bathroom. As she squatted, she closed her eyes and listened to the wind rustle the branches of the creaking trees, the birds calling above her. The duct-taped urn against her stomach felt heavy when she leaned forward.

She watched a mountain squirrel on a nearby rock study her. The furry little creature with its broad and long bushy tail stayed perfectly still as their eyes met. "I'm not going to hurt you, little guy," she said, but the squirrel twitched and scurried off into a slim crack between two rocks.

She pulled up her pants and trudged back up the hill toward her cousins, and as soon as she'd reached enough elevation to see them, she spied Dalton bent over her pack, rustling and digging. She'd expected this, but still, her breathing became faster as her heart pumped.

"Dalton, what the hell?"

He stood up and stared, no longer embarrassed as he'd been the first time she'd caught him.

"What are you doing in my pack?" she said as she narrowed the distance between them. Watching the cold expression on his face sent a lump into her throat that threatened to choke her. *I can't stop him*, Charlie had said. The words echoed in her head.

"Nothing. Just looking for something."

"What were you looking for?"

He didn't answer, only stood over her opened pack and blinked. A shudder ran through her as he flexed his hands as if preparing to punch someone. She now saw that whatever reason he'd come here, he wasn't going to feign support anymore. He was going to push harder now.

"Stay the hell out of my pack."

He backed up and raised his hands in mock surrender. "You got it, cuz."

She waited until he'd moved away, zipped up the pack, slung it over her back, buckled the shoulder strap and cinched the hipbelt. She started the descent for Nokoni, now sure that Dalton was going to do something terrible, with no idea what to do about it.

***

11:45 am

They spent no time at Lake Nokoni, instead pushing straight past the lake toward the next destination. She didn't stop or look at her companions, didn't ask them if they needed a break.

The rising switchbacks between Nokoni and Nanita were even less forgiving. The dirt trail often broke into tall rocky steps, and sometimes she had to lean on hiking poles to keep balance.

Reagan kept running through the possibilities. Dalton knew about the key, she was sure of it now. If he couldn't find it in her pack, he would eventually realize that she was carrying it on her instead. Either he would try to take it from her by force or he would wait until she slept and then take it from her. How could she possibly set up camp next to him tonight, knowing he might come into her tent?

How far would he go to get this key?

In high school, she'd once witnessed Dalton fighting another kid in the parking lot after school. Something about the kid bumping into Dalton's car, scratching the paint. As a crowd gathered, Dalton held the kid by his hair and punched him in the face so many times that blood from the kid's shattered nose sprayed Dalton's shirt with red polka dots. If the Economics teacher hadn't intervened and pulled Dalton away, who knows what he would have done.

If it came to it, the Swiss Army knife in her pocket was hardly a great tool for self-defense. The longest blade was maybe three inches, and likely never sharpened in its life. Plus, the idea of stabbing her cousin was more of a fantasy than telling herself they wouldn't come with her to the lakes. She'd known him his entire life. They had grown up in the same neighborhood, played as kids, partied together when they were older. Facing off against him in some kind of high-noon draw-first Western duel seemed ludicrous.

But, then again, here they were. There was a real danger here, even if she didn't fully understand it. Either she would do something or he would do it first.

A boy scout group approached along the same trail, single file in their tan shirts and shorts. Reagan, Dalton, and Charlie stood to the side of the trail as a dozen of these kids and three adults passed. Charlie offered them salutes, but Dalton said nothing. The flushed and sweating adults mumbled some words of encouragement about how close they were to the next lake.

Reagan smiled politely, taking in the faces of these kids who looked at her and saw an adult. She didn't feel like an adult. More like a panicking child who wished she could trade places with them and be innocent again.

After the scouts passed and she continued again on the trail, another ranger appeared over the crest, hiking toward them. Reagan's heart soared at the sight of this tall and slender man in a Stetson hat. She could grab him, explain the situation, and he would help her. He would make her safe.

But that was crazy. She had no evidence of anything. Dalton had rummaged in her pack twice, had acted like a jerk, and had said some suspicious things on the trail. He'd made no direct threats about anything. Without evidence to convince him, the ranger might as well have been another boy scout.

Didn't matter. She had to say something.

Dalton seemed to sense her anticipation because as the ranger approached, he pulled close to her.

"Excuse me, sir," Reagan said, so nervous that her knees started to buckle.

154

"Morning, ranger," Dalton said, placing a hand on Reagan's back. "How's the lake today?"

The ranger stopped walking and sipped from a water bottle slung over his shoulder like a canteen. "Good, good. Forecast says no rain, thankfully, so you've come on a great day."

Dalton produced a hearty laugh. "Ah, that's great to hear. You have a wonderful day, now, and take care of yourself."

The ranger smiled, waved, and continued past them.

Dalton's fake-enthusiasm jabbed at the back of her neck. He'd meant those words for her as some kind of warning. Her hands felt slick with sweat, and the oatmeal bar she'd eaten for breakfast crept back up her stomach and perched at the base of her throat. Her body felt out of control. Something bad was going to happen, and soon. The future was in motion and Reagan now had to decide what part she was going to play in it.

Dalton eyed her. "You should smile more. You'd be a lot prettier if you smiled more."

Red flared. "Why should I care if you think I'm pretty?"

He shrugged, cinched the shoulder straps on his pack, and hiked past her.

She stole the Swiss Army knife from her pocket and concealed it in her hand as they hiked the last switchback to the crest of the hill to Lake Nanita.

CHAPTER TWENTY-THREE

1:00 pm

The second time Reagan caught him going through her pack, Dalton knew he'd taken it too far. Tricky bitch returned only about ten seconds after she went off to piss. He backed off at first, hoping she might chalk it up to him being his usual snarky self, but the look in her eye said she had some kind of clue what was going on. Maybe not all of it, but she knew enough to be suspicious. Or maybe she'd been aware the whole time and had been playing it cool. Difficult to tell; she could be secretive.

One thing for sure: he was tired of playing the game, being subtle, letting her take her time.

As they pressed along up the steep trail toward the crest of Lake Nanita, Dalton became increasingly sure he was going to have to take action soon. If she'd found the money, she'd been super-secret-agent about it. Not in her backpack. She'd barely left his sight over the last three days, so if she'd tried stashing it somewhere, he would've seen it.

No, Reagan was purposefully hiding something. And if his spying couldn't reveal it, he would have to try a more direct approach.

The problem was Charlie. He still hadn't committed to the cause.

Dalton had no doubt that if he stood tall to Reagan and demanded she tell them where the money was, she would do it. Maybe all she needed was a good hard slap to the face. But with Charlie's help, he stood a better chance of convincing her of the seriousness of the situation. If Charlie sided with her instead, that would add some new elements of complication.

He watched Charlie hike, grumbling, coughing, grimacing in pain from the ankle he'd twisted the day before. Dalton wished he could pull him aside and make one last plea, but there was never a good time. Reagan watched him like a motherfucking hawk.

She kept pushing up the trail, her breaths in time with the alternating clicking of her hiking poles against the rocks.

After they passed the ranger, they trudged toward the crest, with Reagan in the lead, as always. When they hit the rim of Lake Nanita, she stopped. She stared down at the lake below, in the shadow of a giant mountain peak on one side, with smaller mountains surrounding two other sides of the water. Nanita was by far the biggest body of water they'd seen in the park.

The anxiety of the moment gripped his chest and twisted him like a pretzel. He looked behind them and the ranger had disappeared from view. He could also see down the trail that led to the lake, and there was no one approaching. This was the clearest view of either side of the trail he'd had all day. If he was going to do something, now was the time.

"Reagan."

She looked at him, and for a split second, he saw the high school junior who'd taken him under her wing when he was entering school as a freshman. The same girl who'd told him which teachers were the toughest, which upperclassmen kids to avoid because they were going to bully him. She'd been good to him, and in that split second, he regretted what he was about to do.

If he had to get violent, would he even be able to do it? This was his flesh and blood.

Didn't matter. Tyson would not allow him to prioritize nostalgia over a debt, and if Dalton came back empty handed… no telling the punishment that would be waiting for him.

Her eyes held nothing but contempt for him. No mistaking it. She didn't reply, only continued staring at him while she unbuckled the shoulder strap from her pack, then untied the rope hipbelt, and let the pack fall to the ground. She rolled her shoulders and let out a groan, all the while locked onto his eyes.

She had something clenched in her right hand, but he couldn't make it out.

Charlie finally caught up with them, huffing and puffing. "Are we taking a break? That upwards part may have been the steepest one yet. I can barely breathe up here." He started to take off his pack.

"Yep, let's go ahead and take a break," Dalton said as he removed his own.

"Did you want something?" Reagan said. Her lip trembled, but her eyelids were low, like a cat ready to pounce.

"You know what I want, cuz. It's time to stop fucking around. I know why you're out here. If you found it, I haven't seen it. So instead of all this back and forth and spying and shit, why don't you tell me where it is and save me a lot of trouble."

She drew in a sharp breath. "I don't know what you're talking about."

He reached into the side of his pack and withdrew the folding knife Tyson had given him. He'd kept it secret so far, but now was the time to put everything out in the open.

Reagan glanced at the knife but kept her chin held high, hands at her sides and fists balled.

Charlie gasped. "What are you doing with that thing?"

"Shut the fuck up, Charlie."

"I don't care what you say," Reagan said, "or how you threaten me, or what you do with that knife. You're not going to get that key."

Dalton took a step backward, his thoughts now swimming. He hadn't expected this. "A key? What key? What key do you have? What does it open?"

She said nothing. Then it made sense to him, like the twist at the end of a movie explaining all the mysteries at once. *Of course*, it had to be a key. It's not as if uncle Mitch would stash two hundred and forty large out here, where it might get wet or some other asshole might stumble on it. But a key would be easy to conceal, and Reagan could have gotten it

158

from any one of a million hiding spots along the trail. That explained why he hadn't seen her sneaking off into the woods to retrieve a package to stash in her backpack. The whole scenario seemed so clear and simple that he almost laughed.

The course was now clear. Dalton had to get this key and give it to Tyson. The old fat bastard would know what to do with it.

"I think you should leave," she said, pointing back at Lake Nokoni. "You and Charlie just go that way. I'll go on from here and have my own trip. We can pretend this didn't happen and never speak about it again."

Charlie waved his hands and positioned himself between them, off to the side. "Everybody just calm down, please. This is getting way too crazy and we need to take a step back and think about this."

Dalton opened the folding knife, exposing the silvery blade within. "I can't walk away, and I think you know it. You don't understand, cuz, I need that key. Your degenerate-gambler dad took something that wasn't his, and I'm supposed to make sure that what's messed up about all this gets fixed."

"Don't call him that," she said as she retreated a step. She'd moved closer to the edge of the crest. Two feet behind her was a steep decline, with few trees to break the fall on the way down.

He moved closer, edging her up against the drop-off. Making her think he was going to push her might scare her into giving it up. "We just want what's ours, right Charlie?"

"I don't want any part of this, and I told you that. Leave her alone, please. Let's go, like she said."

Dalton squeezed the knife but kept his eyes on Reagan. "I'm disappointed in you. I'm your brother."

Charlie puffed out his chest, in some perverted show of bravery. He stepped directly between Dalton and Reagan. "You're acting like a jerk, and I'm not going to let you do anything stupid. Cut it out, right now."

Dalton whipped his non-knife hand toward Charlie to slap him, but his little brother ducked the blow and jabbed Dalton in the mouth with a closed fist. He hadn't seen it coming. Stinging pain shot through his jaw, and his eyes watered, turning his brother and cousin into a blurry mess. For a half a second, he was too shocked to react.

Then Dalton jumped forward, grabbed Charlie, and pulled him to the side. He'd meant to yank the kid away from the edge, but Charlie pulled in the opposite direction and tumbled down the crest.

Dalton's little brother folded into a ball and rolled down the steep side of the mountain, thirty feet, then sixty, finally coming to a stop when he bumped into a tree. A miniature landslide of dirt and rock cascaded down the mountain after him. He yelped and moaned, grabbing his leg with both hands.

Dalton heard a *snick*, then a glint of light flashed in his eyes as Reagan's hand came toward his face. He put up his own hand in time to block a knife from slashing him. He felt a tearing as the blade connected with his palm.

Red-hot stinging pain seared his hand as blood gathered at the site of the wound. In the mountain air, his blood immediately cooled, and he shuddered. Less than a second had passed since Charlie fell, but the chain of events played out in distinct moments. He couldn't believe what was happening.

She stood there, knife in hand, chest heaving.

"Motherfucking bitch," he shouted as he examined the wound. He staggered at the sight of the blood, now dizzy.

Time slipped by as his vision cleared of stars and he regained his bearings. He blinked a few times as his ears filled with the sounds of Charlie calling for help.

Then he looked up and Reagan was gone.

"Oh, you sneaky bitch."

Folding blade in hand, he ran down the trail. In front of him, the path descended to the lake, steep hill on the left and thicket of trees on the right. A collection of boulders, shrubs, and broken log carcasses clogged up the space between the trees.

She could be hiding anywhere out in that mess to the right of the trail. How long was he not paying attention? Five seconds? Ten? How far could she have gone?

"Reagan? I know you're here somewhere," he said, focusing his eyes to spot movement between the trees.

Charlie's wails came wafting up the hill. "Dalton, help me, please. I cut my leg and I'm bleeding all over the place. I can't stand up."

"Charlie, damn it, be still. I'll be there in a minute." Dalton rotated slowly, surveying the trail. He tried to remember what color shirt she'd been wearing, but drew a blank. "Where are you, cousin? Up in a tree? Hiding under a fucking rock?"

He didn't know whether to go left or right. She may have even doubled back and gone back the trail to the other lake. His stomach gurgled, and anger unlike anything he'd experienced in years raced through his body like cars on a track. Anger at her, but mostly at himself. He'd come so far, endured three days of bullshit food and sleeping on the ground in the cold, and he'd almost thrown it all away because he was impatient.

Tyson would not be pleased.

"Reagan, come on out. I'm going to find you, and you know it. Where do you think you're going to go, huh?"

Charlie yelped louder.

Dalton grunted and folded the blade of his knife back into itself. Charlie might actually be hurt. "Fine, you motherfucking bitch, go ahead and run. But I know where you live!"

CHAPTER TWENTY-FOUR

11:00 am

During the return drive from Boulder to Denver, Spoon debated whether he should tell Anne that he'd seen Tyson going into Reagan's grandfather's apartment. Given how dismissive Anne had been about this man with the banana-shaped scar, he reckoned she wouldn't care. Spoon was on his own when it came to puzzling through this situation.

When they got back to the house, Anne said she was going to go upstairs and take a nap.

"Didn't you say you had to get to work?" Spoon said.

She shook her head. "I thought you knew. I haven't worked since after Mitch and I got married. Truth is, I had to get out of there. You understand, right? I can only take Frank in small doses."

"Sure, no worries," Spoon said, pretending to sympathize.

When she went upstairs, he snatched the neighbor's Lexus keys from the dish next to the front door. Drive back to Boulder and ask the old man about his visitor? No, that wouldn't do any good. Frank's opinions were suspect, at best. If Frank even remembered a visit from Tyson, he may not be willing to explain.

Frank had said that Reagan's father was trying to get money to
her somehow. If that were even true, would Tyson know about it?
Because if Tyson knew, then it meant not just *Anne* was mixed up in this.
Reagan was too, whether she knew it or not. Spoon started to consider
the idea that once Reagan came back from her walkabout, Tyson might
want to tail her as well. Maybe he would think she knew the location of
all this mythical money.

Too many variables and options. He couldn't think straight. In
times like this, the best thing Spoon could do for himself would be to
find an AA meeting, refocus on his sobriety, and then let the solution
present itself when his head emptied all the rubbish. Solving a problem
by not solving the problem.

He walked outside and saw no blue Chevy ute lurking along the
street. He slid into the Lexus and searched his mobile to locate a nearby
meeting, and found one at a Baptist church about a half-mile away. The
meeting started in twenty minutes, so he drove with his mobile in one
hand, navigating the twists and turns to escape the neighborhood and
join the main street.

First Baptist sat on a street corner, a nondescript building with a
single steeple reaching the sky from the center of the shingled roof. He
drove into the parking lot, then checked the Denver AA website again
for instructions. AA meetings at churches usually met in the basement,
or in the kitchen, or some other oddity.

He had ten minutes to kill until the meeting started, so he got
out of the car and circled the building, looking for a cluster of smokers.
The pre-meeting AA smoking crowd was something he could count on
to help him find the right entrance. After rounding the building, he
found a man in a Denver Nuggets t-shirt and a woman with close-
cropped hair standing near a set of doors, each of them with cancer
sticks clutched in their hands. Jackpot.

He walked toward them. "Are you two friends of Bill?"

They both smiled at him, and the woman gave him a cheeky
wink. "You bet. Meeting's inside and to the left, through the hallway in
the little room at the end. Coffee's in the kitchen to the right before you
get to the end of the hall."

"Cheers," Spoon said as he shook hands with each of them. The
man snuffed out his cigarette and held the door open. The three of them

walked inside, and Spoon entered the hallway, debating whether to get coffee. If American coffee was weak, American coffee at AA meetings was the weakest going.

Still, he glimpsed the kitchen as he passed it, and something caught his eye. A slender woman was standing next to the coffee maker, swirling a little plastic stick into a Styrofoam cup. He met her sight line and she threw a grin at him, and Spoon's jaw almost dropped. He *knew* this woman. Or he had seen her around, like the way you can start to recognize people at the grocer's if your shopping schedules sync up.

Not knowing nagged at him.

"It's right this way," the male smoker said, pointing to an open door.

Spoon followed his guides into the small space, which he reckoned was a children's classroom, given the colorful walls adorned with crayon drawings and the half-sized furniture everywhere. Someone had placed a dozen chairs in a circle in the center of the room.

The familiar woman followed him into the room and found a chair, and Spoon sat opposite her. He tried not to think about it; tried to chalk it up to a simple coincidence, because approaching some American woman uninvited might earn him a face full of pepper spray. Better to let it go and ignore the unknown worming through him, or else he'd be unable to hear a single thing said during the meeting. And if he couldn't concentrate, that would defeat the purpose of coming.

The chairperson shuffled some papers and started the meeting's opening as everyone else took their seats. At some meetings Spoon had been to, the custom was to ask out of town visitors to identify themselves, and Spoon was waiting for it.

"Anyone here visiting from out of town, or the first time at this meeting?"

Spoon raised his hand, and so did the familiar woman. They stared at each other. She nodded at him to go first.

"Spoon, alcoholic. I'm visiting from Austin."

"Hi, Spoon," murmured the group. A few of them wrinkled their foreheads and stared, given that he didn't have a Texas accent. Happened a lot when he traveled.

"My name is Jules, and I'm an alcoholic," said the familiar woman. "I'm visiting from California, but I used to live in Colorado."

The situation kept getting stranger. Spoon did his best not to gawk at Jules as the meeting progressed, but he couldn't help stealing glances every few seconds. Her eyes, her hair, the curve of her chin... all of them so familiar he felt he must have been going bonkers.

He had an idea, but it seemed so unlikely, he pushed it aside.

She didn't share during the meeting, just sat with her legs crossed and her hands clasped over one knee, intently watching each person as they spoke. To alleviate the distraction, Spoon closed his eyes and tried to listen to the speakers.

When the meeting ended, she collected her things and headed for the hallway, and he saw his chance to learn about this Jules person fading. The uncertainty burned at him, so Spoon followed her. Potential pepper spray to the face be damned. He shook a couple of hands of people who encouraged him to come back again tomorrow, but he did so quickly so he could find her before she disappeared.

In the parking lot, she pressed the unlock button on the remote control, and the lights flashed on a brand-new Kia with a rental car sticker on the back. He walked as fast as the crutches would allow, kicking gravel across the parking lot.

"Jules, hold up, please."

She turned around and raised her eyebrows at him, and in that instant, he knew for sure. Like a smack across the noggin, a simple solution appeared: Reagan plus twenty-five years. This was her mother, the same one who had disappeared a few weeks after Reagan's high school graduation.

"You're Reagan's mum."

Jules' face softened and she smiled. The same smile his girlfriend wore, which started on the left side then evened up to a full, toothy smile.

"And you're such a handsome young man. I'm not surprised she would pick you."

"How do you know who I am? What the bloody hell is going on here?"

She stepped toward him and held out her hand. "I've seen you on Reagan's Facebook page."

He wanted to ask her why she'd appeared at the same AA meeting. But more importantly, why she ran out on her daughter six years ago. Why she never visited, or called, or even wrote Reagan in the hospital. Why she hadn't come to support her daughter on Monday when they turned her father into a pile of ash.

Instead, all he said was, "I'm Spoon." Then, after a few seconds of uncomfortable silence, he regained his wits. "Why are you here, Jules?"

She seemed a little flustered, stumbling over her words. "I was actually about to park and walk up to Mitch's house when I saw you leaving and recognized you from her pictures online. I wanted to see where you were going."

Spoon felt a little embarrassed that he hadn't known he was being followed. Should have been old hat to him by this stage.

She nodded toward the church. "This used to be my home group meeting, when I lived here. So convenient, just down the street from the house."

"No, why are you *here*? In Colorado."

"Because I *can* now."

That didn't make any sense. He leaned forward on his crutches. "You're going to have to explain because I don't follow you."

"I came to see my daughter. It's time I was part of her life again and put right all the things I messed up."

Spoon was too overwhelmed to know how to interpret Jules' words. He said the first thing that popped into his mind, hoping he could keep her talking until he got answers. "Okay, so where were you coming from?"

"Sacramento."

"And did you just get in?"

She readjusted her purse on her shoulder. "Almost. I checked into my hotel, then I made a quick stop-off to see Mitchell's brother."

Spoon jerked his head upwards. "Wait, what? You went to see who?"

"I don't know if you would have met him. He doesn't come around to family functions too much. He didn't come to the memorial service either, apparently. I went to see Reagan's uncle Tyson."

CHAPTER TWENTY-FIVE

2:30 pm

Reagan crouched at the intersection of three large rocks, forty feet from the main trail. She braced herself between them, struggling to get her breathing under control. Her hands felt cold and clammy against the hard surfaces.

I know where you live, bitch.

Dalton's words echoed. Why was this happening? How could a member of her family treat her this way?

She listened as Charlie wailed about the cut in his leg. The sound of his suffering burned her, brought tears to her eyes.

"Fine, Charlie, I'll be right there," Dalton said, his voice distant from her hiding spot.

She craned her neck to try to hear Dalton walk away. In a couple minutes, she heard both of them talking, and their voices were the same volume. Charlie had stopped his pained cries, so he must have been less injured than he thought. Good. She assumed Dalton was away from the trail now, or at least she hoped so. Couldn't sit here forever.

Time to make an escape. She lamented all the things she would have to leave behind in her pack, which was a hundred feet back on the trail above her… her headlamp, sunscreen, hiking poles, *cell phone*. Leaving that last item behind seemed horrific enough that she toyed with the idea of sneaking back up to her pack to take it. But the risk was too great because he could be hiding behind a tree nearby, waiting for her… what was she going to do, have a bloody knife fight with her cousin?

No, she had to get away. Get away and let everyone calm down. Get out of the park, call Spoon, find out what the key unlocks, decipher the note from Dad, find the money… then what? No idea.

This is why she'd stashed the emergency blanket and the food. She'd prepared for this.

As quietly as possible, she crept away from the rock, peering around it, but the steep angle of the mountainside hid her cousins from her. With each step, she focused on the terrain above for any sights or sounds.

Guilt about leaving Charlie behind stung her, but with Dalton brandishing that hunting knife, there was nothing she could do. She had to hope that Dalton would help his little brother and that whatever injury he'd sustained wasn't severe. Maybe they'd stumble on a park ranger who could get him out of the park.

Keeping her body low—which was much easier without thirty pounds on her back—she moved through the trees toward lake Nanita, while edging away from the trail, where she had to assume Dalton would be looking for her. She hiked like this for ten minutes, deeper into the woods. There wasn't the same level of untamed brush as near Lake Haynach, but she stayed mindful of stray sharp limbs and branches. One turned ankle and she'd become useless.

When she saw the lake to her left, she stopped and looked around. There were no other people in sight. Her pulse raced through her like a bass drum, obscuring her ability to listen to the forest. She focused on slowing her heart rate and made the world slow with her. Birds, rustling wind through the trees: she made all of these things change. They became in tune with her body and she felt at peace with them. An odd sense of power moved through her.

But she didn't know where to go next. Andrews Peak was directly before her, Ptarmigan Mountain to her right, and Alice Peak to her left. Ideally, she should double back and pick up her pack. But that's what Dalton would expect her to do, so she had to send that idea to the recycle bin. Returning to the Tonahutu trail was also out of the question.

She closed her eyes and went into Dalton's thinking. She saw what he would see. Dalton would make Charlie stop complaining and they would go down the trail, dragging her pack behind them to use as bait. They would wait somewhere along the trail, perhaps at Nokoni or back on the main trail, and when she passed, they would jump out and take her.

"I can't let them take me. I am my own and no one can have me." Her own voice sounded strange, like listening to a recording. Thick, heavy, not like how she sounded in real life.

The world around her seemed vibrant and more colorful than it had been that morning. She understood now why this betrayal had happened to her, and the knowing made sense. She had a part to play in something grander than what she'd originally anticipated. Foolish that she hadn't seen it before. She was to find the money Dad had hidden and use it for... for what, she didn't know yet.

Degenerate gambler. Degenerate gambler. Degenerate gambler. Degenerate gambler. Dalton's caustic portrayal of Dad coursed through her veins. How could he have been a gambler? Was it possible? Reagan wasn't so sure anymore. If he wasn't, then where had the money come from? Pieces of the puzzle were missing.

Mitchell Darby had carried a life force inside of him until the heart attack had taken it and thrown it inside an empty casket for people to gawk at. The money was his legacy, and he meant for Reagan to have it. This realization hit her so suddenly that she almost fell over. So clear and evident. Finding the money and closing the casket were the same, and she had to find it because nothing else mattered.

"Focus, Reagan, focus," she said as she knelt and looked at the three visible mountain peaks. Alice was too far. Ptarmigan was too rocky and she wouldn't be able to pass it without climbing gear. Andrews was straight ahead. Somewhere on the other side of the peak was the path that went to Lake Verna and exited the park via the East Inlet. She knew that trail, which ran parallel to the return leg of the Tonahutu loop. All she had to do was cross Andrews Peak and find Lake Verna. Then she would be on the right path back to Spoon, back to the money, and back to understanding.

She set off for Andrews, aware that scaling the mountain would take hours and time was short. Without the pack on her back, she became as light as a bird, floating through the trees and over the rocks and feeling the soft nettles of pine crunch underneath her every step. The sensation thrilled her. She wished a mountain squirrel or fox or deer would come up to her and she could share the creature's beauty up close. Deer scared too easily. Twenty feet seemed to be the threshold that made them flee.

A monstrous scree field sat at the base of Andrews. The broken boulders were almost white, like enormous grains of salt in mid-cascade down the peak. But the problem was the lack of tree cover. A few of them littered the mountainside, but not above 12,000 feet. If Dalton was stalking her, he would easily spot her scrambling over the rocks at that height.

She looked back across the lake and to the surrounding area. She didn't feel them. Their energy wasn't here. But if they weren't at Nanita now, they would be soon. They knew she was coming here to release the ashes.

She examined the scree field and plotted a course that would divert to the right of the peak, through a low point so she could cross without having to scale the summit of the mountain. No way to know the exact elevation, but some of the higher portion broached treeline.

She started up the scree, and felt the urn duct-taped to her stomach wiggle against the tape. If it became too slick with sweat, the duct tape would come loose and she'd have to carry it. She'd grown accustomed to having Dad's remains next to her body, sharing warmth.

Commanding her body to stop sweating, she squinted toward the shore of the lake, looking for any movement. Aside from a gentle rustle of trees from wind, there was no sign of anything.

The climb through the scree field dragged on for what felt like hours. The rocks grew bigger and bigger until she had to pull herself up and throw her legs over them to gain ground. Established trails in the park plotted courses between the rocks, but once off trail, you had to find your own way.

Every part of her body ached from the effort, and she often stopped to catch her breath and study the lake. She had to hide for a few minutes when two figures appeared at the lakeside, but she was too high up to tell if they were Dalton and Charlie. No sense taking chances, so she remained out of sight until the figures left.

Climbing, rest, more climbing. Watching the sun move across the sky. Wishing she had water to coat the dryness in her throat.

When she finally reached the notch beside Andrews peak, she looked down at Lake Nanita, at the deep blue water rippling against the shore. That was where Dad's ashes were supposed to go, but it wasn't possible. She touched her shirt and felt the bump of the urn.

"I'm going to find you a new home, Daddy."

In the other direction, toward the southern end of Rocky Mountain National Park, she'd find her day's destination. Somewhere below her was Lake Verna, and if she could find that, she could find the East Inlet trail and hike her way to the trailhead at the edge of the park. Not the trailhead she'd started from on Tuesday, but one only a mile or two south of it. From there, she could find a way back to her car. Back to Spoon, back to the world.

Warnings from Dad about the dangers of going off trail thudded inside her head. She laughed. She was doing just fine off trail. The wild woods of the park were in tune with her, and she was in tune with them. If she kept her focus on being a part of nature instead of being apart from nature, nothing could hurt her. She felt increasingly sure of this and let the knowledge drive her onward.

She eased down the less rocky southern side of Andrews peak as some clouds lifted and the sun baked her. The vitamin D entered her skin, the sun changed her and made her more like the nature around her. The sun touched everything. She was everything. Everything was togetherness.

So many things were suddenly making sense to her that baffled her before. But she also knew that this understanding was not natural. She'd come by this enlightenment, not by the organic method she should have, but some other way. How? She didn't yet know.

A lake came into view and she didn't know the time because she'd left her phone back with her pack. The position of the sun indicated late afternoon.

She wished she owned a topographical map. With her eyes closed, she tried to feel the elevation, but the signals crossed and as the lake below her grew in size with each step toward it, she wasn't even sure which one she'd found. Spirit Lake? Lake Verna? Hopefully, Verna. Spirit was too far east along the trail. Verna would put her at seven miles from the East Inlet trailhead. She could hike that tomorrow, easily.

She reached an even level with the lake and found a path through the dirt. When she saw it, she dropped to her knees and kissed the grainy and damp surface. The universe was guiding her where she needed to go. There could be no doubt about that.

She walked by the lake, found a rock that jutted over the edge, and sat. For several endless minutes, she watched the calm waters as darting fish and frogs made ripples that grew and receded. She understood the fish and the frogs and the mosquitoes that buzzed around her. She didn't even mind the mosquitoes feeding on her life force. They were all a part of nature.

When the sun began to set, she shivered, so she took the emergency blanket from its pouch and unfolded the crinkly piece of Mylar. She stuck her legs inside of it, then emptied her pockets and set the items next to her on the trail. Pocket knife, a few granola bars, car keys, the pouch for the blanket.

She removed the duct tape from her stomach and set the urn next to her. She picked up a granola bar and had no desire to eat it, despite not having eaten since breakfast. Or did she have lunch? She couldn't remember. Either way, the thought of chewing and swallowing didn't appeal to her at all.

Guilt over leaving Charlie behind fluttered in her head, but she wouldn't let it take hold. The park would care for him and prevent anything bad happening to him. The park would work through Dalton and ensure safe passage for her innocent cousin.

She wrapped the blanket around her and closed her eyes, but sleep didn't come. Her heart raced and her brain fired countless neurons simultaneously, flooding her thoughts and driving ideas faster than she could understand. At first, this confused her, but as her mind kept processing faster, eventually the answer came to her.

Manic.

Friday

CHAPTER TWENTY-SIX

The first glimpse of illness came to her in high school, although a much milder version than the situation that led to the mania, crashing depression, and subsequent suicide attempt at age twenty-two. As a teenager, the mania might last a few days and she would feel vibrant and passionate, would stay up for one or two nights and drink coffee and discuss philosophy and brazenly tell cute boys exactly what she thought of them.

Following the high came a couple weeks of lowness and anger, trouble concentrating on schoolwork, and lack of interest in after-school activities. The drama teacher begged her not to quit, but Reagan couldn't imagine herself going on stage anymore.

At the time, she was convinced the mood swings were natural, but Mom and Dad insisted she see a shrink anyway. Reagan was clever to convince the shrink she needed no medication. She spent the next few years in and out of therapy, and any time the word "bipolar" crept into conversation, a wall went up.

This trend lasted throughout college in Austin, until her fourth year. The week before classes started, Reagan was leaving a bar on 6th street as a man on the sidewalk pulled a pistol and shot a woman in the head. The chaos of the aftermath of that moment created her first serious manic episode, which trampled the course of her life for the next several months.

At first, everything was right in the world as the mania grew. Her voice exuded confidence and passion, and she often became impatient with others and their lack of insight. She spoke with subtext and poetry and she lashed out when people didn't appreciate her gift. Every word that came out of her mouth would be quoted by a team of scribes following her someday, recording everything for the sake of history.

All her actions were part of a great intellectual revolution, and she held a key role as a kind of secular spiritual leader. She studied Kerouac and the works of Richard Bach, particularly *Illusions*, an allegorical tale about a pilot who meets the messiah reborn in the cornfields of Illinois. With each reading, she further unlocked the mystery of how she might become a new version of this same messiah. But not a religious messiah, because they'd done nothing but lie and use people. Religion was a set of rules, and spirituality was a way to understand the inner self. She would be a new kind of messiah who could lead people away from the lies and hypocrisy of religion and toward the light of truth and realization. A true messiah.

She was a teacher who could dissolve fear and show people their true selves. Unique insight allowed her to glimpse the real psychology and spirituality that formed the universe. The universe chose her to illuminate and enlighten and help those addicted to the material world of illusions and attachments.

She worked part-time in a bank to supplement her student loans, but the job became a limitation. She was able to interact with people superficially, but not allowed to help them. The job prevented her from giving them education about the prisons they had constructed for themselves.

When her boss fired her from that job, she took it as a sign. She went to work dancing in a topless bar, and that opportunity unlocked many new doors for her. Sick people came to her for healing, and she moved her body and gave them energy and freed them from the shackles of their captive lives.

Sexuality blossomed through dance. Having slept with only four boys in all of high school and college, she realized how she'd deprived herself of the truth of connectedness. In *Illusions*, Richard Bach wrote that learning is rediscovering something already known. She rediscovered how to talk to men in order to create the symbiotic relationship required for healing. Strong and seductive, or meek and needy, or intellectually mysterious and clever, or whatever was necessary to establish the connection. The men she took to her bed became healed and enlightened more than the ones she healed from the stage.

She made piles of money moving her body onstage but never seemed to save any of it. Whatever she made, she gave away or spent on extravagant dinners with her friends. Chunks of time evaporated, and when she would come out of a blind spot, there would be pages of new apps on her phone she had no memory of buying and downloading. She would purchase forty or fifty books at a time for her Kindle.

School lost its value. What was the point of education when she already knew everything, she just had to rediscover and unlock it? She argued with professors in class about their teaching methods and their inability to interpret the textbooks with the same insights she possessed. Her Psychology of the Elderly professor asked her to leave class one day, which she did gladly.

Not everyone was willing to be enlightened. Her friends stopped asking her to come out to coffee and lost the willingness to hear about truth. She needed to try harder. Beatrice would rarely stay in the same room of the apartment with her as the fall semester progressed. Beatrice only seemed to care about whose turn it was to do the dishes, clean the toilet, or take the rent check to the landlord. Reagan didn't understand the refusal to see the larger beauty of the universe.

The crash came three months after it began, but it wasn't sudden like a light switch flicking. If she had to pinpoint a single event that sent her from mania to the depression that would change everything, it began two nights before Thanksgiving. She'd called Dad and explained that she couldn't come home for the holidays because she had too much schoolwork. He said he understood, but his tone dripped with concern and unease. Her thoughts were firing so fast, her mouth started skipping over words as she tried to explain why she needed to stay in Austin, for the benefit of everyone. So many things to do and so many people to help. She could barely keep up with it all.

She tried calling a few friends, but no one answered their phones. They usually hung out at a particular coffee shop, so she drove there and walked in to find a group of them at their regular table in the back.

They turned and looked at her as she called to them, but then they all averted their eyes and went back to their own conversation. They closed the circle.

Just like that, they excommunicated Reagan from the group, and the questioning and criticism began to overtake joy. Why did no one like her? What was the flaw in her that pushed her outside the circle?

At first, she tried to shrug it off, but self-examination became self-criticism, and within a week, she no longer wanted to get out of bed. Within a few months, she was swallowing a handful of Valiums, looking for a way to silence the ruthlessness of her own mind.

***

5:20 am

Reagan doesn't sleep. She stays in the emergency blanket because of the frigid park air, but she keeps her eyes open, watching the stars appear and disappear as clouds roll in front of them.

She thinks about Spoon and the money and the key and Dad's note and the possibilities of all things. The key opens something, but no telling what. It looks like a safe deposit box key, but Dad never had one of those. As far as she knows.

The key unlocks the money and the money unlocks many options. With the money, she and Spoon can open some kind of school where professors and wise people from all around the world can come to teach for free, to make the world a better place. They will teach men how to love women without hurting them. They will teach parents how to raise their children without the shackles of religion. They will fix the world.

The casket is empty, but there is a means to an end.

Cold. She shivers inside the emergency blanket, which crinkles with every movement like shiny Christmas wrapping paper. Must stop making so much sound. She thinks about bears, and wonders if one were to come along if it might stop and sniff her.

She would feel safer inside a tent. But that's ridiculous, because A) a tent provides a millimeter's-thickness of protection between the inside and the outside world, and B) the bear will not harm her because they are the same. They are both of understanding and they are both of nature.

When the sun starts to rise, the reflected hue of the mountains around Lake Verna changes from gray to yellow and it's the most beautiful thing she's ever seen. More special than the Grand Canyon or the sheer cliffs of Yosemite... this is it, this moment.

She climbs out of the emergency blanket and takes her clothes off. The cold tickles her naked skin, but she needs to experience nature uninhibited. The makeshift rope hipbelt has left red welts all over her hip, and Arnica or Tiger Balm or at least aloe would help, but she doesn't have any of those things. She will have to heal herself with sunlight and oxygen.

Deep breath in. Exhale. The world enters, she takes what she needs, and lets the excess return.

Her arms spread out wide as the sun lights the trees to the east and then passes over her, warming her from the outside in. The day is colored green and glorious.

She looks down at her exposed flesh and imagines Spoon standing behind her, wrapping his arms around her waist and gyrating back and forth, the slow dance he does with her sometimes in the kitchen of their tiny Austin apartment when she's making dinner and a good slow song comes up in the rotation. She can almost feel his flesh against her flesh and it tickles her like cat whiskers against bare skin. She's horny, for the first time in what seems like forever.

Spoon. Have to get back to him.

She puts her clothes back on, folds the emergency blanket, then stuffs it in her pocket. She sits and cradles the urn in her hands, gliding her fingers over its smooth surface. Where did Dad get this? South America? Africa? She can't remember. She thought it morbid when he'd presented it to her for the first time, but now she sees the incomparable beauty of the design. The wood varnished to a deep brown, and the surface so smooth, like one continuous piece. Did he know there was a hidden compartment when he bought it? Did he have someone make it, or possibly build it into the urn himself?

She carries the urn down to the edge of Lake Verna and opens the top. "I know you wanted to be in Nanita, but I hope you can see how much better this is. The beauty, the nature... it's all here and it's perfect and nothing will be able to separate you from that once I have joined you with the world. I don't know if you were who they say you were, but I know you are my father and no one else helped me when I was sick. No one else bothered to take me camping, even though I didn't want to go, the guidance you gave me then helped me get better, and now I can give that peace to you and the park and to Spoon and to anyone else who is ready to feel it."

She tilts the urn until a mist of pebbly ash spills from the opening. The powder coats the water, slowly rippling on top of gentle waves. Smells like a neglected fireplace. It mixes with the liquid and becomes darker, like charcoal, and she dips her hand into it, mixing Dad into the park.

Her reflection in the water tracks and mirrors her movements back to her. A rush ascends through her feet, like an orgasm but not sexual, more like a warm meal on a cold day when the mass of energy worms its way from your mouth down your throat and into your stomach.

She shudders. This isn't the goodbye she wanted, but it is the one she has, and it is beautiful. Maybe even better than what she planned. Someday she will come back to Nanita and say goodbye properly, but she can't imagine a more perfect moment. This is it.

A twig snaps. She jerks back into awareness and covers herself, having forgotten she is no longer naked. She turns around and around, looking for the source of the sound, but there's nothing to indicate anyone nearby.

Dalton. She has almost forgotten about the cousin who threatened her life the day before. She tried to heal him on this journey, why did she fail? She needs to work harder. But not here. Not in the park. He obviously can't see the intrinsic power of beauty and they must return to Denver. If she tries to heal him here, nothing good will come of it. He's too sick with grief and she needs Spoon's help. Together, they will set right the world.

She has to get back to Spoon. While what she has done here is important, the critical tasks are back in the real world of cars and buildings and people and verbal communication.

With no camp to pack up, she starts walking along the East Inlet trail toward the western edge of Rocky Mountain National Park, ready to experience more joy and beauty of the world.

CHAPTER TWENTY-SEVEN

10:10 am

Spoon had spent the first few minutes after returning to Anne's house in shock. Not only was Jules from the AA meeting Reagan's mother, she had also named that loud-mouthed, henchman-slapping bloke Tyson as Reagan's uncle. She'd said these words so casually, like no big deal. Common knowledge.

Spoon hadn't realized he was in the middle of a grand family reunion. If Tyson was her uncle, why hadn't Reagan ever mentioned him before?

The parking lot convo had ended shortly after this revelation, and Spoon didn't draw any more helpful information from Jules. She said she would 'be in touch' with Reagan after her backpacking trip.

But now, at least, Spoon had some dots to connect, and a theory about why Anne had been so dismissive. She didn't want it known that this Tyson thug who'd been harassing her was one of her relatives.

Tyson was after the money that seemed to be missing from the will. Or maybe the money wasn't an inheritance… he'd never actually said that's where it was supposed to be. Anne was the one talking about the will.

Tyson assumed the missing money was rightfully his. His and Mitch's father, Frank Darby, had claimed that Reagan's dad had socked it away somewhere in a safety deposit box, but Frank offered no information about where the money was or how it came to be hidden. Frank believed that Reagan knew something about it, or at least Mitchell intended for her to know. And if Tyson knew that—which he probably would since he'd visited Frank—then Tyson might hold her accountable.

There were still pieces that didn't fit. Was the money real? Where was the safety deposit box? How much did Tyson know? Why had Reagan's mother made such a sudden and surprising appearance? Jules tied into the whole mess somehow.

Spoon had spent the last three days thinking Anne was in trouble, but what if Tyson was actually after Reagan?

The last question plagued him the most, and on Friday morning, he decided to do something about it. He had to keep Reagan safe. If only he could talk to her, he could tell her to get out of the park, to come home so they could leave. But her mobile was off, or dead. He was on his own.

When he woke, Anne was gone, so he took a quick wake-up shower and decided to use the neighbor's Lexus to drive north through Denver to the lawnmower shop in Broomfield. Answers should be coming soon.

No blue Chevy ute waited outside to follow him today, so he didn't bother with the careful driving. He did have to refill the gas tank at the servo, which made him painfully aware that he was now unemployed and needed to be cautious about money. There had still been no word from the job prospect about rescheduling the New Orleans interview. That seemed like a lost cause.

As he approached Tyson's shop, he parked behind the Slinky Grape across the street and walked in a meandering arc behind his destination. His knee throbbed with every click of the crutches.

The little shop had front, side, and back doors. The side and back doors both opened to fenced-in areas. The side looked like some kind of lawnmower storage area/graveyard, and the back door's chain-link fence area was much smaller. Like a porch, almost. The side door seemed to be the best bet.

182

There were two cars out front: the blue Chevy Tahoe and an aging red Corvette. Tyson and a customer? Tyson and one of his associates?

Spoon rounded the shop and checked out the side fence, secured with a weighty padlock. Made sense, since hundreds or thousands of dollars of lawnmowers were sitting inside. The fence was three meters tall, and with his bad leg, no way Spoon was going to scale that thing. The rattling of the fence might be enough to draw attention.

The gate on the back fence wore no padlock to protect it. As he lifted the latch holding the gate in place, the metal creaked as it swung open, and his throat tightened until he couldn't swallow. He was doing this. He was breaking into a place of business. Not exactly what his AA sponsor would call *living a program of rigorous honesty.*

Exceptions had to be made. His future wife might be in danger and the only person who could give him answers was probably inside this shop right now.

He inched toward the back door, hand shaking as he reached out to touch it. The door had no knob, instead opened with a handle like one on a tea cup. Not locked, which was a shocker. He immediately released his grip on it. What if the door squeaked when he opened it? Would someone come at him with a shotgun? Americans loved their firearms, especially shopkeepers. And the shop looked no bigger than the living room of his apartment; maybe 150 square meters total. They'd be on him in a flash.

He stared at the door, licked his lips, unsure what to do.

Every second standing here was another second they might accidentally find him. Time to take the risk.

He placed both hands on the handle and pulled as slowly as humanly possible. It opened with no squeak. He stopped when the crack was big enough to stick his head through and he peered inside.

Then he understood why they'd left the back gate and door unlocked. Something obstructed the door. Some kind of metal shelving littered from top to bottom with objects that looked like motors, engine parts, tubing, valves, and gaskets. All of these objects projected mustiness, and the overwhelming odor of dust and grease almost made him gag.

183

Between two engines, he glimpsed the interior. Rows and rows of similar shelving cut through the tiny shop, arranged like a maze.

"No, no, no," came Tyson's booming voice.

Spoon almost released his grip on the door, but steadied himself.

"What? What did I do?" This new voice sounded nasal, like someone with a cold.

"We need to keep the Hondas and the Briggs & Strattons separated. You keep them on the same shelf and customers can't tell them apart," Tyson said.

"So we're putting stuff by brand?"

"Look, I know where everything is. Honda over there, Briggs & Stratton over there, Kohler in the back. You move shit around, I won't know what's what. And if you break anything, it's coming out of your check. Inventory's tight this quarter, so don't you mess it up."

"Sorry, boss. I'll be careful."

Spoon's arm started to ache. The door was heavy and attached to some kind of spring that wanted to pull it closed.

He waited through two more minutes of lawnmower inventory discussion until they finally got around to something interesting.

"How are we with the other thing?" Tyson said.

"I'm trying to follow up on what your dad told us, but he don't know the bank or anything, so there ain't much to do. I was thinking we should go and hire us a private investigator. Those guys can look at financial records and all that stuff. Find out when and where he rented a safe deposit box."

"Ok, genius," Tyson said, "how exactly does that work? What do you think he's going to do when he finds out there's almost a quarter-mil in cash in there? Do you think he's *not* going to tell the police about that? And then they come by the shop and start sniffing around what we do here?"

"Are you saying he'll tell the cops?"

"We can't take that chance, dumbass. Use your head."

"I thought once you hired them, they had… what do you call it? Immunity or whatever. Like how your lawyer can't say shit."

Tyson let out a long sigh. "Dalton will be back later today. We'll see what he got."

184

Goose bumps broke out over Spoon's flesh. Where was Dalton and what was he going to get? Then it occurred to him that if Tyson was Reagan's uncle, he must be Dalton and Charlie's father.

He leaned closer to the door, but the shuffling feet were going away from him. Tyson and his associate continued to talk, but their voices became muffled.

The front door opened. They were going outside.

Spoon panicked. If they were talking about Dalton, they could also be talking about Reagan. And if they were going to the front of the shop, he couldn't stroll around to the entrance to get a better listen. These people had been following him, so they weren't exactly his mates.

Spoon limped backward and let the door close. His eyes darted around the back porch, searching for a solution.

Then he saw it. A jumbled stack of plastic crates up against the fence. They looked sturdy enough, and if he could make a pyramid of a few, he could access the roof.

He went to work stacking a row of three crates, with two on top of that and one to complete the pyramid. The height placed him within a meter of the roof. He set his crutches on the ground and hopped onto the first row, using the fence to steady himself. The crates seemed sturdy enough.

Onto the second row, then the top container. He was close enough to the storm drain jutting from the edge of the roof that he could touch it. He planted each hand above the storm drain, grasping rubbery shingles. With the blinding sun above, the shingles nearly burned his hand, but he resisted the impulse to yelp and let go.

He pulled with all his might until his head was above the storm drain, then pushed against the shingles. He held his breath so he didn't grunt with all the exertion. Once he had reached the extent of his arms, his waist was even with the rooftop. He kicked his good leg up and his foot landed in the storm drain. One last push with his hands vaulted his body on top of the roof. Too much noise.

The roof angled upwards to a peak, and he crawled toward it, one side at a time like a soldier crawling through muck under barbed wire. When he reached the top, he peered forward and again heard the voices. He started to crawl down the other side, careful about the

185

swishing noises his trousers were making against the rooftop. Smoke wafted into the air from the front of the shop.

He stopped when their heads popped into view. They were both smoking cigarettes, Tyson pointing a finger at the other man's chest. The nasally-voiced man had plastic hearing aids encircling both his ears.

"That's not your goddamned problem," Tyson said. "You let *me* worry about retribution for what my brother stole. You focus on finding the money."

"I know, boss, I'm just saying," the other man said.

Spoon inched forward to get a better look at the two men. His brain raced to catalog all this new information.

"When she gets back, I'm going to talk to her. Your job is to follow her if talking to her doesn't help. For all we know, the money isn't in a bank somewhere, Mitch stashed it out there on the trail. Dalton and Charlie could be coming back with a big suitcase and then this whole thing will be over. If it's not, then we got to worry."

Spoon stopped himself from gasping. Were Dalton and Charlie in the park with Reagan?

"I need to know how far you want me to take this, boss. I need to know where the line is at. This could go a lot of ways."

Spoon lowered himself and inched forward again, and his belt buckle scraped a shingle. The *scrack* was like thunder.

Tyson and his associate both snapped their heads upward, right at Spoon. Looks of confusion quickly bled into anger.

Spoon tried to scramble backwards, but there was nowhere to go. They'd seen him. The breadth of Tyson's scowl sent a shiver down Spoon's backside.

"You," Tyson said. "Why do I always seem to find you hovering above me like a goddamned cloud?"

"That's the guy staying at Anne's house," the nasally bloke said.

"I know who it is, genius. Liam Witherspoon. Why don't you come down off my roof, Liam? You and me need to have a talk."

CHAPTER TWENTY-EIGHT

11:00 am

With each step along the rocky path, another jolt from the ground shocks Reagan's foot and spreads to her calf and to her thighs. Muscles have been drained the last four days, in ways she hasn't anticipated. Saturday morning bike rides with Spoon in Austin are measly outings compared to hiking thirty miles at 10,000 feet.

Escape from Dalton and Charlie has taken her from the Tonahutu loop to the East Inlet trail, which is a parallel route a mile to the south. Separating the two trails are a series of mountain peaks. East Inlet also leads to a parking lot on the west side of the park, but a different lot than the one where she parked Dad's car. That's a worry for later this afternoon, when she's done with the trail.

As the sun rises above the mountains and she's hiked enough to work up a sweat, she stops shivering. She crosses wooden bridges over streams next to pulsing waterfalls. The trail sometimes curves around boulders as big as houses.

The trail becomes a jumble of mud and tree roots and little rocks, and often her feet land at odd angles, creating slashes of fear that she's broken her ankle. But she presses on.

A laminated sign nailed to a tree:

Trail condition warning. Due to a recent fire various travel hazards exist in the next several miles. Use caution and good judgment when crossing the affected area.
Potential hazards include:
Falling trees
Slope instability & mud slides
Collapsing trail tread
Difficulty following designated trails due to fire damage
Damage to bridges
Possible re-ignition of fire.

While she's studying the text, voices drift from up ahead, around a bend in the trail. Multiple people are talking. Several options occur to her at once. She can ask them if they have a camera. She can ask them if they understand about loving everyone equally. They won't. No one understands love. It's her job to teach them.

Darker options also come to mind. These people might not be friendly. They might be some of the unenlightened people who are sick and need healing. What if she is unable to heal them? She hasn't been meditating and studying healing for a long time. What if she doesn't remember how to do it? What if these people ahead are Dalton and Charlie? Dalton wants to hurt her. Dalton wants to take the key and the note and find the money and shame Dad's name by not letting her use the money to open the educational center.

The center needs a name. What should she call it? Approaching Awareness? No, that's cheesy. Something like that, but profound.

She shakes her head free of the mess. Need to focus. The voices are getting louder. There are too many possibilities and not enough time. Hide. It's the only option.

She scans the nearby area. To her right is a hill littered with skinny tall trees. To her left is a valley, which quickly becomes steep as it drops to a creek below. Uphill. The best choice.

A second of panic. Is she still naked? She looks down. Keeps forgetting that she put on her clothes before she left Lake Verna.

She darts up the hill and traversing the incline burns her quads. The trees are too skinny to hide behind. A pile of them up the hill might provide cover, but it's too far away.

Maybe she can make it. She has to make it.

The voices pulse below her as she lunges toward the pile, chest heaving. The collection of fallen wood lies sad and dead on the hillside. She feels pain for the trees, but it's just another part of the rebirth of the forest.

She scrambles behind the pile and peers over. Two males and a female hike below on the trail, all three of them young and glowing with energy. Reagan forgot about seeing auras. Light practically radiates from their heads as they climb uphill, tapping their hiking poles against the ground.

Reagan squints to get a better look at them. One of them is wearing an enormous black pad on his back, like a mattress folded in half. It's a bouldering crash pad. These kids aren't part of Dalton, they're here to rock climb.

Still, Reagan has committed to her hiding place. She can't leave it now.

"Don't trouble yourselves," she whispers to the log.

In a minute, they pass, the youthful energy of their voices fading. She waits until they are definitely gone and then returns to the trail. Part of her feels silly for hiding, part of her thinks she did the right thing. No way to know.

The trees sigh. The breeze takes the sounds and massages them. The rocks bleed minerals into the air, and Reagan's lungs pull in the minerals. She exhales the elements she doesn't need, now understanding how the universe works. What if no one else understands? Spoon will understand. He is so much smarter and more talented than he realizes. He is a beautiful Australian boy and she loves him, even though she hasn't shown him properly for too long.

A couple minutes along the trail, she finds the truth of the warning nailed to the tree before. Several thousand square feet of trail have been burned to a crisp. Apparently, an avalanche has come through recently, because the trail appears broken, sections of it vanished and cratered like canyons. Feelings mix as she looks over the devastation of the fire zone… sadness at the loss of life, but hope in the renewal of the forest.

All around, burned tree limbs litter the ground. The husks of these burned limbs shimmer like scaly snakeskin under the force of the sun. The trees that haven't fallen stick up from the earth like chopsticks, wearing grungy black coats of amber and ash.

At the end of the burned area, another tree wears the same laminated warning card. She touches it as she moves past the devastation.

Within two hours of starting her hike, as the sun begins to toast her skin, she reaches One Pine Lake at the bottom of a steep trail. She knows this place now, and she's oriented. She hiked this trail the summer after her first year in college. But she was only two-dimensional then, or closer to it. She didn't understand it as she does now.

At the lake, she pauses to splash water on her face and consider her options. She reads the rain-blurred letter from Dad again.

Dearest Reagan,

I wish I had time to write everything I want to say, but … I had hoped that you … I made some mistakes. I was selfish. And I'm sorry … what the key in … farmer's market. You'll understand when you get there. Your grandfather … I hate to be so vague, but I … to say I'm sorry, other than to tell you that I'm proud of you and I love you. I know that's not good enough.

Dad

You'll understand when you get there.

"What were you selfish about? Where will I understand, Dad?"

All the terrible things Dalton said about him. Degenerate gambler. Empty casket. Or is the casket no longer empty? She spread the ashes into the water. Did it work?

And what does her grandpa have to do with anything? He is slipping away in an old-folks home in Boulder, his life slowly extinguishing. Is she supposed to take him to the educational center? Maybe that's the answer. Maybe he is meant to be a teacher and help spread awareness of love, with whatever time he has left.

The lake has given her some answers, but not enough. She removes a granola bar from her pocket and reads the ingredients. High

Fructose Corn Syrup. Partially Hydrogenated Soybean Oil. Poison. She almost throws the bar into the lake, but that's a terrible way to repay the lake for helping her understand some of Dad's letter.

As the sun rises overhead, she reaches the East Inlet Falls. Her skin begs for sunscreen, but she has none. There are a number of people watching the falls, and none of them scare her until a little girl waves. Why is she waving? What does she know? Reagan decides not to find out. She must leave.

She follows the falls to the East Inlet river, which will take her to the trailhead. What will she do there? She'll still be a few miles from her car. Can't worry about that now.

The river winds and bends next to the trail and it whispers that she is doing the right thing, that her cause is noble and just. That no one can hurt her as long as she remembers that.

But what if the river is lying?

Degenerate gambler.

Charlie. She left him behind. He was injured and hurt and scared and she ran away. He needed healing almost as much as Dalton and she abandoned him. That was wrong. But what can she do about it now? He is with Dalton and Dalton is sick and so Charlie is suffering. When Reagan gets stronger, she can heal them all.

She comes to a broad open meadow on one side and a hill reaching a small peak on the other. Grunts mix with the whispers of the aspens and the river. The grunts don't fit. They are not trees or river or wind or bird calls.

The grunts belong to a moose. A baby calf, no bigger than a golden retriever. Its coat is the color of rust. The grunts are the sounds it makes as it yanks leaves from the twigs of a freshly-fallen tree.

The baby is beautiful. It is not the trees or the river, but it is nature too. Its grunts *do* fit and Reagan can now categorize them among the rest.

"You are beautiful."

The calf stops chewing and stares at her. It looks into her eyes and it is not afraid. It does not run away.

"I understand you," Reagan says. "I am of nature too. Maybe you can't see that but you and I are the same. I'm here for the same reason as you."

The calf now retreats a few steps. It's looking past Reagan, looking for something else.

Louder grunts. Two hundred feet higher on the hill, another moose roots through a disintegrated log. This one looms larger, its coat a husky gray. No horns sit atop its donkey-like head.

This is the baby's mother.

"Hello, mother," Reagan says. "There's nothing to worry about. I'm not going to harm your child. If I harm her, I harm myself. Do you understand?"

The mama moose, which has been chewing, stops. Her angular head points at Reagan, eyes black and devoid of emotion. Her fuzzy brown ears flatten against her head. The moose eases down the hill toward her. Slowly at first, then with increasing speed. The sound of hooves tromping the hillside grows louder.

Only a hundred feet separate Reagan and the mama. "It's okay. I'm not here to hurt your baby."

Mama grunts. She's closing the distance between them.

Danger. This is danger. Needles dance all over Reagan's sunburned skin and she feels like she's falling. The moose is going to kill her because it doesn't understand. It doesn't see how they are all the same and must hear it out loud.

"You'll be killing yourself," Reagan shouts. "Why can't you see that?"

Thirty feet between them. The moose stops, its hooves digging into moist earth.

Reagan looks left and right. There are trees to climb, but they are too skinny. The branches won't support her, and the moose will ram any tree she climbs to knock her out of it.

"Don't do this," Reagan says, widening her stance and holding out her hands.

The moose lowers its head and charges. Hooves like thunder against the grass.

In a flash, brown and gray rush toward Reagan. She wants to run, but she knows the moose is too quick. She can't outrun it. So she waits.

Twenty feet. Ten feet. The moose is upon her.

Reagan ducks and rolls to the left while the moose runs past. Reagan's shoulders crunch against the ground as she tumbles. Pain sprinkles along her back.

This freedom won't last. The moose scrambles and turns back to her, nostrils flared and eyes on fire. Only five feet away, the moose lowers like a cat readying to jump.

Reagan tries to stand, slips, and she's on her back. Above her, the moose raises its front hooves and emits some kind of awful scream as it thrusts them forward. The wind moves, then she feels the horrible sensation of being punched in the stomach, but harder and more painful than anything she's ever experienced. The moose's hooves have dug into her ribcage.

If Reagan had eaten anything today, she would have spewed it all over herself. She gasps for breath as the moose removes the hooves from Reagan's belly. Can't breathe. The moose has stolen her air. Reagan's vision turns spotty and full of pinpricks of light.

The moose rears back to attack again, but this time, Reagan reacts. When the moose's body falls, Reagan twists out of the way, and the moose hooves slam into grass. Pushing off the ground, Reagan thrusts her shoulder into the furry belly, which knocks the moose off-balance, its body twisting in midair. With a wail, it falls on its side, thudding against the ground.

The beast shudders and moans. It kicks hooves through the air.

Gasps turn into coughs, and Reagan's eyes land on the trail.

She jumps to her feet, vision swirling, as the massive creature struggles to get its legs under it. Reagan's breath comes in interrupted gasps and hitches as if she's choking.

She hurls her body forward with all her might toward a cluster of aspens, her vision jerky and her chest on fire. Her heart might explode against her ribcage. She has never felt danger like this before. All of her senses come alive at once and she can't tell the difference between the sounds of the birds and the feeling of the dirt beneath her feet. Sensation is realization and the world is burning.

She reaches the aspens, into a cluster of three trees close together. Close enough that she can wedge herself between them. It's cover, but if the moose charges again, it can probably smash through, and then Reagan will have nowhere to run.

The moose stands still, a massive bulk rising and falling with each labored breath. The beast shakes its body like a dog drying off after a bath.

Reagan and the moose look into each other's eyes, silent. Knowing. Understanding.

The calf tumbles toward its mother, little skinny legs moving awkwardly as if they are working independently from each other. The calf bumps against its mother's leg. Mama pauses, then lowers her head and nudges the calf away.

Reagan stays motionless. Is the moose's vision based on movement? She can't remember.

The calf mewls and the mama nudges her again, stamping a hoof against the ground. The baby trots toward the meadow and the mama follows. They are leaving.

Reagan spends thirty seconds—or maybe thirty minutes— bracing her hands against the aspens and letting her breath return to normal. Her heartbeat becomes regular, and the danger drains from her senses. She had to hurt the moose, and for that, she feels terrible. But what else could she have done? There was no time to create a better reaction. No time.

Did that really just happen? Seems impossible. The world bends and twists and oozes reality, or lack of it.

She lifts her shirt and examines the reddening circle across her midsection. Doesn't seem like her ribs are broken, but it's hard to tell. Breathing hurts, but she can move without too much pain. Just a low throb.

She looks back at the trail. Maybe three or four miles to the East Inlet trailhead. Then somehow, she has to get to the *North* Inlet trailhead where Dad's car waits for her.

She staggers from her hiding spot, one hand caressing the thudding ache forming in her stomach. Keep going. Whatever else, have to keep going.

Then a new thought materializes: what if Dalton is by her car, waiting for her?

CHAPTER TWENTY-NINE

11:15 am

Spoon looked down at Tyson and his associate from his perch atop A1 Lawnmower Repair. The surveillance mission had gone from promising to complete disaster. Chances of convincing them he wasn't up on the roof to spy on them: slim to none.

"Get your ass down here," Tyson said. "I'm not going to tell you again, and I'm not coming up there to get you. You're trespassing. I don't even have to call the cops, I'm just going to shoot you." Then, to his associate: "Gus, go inside and get my revolver."

Spoon raised his hands as panic shuddered through him. "Whoa, hey now, reckon that's not necessary, yeah? No need to do anything rash that some of us might regret later. I'll come down and explain all this."

Gus evolved his smirk into a full-on smile. Spoon had no desire to find out what the bloke thought was so amusing.

"You can explain?" Tyson said. "What I really want to know is if you can tell me where my money is. And don't even try to tell me that you have no idea what I'm talking about. I am so unbelievably sick and tired of everyone filling my ears with horseshit."

Spoon shook his head. "Honest truth is that I'm afraid I don't know where it is."

"We'll see," Tyson said.

Spoon inched toward the edge of the overhang. His crutches were in the back of the shop, but if he met these two men on that side, there would be no other people around. At least out front, they were close to a street full of cars whizzing by. They couldn't do anything out in front of a place of business, in plain view of anyone who might see. Could they?

He slipped his legs over the edge and let his body ease forward until he was hanging from the roof by his hands. The trick was to fall on his good leg by keeping his bad leg bent, even though flexing those muscles was painful.

But he didn't get a chance. Hands grabbed his legs and yanked him from the roof. Searing pain bubbled up from his knee to every part of his body. They spun him around. Tyson stood centimeters from his face, close enough that Spoon smelled rotten breath leaking between yellow teeth.

"Look, mates," Spoon said. "If you'd listen to me for a moment so I can tell you my side of things. Two switched-on fellows like yourselves, there's no reason why we can't be civilized about this misunderstanding."

Tyson's fist launched into Spoon's stomach, and all of the air whooshed out of his lungs. As he gasped and coughed, he felt Gus dragging him toward the shop, then inside, away from the eyes of the outside world.

CHAPTER THIRTY

1:40 pm

Reagan's day, which began as green and beautiful, is now fading to black. Black is fear and despair. Black is the unknown. She has survived a moose attack, something she's never dreamed she would even need to face. Her stomach throbs from contact with the moose's hoof, like cramps after a bad meal.

Optimism is dying. Its hope is fading. Now she has only possibilities that flash before her like flights on an analog airline terminal display, changing and updating every few seconds. Tick. Change. Tick. Change.

The terrain on the trail challenges her. Even though she's progressing downhill and it's not as strenuous as going uphill, she's exhausted. Her body is weary and needs to stop this forward motion, but her mind carries on, never stopping, never relenting. The trail has moved into the grassy meadows of the western edge of the park. Soon, she'll reach Adams Falls, and that's near the trailhead. The end will come.

Sometimes, there are large tree limbs blocking the trail. This should mean that the trail is closed, and to divert. But it may mean that a tree fell here and no one has come yet to clear it away. Hard to tell.

She approaches a lone hiker, an older man with long blond hair. She tries to pull her thoughts back inside and focus so she can run if she has to, but there's no energy left to run. Only forward.

He's shirtless, and his skin seems bronzed and taut for a man closer to Dad's age. He nods and waves. "Afternoon. How's the trail up there? Muddy?"

"Moose," she says, and speaking turns a vice grip inside her stomach.

"What's that?" His face changes as he looks her up and down. "Oh my, are you okay? You don't look okay."

"Raised up against me, but I defeated it. All I wanted was to heal the poor thing, and it refused. So I had no choice. I feel awful about it, like it was all a communication problem. Spoon will understand. He's the only one who can understand."

"You're not making any sense," he says. "Are you dehydrated? Do you not have a water bottle?"

She tries to swallow, realizes she hasn't had anything to drink all day. Saliva wells at the back of her mouth, begging for water to cool her throat. She eyes the drinking tube hanging from his pack and shakes her head.

He offers it to her. "Go ahead. Have a sip if you need it."

She looks at him, his smiling face, and sees the deceit behind his eyes. What's in the water? Could be anything. Could be poison, the same or worse as the poison in the granola bar she carries in her pocket.

She takes a step backward.

"Miss, are you in some kind of trouble?"

"Stay away from me," she says, moving further back.

He watches her retreat, frowning. "Do you want me to go find a park ranger? If you're in trouble, I can get you help."

Lies, all of it. She looks to her left to distract him, then breaks into a run down the trail to escape. Every muscle resists the exertion, but the pain is a valuable lesson. Don't talk to strangers. Who knows whom Dalton may have infected and the extent of the sickness inside the park? The moose had it. This stranger has it.

She pauses when a stream crosses the trail, dips her hand in the water, and splashes the cool liquid on her head and down her back. She steps gingerly across the rocks that rise above the water to get from one side of the stream to the other.

After a lifetime, she reaches Adams Falls, which is near the official park boundary. There are a dozen hikers and tourists milling about, holding out phones to take pictures, chatting, gawking at the bedraggled young woman heaving and wincing as she refuses to make eye contact with them.

She weaves through the crowd, holding her body close together so she will not have to interact with anyone against her will. She comes upon a tall tree, half-burned and failing. Streaks of black and rust color twist around the barkless shell. Deep channels from knife carvings of the initials of graffiti artists scar the base of the tree.

She blinks, and now finds herself in the dirt parking lot next to the East Inlet trailhead. The last few minutes seem to have vanished, but she's finally at her destination.

She is so physically drained she can barely move. With a thud, she sits in the middle of the lot, surrounded by a half-dozen dust-drenched cars. She should feel excited to have reached the end of the trail, but she's still not home. Too tired. The brain keeps moving, the body wants to stop.

What does she do now? She can walk the road next to Grand Lake, but it's still two or three miles to the other trailhead, and she doesn't know if she can stand again. Regardless, she's not sure if she knows the exact way to get to the dirt turnoff that leads to the North Inlet trailhead, without the GPS on her phone to guide her.

"Oy." A voice from behind her.

She twists her body to look, which drills the pain in her stomach so hard she almost vomits. There's a tall man fifteen feet behind her, with a large camera on a tripod, slung over his shoulder like a spear. He's wearing the same kind of utility vest that fishermen wear, except instead of lures, camera lenses poke out of various pockets.

"That's maybe not a great place to sit," he says.

His accent sounds like Spoon's. Reagan notices the hand holding the camera steady has a wedding band on the third finger, gleaming in the sunlight. She trusts him but doesn't know why.

"Are you Australian?" she says.

"Not quite, but pretty close. New Zealand. Queenstown, exactly."

"My boyfriend is Australian."

"Sweet as. He a Union-man or a League-man?"

Reagan pulls her body to face the New Zealander, grimacing from the effort. "Huh?"

"Rugby. Rugby Union or Rugby League. Which one does he support?"

Thoughts flash and speed by. "He likes AFL. Says rugby is 'for tossers,' or something like that."

The New Zealander lets loose an unrestrained belly laugh, and the sound is glorious. Reagan then notices how handsome this man is. Square jaw, broad shoulders, tanned skin.

He rests the tripod on the ground in front of him. "You waiting for a ride, Miss AFL-boyfriend?"

At first, she doesn't know how to answer. She trusts him, but she's been wrong about that before. Her head shakes, back and forth, and she's not sure why she's doing it.

"Does one of these cars here belong to you?"

"No. My car got lost along the way. Part of the journey but all that has changed. I need to get back to my car so I can catch it. Not even *my* car, actually. My dad's car. He's gone too, not in the world but somewhere else. He was supposed to go into Nanita, but I left him in Verna. Not what I wanted, but circumstances change everything. That's what I'm learning."

He twists up his face, looking puzzled. "Did you need a lift?"

She stands, nearly yelping from the sizzling pain in her stomach. "Yes."

He points to a small green car and starts walking. She follows him, now fully aware of the blisters and bruises on her feet. The trail hides much of the pain.

In his car, he turns on the air conditioning, and the cool air on her hot skin is the most amazing thing she has ever felt. Then she becomes aware of how bad she must smell, after thirty miles trekking without a shower.

On the way to the other parking lot, he tells her a story about going to university in Sydney, how fickle Australian girls seemed to him.

But now that he looks back on it, *he* was the one that was fickle. He often laughs while telling the story, and Reagan finds his words comforting, but he frowns at many of the things she says in reply. She doesn't know if it's a cultural barrier or if there's something else going on. She forces herself to say as little as possible, although the temptation to interject plagues her every few seconds.

When they pull into the North Inlet parking lot, a cloud of dust obscures the cars parked there. When it settles, she opens the door, gives her thanks to the New Zealander, and steps out. Dad's car is unscathed, unchanged since she left it on Tuesday.

But Dalton's car is already gone.

CHAPTER THIRTY-ONE

3:15 pm

Spoon sensed something hard pressing against his face, his hands, his hips, and his legs. Reminded him of the rigid wooden pews he sat on at church when he was little, how he fidgeted and shifted but could never get comfortable.

As he drew in a breath, the ache in his chest revved like a motorcycle, and he remembered someone punching him. Gus, that was his name. Tyson Darby's associate, or employee, or hired-muscle… one of those. Spoon had endured a stream of punches by two fat blokes inside a lawnmower shop and hadn't landed a single blow on either of them. His old boxing coach wouldn't have been pleased with that outcome.

He opened his eyes, but the left one refused to cooperate. Something held it closed, something painful. As the right one opened, yellow beams became overhead lights and it dawned on him that he was staring up at floodlights hanging from some kind of carport. No, that wasn't right. Much taller than a carport.

He angled his head and the yellow beams turned into a flashing red and blue. Ambulance. Across the parking lot, idling, its lights rotating and alternating.

He pushed his hands against the ground and lifted his body a few centimeters. He was in front of a hospital, crumpled on slick concrete. Had it rained? He wasn't sure.

He hadn't felt this bad since the morning after his eighteenth birthday, when he'd drank so much he woke up sprawled on the hood of his mate's car with his grundies around his ankles, the cold morning air having shrunken his old fella to the size of a thimble.

As he turned, he noticed his crutches on the ground next to him. Someone had put them there. Someone had put *him* here. Must have done, because he had zero memory of driving himself anywhere. He dug a hand into his pocket and found the Lexus keys, but the car was not within sight. Neither was the blue Chevy Tahoe. He clicked the remote lock button a few times and listened for the horn honk, but no car gave any response.

The other objects he'd stashed in his pocket this morning were still there, so he breathed a sigh of relief for that.

A set of massive glass doors opened with a *swish* and a man in blue scrubs rushed to him. "Sir, are you okay? Are you injured?"

Why had Tyson and Gus dropped him at the hospital? They obviously weren't around. "I don't know."

"What happened to your eye?"

Spoon touched his closed eye and felt a swelling as if the lid above had ballooned to twice the size it should be. "I had an accident."

"Do you need medical attention?" the man in scrubs said, enunciating each word.

Spoon shook his head, which felt like jelly wobbling inside a bowl.

"I think you should come inside and talk with Security. If you've been assaulted, they'll want you to speak with the police before you see a doctor."

The idea of explaining everything to the police had some appeal, but they would want him to go to the station, give statements, tell the story a hundred times, and meanwhile, Tyson would be looking for Reagan. Spoon had to talk to her first. She should be on her return from her backpacking trip now, and she might have no idea what trouble awaited her. Had Tyson said something about her cousin Dalton going with her, how he had some kind of plan? That sounded familiar.

"No," Spoon said. "I was just walking and I slipped here. I'm fine, thank you, but I don't need to see anyone. Sorry to have caused so much fuss."

He pushed himself up, then grabbed his crutches and stood. He had so many aches and pains in his body he couldn't separate them all.

The man in scrubs crossed his arms. "You don't seem fine."

Spoon had only been to American hospitals in Texas, not in Colorado. He knew that sometimes the laws were different in different states. Could they compel him to go inside? Better to avoid any hassle by getting out of here as soon as possible.

He gave the man in scrubs a nod and limped toward the parking lot. A thousand cars littered the lot in all directions, with a handful of businesses lining the edges and across the street. He set his sights on a Subway restaurant at the edge of the lot and changed direction.

On his mobile, he tapped until he'd found out his location. Still in the suburb of Broomfield, at the Exempla Good Samaritan Medical Center. He checked his missed calls and voicemails, but there was nothing from Reagan. He phoned her, but it went straight to voicemail, just as it had for the last three days. Staggering through the parking lot, he grunted as slashes of pain wriggled from his knee up through his leg.

He opened the door of the Subway and went inside, at first blinded by the strength of the fluorescent lights bearing down on him. He walked straight to the bathroom while pretending not to notice the stares from the workers behind the counter.

Inside the loo, he groaned at the mess looking back at him in the mirror. One eye was bruised shut, and several small cuts crossed his cheeks and forehead. Gus or Tyson must have been wearing a ring. Seeing his mug in this horrible state made the injury start to throb, as if his face were a bass drum.

"Alright, Spoon. Get ahold of yourself. She'll be done with the walkabout soon and she'll ring you. You have to be patient."

He left the bathroom and limped toward the counter, now feeling dizzy and nauseous. The two teenage girls in their matching uniforms and visors went slack-jawed.

"Oh my God, what happened to your face?" one of them said.

"Do you reckon I could have a plastic bag or something?"

The other girl scrambled to grab a sandwich bag and thrust it over the counter. He filled it with ice from the soda machine, chunks thunking into the bag. The ice stung as he pressed it to his face, but it also soothed his skin and eased the bass drum from heavy metal to jazz.

He returned to the seat where he'd left his crutches. Sitting pulled his stomach muscles like shoelaces stretched to the breaking point. The dizziness abated, but his breaths came in short snatches. They'd seriously kicked the shit out of him.

He took out his mobile and stared at it, trying to decide what he would tell her if she called. Where to start? Some things, she maybe shouldn't hear, like her drunken stepmother trying to seduce him. And what to do about losing his job? With everything else going on, his sudden lack of employment seemed insignificant.

Then his mobile lit up and started to vibrate.

CHAPTER THIRTY-TWO

4:30 pm

Reagan speeds out of Rocky Mountain National Park and connects with highway 40 toward Winterpark. She bounces in the seat as she drives, distributing some of the energy from her body into the car, helping it seek its purpose of propelling her along. She's no longer tired, having drawn from the energy of motion to refuel her stores.

The steering wheel wears a thin layer of grime, still containing Dad's DNA through the years of his sweat and skin cells accumulating on its surface. She touches the remnants of him as she drives.

Spoon Spoon Spoon. She can't wait to see him again, his deep reflective eyes, his adorable accent, his scent, his warm body. The anticipation approaches an orgasmic level.

The lyrics to a Devotchka song repeat in her head and she thinks that she now fully understands them. She never appreciated the band when she lived here, but now that she's back, she can understand the appeal. That crooning voice over such complex rhythms. Who wouldn't like it? She should start a blog analyzing the music. It would be crazy popular.

But what she wants more than anything is to return to Denver and reunite with her man. At first, she slows anytime she passes a convenience store, but not one of them seems to have a payphone. Do payphones even exist anymore? She wishes she'd left her phone in the car before beginning the trip, but there's no sense in worrying about that now. Sometimes you eat the bear, sometimes the bear eats you.

Maybe she can stop at one of those convenience stores and ask to borrow someone's phone. But there's risk in doing that... since Dalton's car was already gone, who knows where he's been or who he's sullied? Any of the people she may meet could be compromised. Compromised people are unable to accept healing. These people need her educational center.

What should she call it? Opening The Mind? No, too clichéd.

She has to get to a phone. The desire becomes powerful, like a churning freight train. It permeates everything, beginning to wash out all other thoughts. Phone phone phone.

At the edge of the skinny mountain resort town Winterpark, she exits the highway and parks at the office of Grand County Travel Agency. She checks the dashboard clock. It's Friday afternoon. They should still be open.

She sits in the car, watching through the window. There's a lot of glare, but she thinks she can see two people inside the small office building. Two desks and a door between them. Possibly, leading to a kitchenette-type room or storage? She will have to ask. If there are others in the back, they will have to come out and identify themselves. It's the only way she can trust them to speak openly. Secrets spread sickness.

Swinging the car door open, energy pulses through her body, fighting the grit and exhaustion of four days in the national park.

She opens the front door, bell jingling, and a man and a woman smile back at her from their desks. It's a tiny operation. The walls are plastered with the same fake wood she last encountered when visiting some vague relative's house many years ago. Trailer-park walls. She frowns because that's judgmental and it's poisoning everything, and she feels guilty for what she has done to these nice people. They might see the poison already.

"Can we help you?" asks the woman. She has a foofy perm and a billowing blouse that hides any sense of shape of her body underneath.

"I don't care about the walls," Reagan says. "In case you thought I did. Most businesses fail in the first year. At least that's what I heard. Just saying, if you're still here, good for you."

The man and the woman share an uneasy glance.

"I'm sorry, what?" says the man.

"None of that is important. I need to use your phone. It's an emergency."

They glance at each other again. Reagan pauses, wondering why they're doing that. Sharing information without telling her is not a good beginning to this relationship.

The woman nods at a phone perched on the edge of her desk, a green telephone like the one anchored to the wall in Reagan's kitchen when she was little, the one Dad was always talking on as he leaned back in a chair and ran gentle hands through his thinning hair. He was so handsome, and the expression on his face always affirmed the kindness within. Or at least that's what she saw. Maybe she's wrong about that.

Sitting opposite the foofy woman, Reagan smells lavender on her hands. It's lotion or some kind of salve.

Reagan picks up the phone and stares at the keypad. Oh, no. Spoon's number. She's had it stored in her phone for so long, she doesn't know if she can recall the number from memory.

"Is everything alright, sweetie?" the woman asks.

"It's a memory thing. Seven, plus or minus two. Phone numbers, that's why they're all seven digits long. But the phone knows the number, and the phone is in the top panel of a backpack that's either near Lake Nanita or on its way back to Denver."

The man and woman again slant their eyes at each other.

"Please stop doing that," Reagan says.

"Stop doing what?"

A flash of memory hits her after she visualizes Spoon's contact page on her phone. "Never mind. I got it."

She presses the buttons, and some of them feel sticky with something like spilled coffee or the glaze of donuts. The rings blast her ears.

"Hello?" The voice on the other end is shaky but unmistakable.

A rush of excitement whips through her. "Baby!"

"Reagan?"

He wouldn't have recognized the phone number. She looks up at the man and woman at their desks. They're staring at her, waiting, watching, judging.

"Yes, of course, it's me. My baby boy, I've missed you so much. I can't wait to see you. I have so much to tell you. Light, darkness, the moose, the New Zealander. How much do you already know?"

"How much do I know about what? What's this number you phoned me from?"

He doesn't know anything, and she doesn't even know where to start. "My phone is back in the park. It's gone. Lost. Not coming back. Dalton has it, probably. He's sick, baby, and he needs healing. I can heal him but not from here. I need to come see you. Are you at my dad's house?"

"Reagan, are you okay? You sound like you're coked-up."

She purses her lips. He seems to be missing the point. "I'm okay. I can explain it all when I see you."

"Okay. I'm not at your house. I'm in Broomfield, at a Subway restaurant near the Good Samaritan hospital."

"What are you doing there? How did you get there?"

"I got in a fight. It's a long story, but you need to hear it."

She gasps. "I knew it. I felt that you were hurting. I could feel it in my bones as soon as it happened. I'm going to heal you too."

A little rasp escapes his lips. "What has gotten into you?"

"Stay there. I'll come get you."

She hangs up the phone, mildly annoyed that he seemed distrustful. The man and woman are still staring, and she gives them a wave before leaping from her chair. Her muscles scream, but she ignores the burning and rushes to the car.

She starts it up and races out of the parking lot. Broomfield. Spoon. Healing. The course is clear.

Must drive slowly through Winterpark. Cops are everywhere, lurking, waiting, watching. Past the town, she can speed up again, and she has to pay vigorous attention as she passes cars going up the twisty roads that will lead her back to I-70. She wishes she had time to stop at the many pullouts that overlook the severe mountain peaks slicing the sky. But there's no time. Spoon. Broomfield. Hospital.

I-70 eastbound slows her down. Too much traffic. Not as bad as the westbound lanes, though, with the dribble of cars going into the mountains clogging the interstate. Denverites, leaving work early on Friday afternoons to shuttle their families into the touristy mountain towns and escape the city heat. They'll take the kids zip-lining and through mine tours while the grownups drink high-altitude microbrews and listen to real estate pitches. Not the life Reagan ever pictured for herself, but if it makes them happy, more power to them.

When she reaches Idaho Springs, just thirty miles from Broomfield, she finds the source of the congestion. A car has stalled on the shoulder, and the cops have closed traffic to a single lane. Past it, she can pick up speed again.

Healing. Broomfield. Spoon. Dad. Nanita. Grandpa. Healing. Dalton. The Educational Center. Aching knees. Spoon.

As she exits I-70 and turns onto the road that will lead to her boyfriend, the sun begins to set over the mountains behind her. The sparse clouds dotting the sky turn pink, then purple. Snow still caps the tips of some of the peaks, glistening gold as the sun frames the angles. Sunsets always amaze her.

The drive to Broomfield takes another thirty minutes. When the Good Samaritan hospital finally appears next to the road, her heart scrambles into her throat, pulsing the energy of the whole universe into one giant rotating siren. Spoon. It's almost time.

She races through the hospital's parking lot to reach Subway. The ticks of the clock begin to slow as she reaches her final destination, the only thing she's wanted since she left the park those few hours ago. Has it been hours? Seems like only minutes. She glides into a parking spot and gazes through the store window at a set of crutches leaning against a table. He's there, but facing away from her.

She leaps from the car and skips to the door. Throws it open. "Baby!" she says.

He turns, and her excitement bleeds to horror when she sees what has happened to his face.

CHAPTER THIRTY-THREE

4:40 pm

Dalton and Charlie had spent the remainder of their time in the park grumbling at each other. Dalton's little bitch of a brother barely scraped his leg but whined for most of yesterday as if he'd lost a limb. The cut had already scabbed over.

When they left the park and entered cell-phone-service area, Dalton called Tyson. As the phone rang, Dalton's throat turned into the Sahara dessert, which made swallowing difficult. Having to disappoint his old man didn't lead to warm fuzzy feelings.

"What did you find out?" Tyson said, right after the call connected. No *hello* or anything like that.

Charlie opened the glove box, fished out a fast food napkin, and blew his nose so loudly that Dalton switched the phone to his other ear.

"We... uh... she didn't have the money. She did, though, tell us she has a key. She wouldn't tell me what it's for—"

Tyson grunted. "I already know what it's for. Your grandad told me all about it. For a safety deposit box somewhere in Denver, at one of the banks around here. I just wasn't sure that she had it with her."

211

Safety deposit box? That made perfect sense and now seemed like the only real possibility. As if uncle Mitch would hide a bunch of money out in the woods. Ridiculous idea.

"Did you see the actual key?" Tyson said.

"Uh, no, but she said she had it."

"She has it, and you don't. What the hell were you doing out there for four days?"

Dalton tried to speak, but only a sputter came out.

"Are you talking to him right now?" Charlie said.

Dalton cradled the phone between his ear and shoulder so he could free up a hand to smack Charlie on the arm. Then he held a finger to his lips, giving his little brother the death-stare.

"What do you want me to do?" Dalton said.

"Get your ass back here. I'm in Broomfield, in the parking lot of the Good Samaritan hospital off 287. West end of the parking lot. I'm watching the boyfriend lick his wounds at a sandwich shop, so she'll come around looking for him eventually."

"Spoon. His name is Spoon," Dalton said.

"I know what his goddamned name is," Tyson said, and then the phone beeped when the call ended.

"What's going on?" Charlie said.

"He's onto the boyfriend. We have to meet him in Broomfield so we can follow them when they leave. Those clueless idiots will lead us right to the money."

Charlie's face fell as he stared at the dashboard. Breaths whistled through his nose. "Take me back to my apartment."

"Didn't you hear me? He wants us to meet him."

His brother looked at him, tears in his eyes. "I don't want to do this. I never agreed to do anything that would hurt Reagan. You twisted the truth around and made it seem like all of this was okay, but it's not."

"Grow up."

"You pulled *a knife* on her, Dalton."

Dalton slapped the dashboard. "Because it's what he wants. She may be our cousin, but he's our dad. If you're going to claim family, he's higher up the chain."

Charlie looked away, out the window. "Take me home. I'm sorry that I punched you out on the trail, but I don't want to be a part of all this stuff anymore."

Dalton squeezed the steering wheel until his hands ached. "Fine."

The detour to return Charlie home took him twenty minutes out of his way to the Denver suburb of Westminster, and Dalton didn't say a word to his brother for the rest of the trip. Dalton hated this shitty neighborhood. Full of thugs. After pulling into a parking space in front of the apartment, Dalton popped the trunk but left the engine running.

Charlie looked at him, desperate sorrow in his eyes. Dalton didn't care because the whiny bitch had brought this on himself. Dalton waved the back of his hand toward his brother, flicking him away with a single gesture. No teary goodbyes, please.

Charlie hefted his backpack from the trunk, stepped aside, then Dalton squealed the tires as he slammed on the gas.

Now alone, he started to worry about seeing his dad for the first time since after uncle Mitch's funeral. Dalton had a definite goal and he failed. He didn't know anything that Tyson didn't know and had nothing useful to provide. He'd have to do something monumental to atone.

Every mile closer to the hospital was another hitch in his anxiety level. He drove too fast, took the turns too sharply. When he pulled into the hospital, his stomach lurched and he had to pull over and open the door. He didn't puke, but he spent a couple minutes waiting and spitting the excess saliva pooling at the back of his mouth. Eventually, the feeling subsided and he started searching the parking lot for Tyson.

He was going to have to do better. Try harder. Be more cunning. Never again would he disappoint the old man like this again. He spotted the blue truck in a corner spot, under the shade of a massive tree. As he pulled into the empty spot next to it, they both rolled their windows down.

Tyson sat in the driver's seat, which was odd. He usually had a driver. Country music twanged from the truck's speakers. "What took you so long?"

"I had to take Charlie home. He didn't want to come."

Tyson mused on this for a second, then nodded. "Okay, that's fine. He'd probably get in the way, anyway."

"Dad, if you'd give me a chance, I can explain what—"

"I don't want your goddamn explanations. I gave you one job. One job. Whatever you were doing out there in the woods for the last four days, it doesn't matter now. All I want to know now is: how far are you willing to go to make this right?"

CHAPTER THIRTY-FOUR

7:30 pm

Reagan lets the door to Subway close behind her. Spoon's face is battered and bruised, plastered with cuts that have colored his face black and blue and yellow and red, as if he's wearing makeup applied by a kindergartner. One of his eyes is swollen shut.

She walks to him, cradles his face in her hands. "Oh baby, who did this to you?"

He smiles at her through his injuries.

She wraps her arms around him, and the joy and sorrow and excitement wash over her. She's been dreaming of touching him for days. Her skin warms, and she wants to touch all of him. The pink of passion almost outweighs the yellow of confusion, but it's competing with a dozen other feelings wriggling and swirling through her head.

One of the Subway workers behind the counter clears her throat. "Are you guys gonna order something?"

Reagan wants to lash out at them for interrupting this moment... what should have been the most romantic and spectacular moment, but one marred by their petty comments.

"Let's go," he says. "I'll explain in the car."

They exit the restaurant and she leads him to the car, helping him take every step. His crutches gingerly click against the ground as his face contorts in pain.

She helps him into the car and rushes to the driver's side. "Baby, what happened? Do we need to go into the hospital? Have you already been?"

He shakes his head. "No, we need to get out of here. I don't know where they are, but I reckon they could be looking for us or waiting for us somewhere. We need to find somewhere to hide."

"Why? What's going on? Who did this to you?"

His eyes flood with dread. "Do you have an uncle named Tyson?"

She nods, and his face falls. "Him," he says. "Your uncle did this to me."

Uncle Tyson? Doesn't seem real, but there's nothing but conviction in Spoon's eyes.

"Why haven't you ever mentioned him before?" he says.

"I don't know, he hasn't been a part of my life for years now. Different when I was a little kid, you know, before I found out how he makes his money. He sells drugs, I don't even know what else he gets into. None of my business."

Spoon sighs. "I'm sorry that you had to find out like this. He's looking for some money he thinks your dad hid away." He points at the ignition. "Please, sweetheart. Start the car. We need to get out of here."

She snaps out of her daze and turns the key. She backs out of their parking space and heads for the highway, mind racing, filing new information, firing synapses. Axon to dendrite to form new memories and slip them into the appropriate folder.

"He thinks your dad had a safety deposit box."

Reagan nods. "He does. I have the key. I don't know where it is, though."

"You have the key?"

"Yes," she says. "It's for the center we're going to build. The money is, I mean. I've already worked it out and talked to many great teachers. It's all a part of the plan… my dad must have known about the center, and the money is a gift from the universe, through him."

His forehead wrinkles. "What are you talking about?"

216

"I wasn't sure at first, but I understood it when I saw the moose with her calf. Mother and child, teacher and student. It all became clear right then."

"Are you feeling okay?"

"I've never seen things this clearly before," she says. "All of the suffering we've been through, it's all supposed to happen. My dad dying, Dalton doing what he did, my uncle, all of it."

She explains the last four days in the park, finding the key, reading the note, spreading the ashes. Spoon's expression grows increasingly hesitant as she skips from one topic to another. She keeps thinking he'll turn around and start understanding, but it doesn't happen. He only looks concerned.

He, in turn, explains about Anne's attempts to divert him from Tyson, about meeting her grandfather and his revelations about the safety deposit box. The amount of information threatens to overwhelm her, but she tries to look at each thing individually, as a holistic component of a greater truth.

He looks out the window. "Where are we going?"

"Motel."

"I can't afford that," he says, wringing his hands together. "There's something I didn't tell you yet. I lost my job the other day."

She laughs because she could have predicted the universe placing this piece of the puzzle directly before them. "This is perfect. This is meant to be. I'll quit my job too, and we can start the center. I don't have a name picked yet, but I have a dozen options I'm working through. Everything is falling into place. Couldn't be more perfect."

"Reagan, you're scaring me."

"The truth is sometimes scary. I'm sure you can put all that aside and trust in me. I know what I'm doing."

They park in front of the office of a shabby motel complex. The three-story building borders a single parking lot. Rooms on all three stories face the lot, with outdoor staircases on each end.

She checks her face in the rearview. Having no makeup on feels liberating, as if there's no disguise between her and the rest of the world. "I'll take care of this."

Before he can respond, she's out of the car and walking into the office, flipping her purse over her shoulder. Her knees ache. Her hips are throbbing. But it feels good to have a plan to set in motion. Despite the awful scare she got when she first saw Spoon, the future now looks bright.

She steps up to the counter, which is so tall she can barely fit her elbows onto its laminated surface. Her finger taps the bell once, and she waits for someone to come out.

In a minute, an emaciated man shuffles from a back room to take her name and information. She chats with him while filling out the form, and he gives her strange looks as she hands over the cash for the room. Why does everyone keep looking at her this way? Maybe it's because she pays with one dollar bills, a casualty of waiting tables. Like dancing at a topless bar. She laughs because she's never drawn that parallel before.

He says nothing as he records her name and car information. She gives him nothing but fake details, which seems the smart move after all the untrustworthy people she's met in the last couple of days.

Room key in hand, she returns to the car.

"We can't park here," he says. "They'll be looking for us. We need to park somewhere else."

She opens his door, helps him out of the car, and presses the key into his palm. "You are absolutely right, baby. You open up our room and I'll park down the street."

As he limps toward the stairs, guilt stabs at her for getting him involved. Destiny or not, seeing him hurt like this is agonizing, and it's all her fault. She should have insisted he stay in Austin instead of coming to Denver for the memorial service, but they'd planned to travel on to New Orleans the following day. Only four days ago, but so much has changed.

She'll find some way to make it up to him.

Across the street, there's a gas station, and a spot behind the dumpster that she can fit the car into. She's proud of herself. This is going to work.

She crosses the street to the motel, knocks on the door of the room, and when he lets her in, she suddenly realizes she can shower here. Get clean. She hasn't showered since Tuesday morning, and the idea of washing four days of trail muck off her skin is the most heavenly thing she has ever considered. Shower, make love to Spoon, then they can talk about the key and the note and the next steps to setting everything right.

Spoon reclines on the bed, wincing as he arranges his knee brace.

"I'm going to take a shower," she says, glancing around the room. There are visible water stains on the ceiling, drab art nailed to the walls, an ancient mammoth television bolted to the only dresser in the room. Get what you pay for, and this place is cheap.

"Wait," he says, raising an arm. "There's one thing I haven't told you yet. Can't believe I almost forgot about this."

She sits on the edge of the bed next to him and places a hand on his thigh. "Go ahead."

"Your mum. She's in town and I met her yesterday."

CHAPTER THIRTY-FIVE

8:00 pm

Dalton still couldn't get used to seeing Reagan drive uncle Mitch's Honda. Even though maybe not technically his anymore, still seemed freaky. Uncle Mitch had been a decent guy, and Dalton didn't like to think about it, not after what he'd seen at the end.

He had been impulsive and callous to lecture Reagan about Mitch being a degenerate gambler right to her face. Dalton knew that losing his temper was something he needed to work on if he wanted to achieve his career goals. Maybe Tony Soprano and Scarface could flip out and get away with acting all crazy in the movies, but in real life, keeping your head was the key to handling stressful situations. The right path always seemed obvious looking back on it.

All this introspection almost made him lose Reagan and the Aussie boy as they drove down Highway 287. They turned, and Dalton didn't approach the turn fast enough, so he had to stop at a red light. He considered jumping the median, but a cop was idling two cars behind him.

Then he had a brilliant idea. He whipped out his phone and searched the Maps app for nearby hotels. Came up with four within a mile. He texted Tyson, who was supposed to be following him, but had turned off a couple miles back.

In less than a minute came the reply:

Txt me when u know where. DO NOT approach.

The light turned green and Dalton let his phone guide him to the first hotel in the area. Big place, big parking lot. No matching Honda Accords.

He left the parking lot and headed for the next nearby joint. A brief moment of anxiety unsettled him when he wondered if his brilliant idea could be totally wrong. They may have turned off the main road to mess with anyone following them.

He couldn't be wrong. Couldn't mess up again. Not an option.

The second hotel was much smaller, only three stories tall. Shabby and run-down. But he didn't need to search the parking lot because the Honda Accord sat at a gas station across the street. In the rear of the building, but the nose was poking out from behind a dumpster. Not exactly super-spy-quality hiding.

He copied and pasted the address from his Maps app into a text to Tyson and started mentally mapping the layout of the hotel. Three stories, all the rooms facing the street. Couldn't be more than forty units. He could walk by each door, listen, and pinpoint for Tyson exactly which was the one the little lovebirds were in. Probably fucking their brains out.

But Tyson had told him to wait.

He drummed his thumbs against the steering wheel, looking at each of the motel room doors facing him. The cut on his hand throbbed. The whole building remained motionless; the concrete hallways out front empty and quiet.

Fuck it.

He got out of the car and crept toward the motel. Then he realized all this cloak and dagger shit was retarded, straightened up, and walked normally. He wasn't doing anything illegal. Not yet, at least.

He climbed the stairs to the third floor to begin at the far-right end. He worked his way back left, leaning toward each door. Mostly, he heard televisions, muffled conversations, a couple rooms with little kids running around playing, but nothing that sounded like Reagan or an

Australian guy. He had to resist the urge to walk with light feet, because looking like a creeper would be much more suspicious than the sound of footsteps on the walkway.

At the last room on the third floor, as he leaned close, the door opened and he nearly fell over the balcony railing. He stopped himself as a woman with a big fat pregnant belly and her hair up in curlers threw the stink-eye at him.

"Excuse me. What are you doing lurking outside my room?"

He averted his eyes and said nothing, then hustled down the stairs to floor two. No luck there, either. He started to descend the stairs when his phone vibrated.

The fuck r u doing up there?

Dalton surveyed the parking lot and saw Tyson's blue truck backed into a parking space. He raced down the stairs, trying to think of what he would say to his father. Four days of backpacking had left him with sore knees and hips, another reminder of his failure.

The tinted window lowered as he approached the car. "I told you to wait."

"They're here, somewhere. I know it."

"I don't see Mitch's car," Tyson said.

"It's across the street at that gas station. They've got to be here, for sure. I just don't know which room."

Tyson rolled up the window but unlocked the car doors. Dalton rushed around to the passenger side and jumped in the car.

"We wouldn't have to be here if you'd taken the key from her in the park, like you should have."

Dalton ducked his head. "I know. I'm sorry, Dad."

"You're sure it's this one, though? Are you A-1 positively sure?"

Dalton nodded, still looking at the dashboard. "Do you know which bank has the safe deposit box yet?"

Tyson tugged at the scruff jutting from his chin. "Not exactly. Mitch had an account at FirstBank, but I called them and he doesn't have a box there. Your grandad doesn't know."

"You think Reagan knows?"

"Maybe. But even if she does, that doesn't mean we can get in it. I did some research. The bank or the state might seal it for weeks or months until they see death certificates and all that horseshit. But we don't got to worry about that yet. Step one is finding the god damn thing."

"As soon as she tells us where it is," Dalton said, taking his knife out of his pocket and then waving it in the air, "I'm going to gut that bitch."

Tyson whipped his head around, the whites of his eyeballs flaring. "You're going to *what?*"

Dalton put away the knife. "I just… I don't know. What do you mean?"

"That's your cousin, and you're going to slice her open like some crackhead?"

"I thought that was the point. Get the money and get her out of the way. You asked me what I was willing to do to make it right, and all that."

Tyson sat back and rubbed his temples. "You stupid little asshole. That's why she got away in Rocky Mountain, isn't it? You pulled some shit, freaked her out, and she ran."

Dalton didn't know if he should answer the question. He was confused, since Tyson had never told him one way or the other what he was or wasn't supposed to do in the park. Just get the money.

"You ever know anyone with a cat?" Tyson said.

"Sure."

"If you want a cat to pay attention to you, you can't go chasing it around the house. You sit back in a chair, then scratch on the side of the chair for a few seconds. Then you stop. In a minute, the cat's going to get curious, then *bam*… it's in your lap."

Dalton searched the roof of the truck, rehearsing the words of Tyson's story. "So… we're supposed to ignore her?"

"No, goddamn it. I'm trying to tell you to be subtle." Tyson took a toothpick from his pocket and picked something from between his front teeth. "Listen to me very carefully. We may have to get physical, but you are not going to take out that knife or do anything like that unless I tell you to, got it?"

223

Dalton nodded but wasn't sure if he meant it. That bitch had cut him. There had to be payback.

"Tell me you got it," Tyson said. "I need to hear you say it out loud."

"Okay, okay, I get it. So what do we do now?"

Tyson popped the glove box and removed a piece of cloth. He unfolded the cloth and showed Dalton a device, about two inches by two inches, with a set of LEDs lining the front. He opened the truck's center console and snatched a package of AA batteries, then held them both out to Dalton. "Do you know what to do with these?"

Dalton puzzled over it for a second. Then he nodded.

"You go take care of that, and then come back and we wait. They can't stay in there forever."

CHAPTER THIRTY-SIX

8:00 pm

Reagan steps backward until she bumps into the combination mini-fridge/microwave bolted to the motel room wall. Spoon's revelation has filled her veins with ice water. "My mother?"

Spoon casts his eyes to the floor. "Her name is Jules, right? She followed me to an AA meeting yesterday."

Six years. Six years since Jules Darby left, and not a single word since then. Not a word at her first day of college, not a word when Reagan attempted suicide, not a single letter or phone call the whole time she was drugged up in the hospital or recovering afterward. Not even for the funeral of her husband of more than twenty years.

"What happened?" Reagan says.

"Not much. I didn't know who she was until after the meeting. We chatted in the parking lot, she said she was here to see you."

The possibilities spin Reagan's brain. The money, Spoon losing his job, Mom returning. "This is all part of the plan. I'm sure of it now. She's here and now she can help us find our way and open our educational center that's going to heal the world. But not in the usual, *come-here-and-find-Jesus* kind of way that always turns out to be some scam where the priests molest little boys and the guys at the top skim all the donation money. No, this is going to be true, and full of enlightenment and people who pay things forward because it's the right thing to do. Mom will help us. She has to. Why else would she be here?"

"Reagan..." he says, slipping his hand into his pocket.

Something about his hand in his pocket feels wrong. "What are you doing?"

"I looked in your nightstand on Wednesday and found some pill bottles. I'd hoped they were extras that you didn't need, but I can now tell by your voice and how you never stop fidgeting that you haven't had any meds. You've gone round the bend."

"I don't need them," she says. "There's no point in diluting the world now because I can see everything clearly. I've never been this clear before."

He inches his hand out of his pocket, and he's clenching a plastic baggie with a dozen pills of different sizes and colors. "I took these from the bottles this morning, since I knew I'd see you. Didn't know if you'd need them, but I reckoned if you did, you'd need them right away."

In his hand, Spoon holds death to creativity. Death to imagination. Lithium, Risperdal, Seroquel. A recipe for flattening Reagan into a conformist pancake, ready to be pressed into a box and shipped out to the world. Stomp her down into a Good Little Girl ready to accept more steaming spoonfuls of the world's garbage.

"I don't want them. I want to live and breathe and understand the universe. I want to have sex. Do you understand? That stuff takes my sex drive and squeezes it into a tiny glass bottle; makes it something impossible to think about. You've said you wish we had sex more often. We *can* now, baby. I want to show you how much I love you."

He fidgets on the bed. He holds the pills at arm's-length, refusing to look at her. "I know what I said, but I think you should take your meds. You're scaring me."

"If you loved me, you wouldn't do this."

"I'm doing this *because* I love you."

She reaches behind her and grabs a stack of Styrofoam cups next to the coffee maker. The day's color bleeds into red, and her face reflects the change. Heat dots her skin, making her feel lightheaded. She crinkles the cups in her hand, and then starts to shred them into little pieces, letting the bits fall to the floor one at a time. "You don't understand me at all."

He won't withdraw the pills, and she can't stand here and watch this anymore. She storms away from him, into the beige bathroom with its mildewed shower curtain and poorly-sanitized toilet. She shuts and locks the door, and within ten seconds, he's knocking softly and calling her name but she doesn't want to hear it.

Can't lose this peak of understanding. She knows that she's manic and the last time she felt this way, a ton of bad things happened, but this time will be different. Maybe all this new self-awareness will change things. Maybe she can control it.

She sheds her clothes and faces the mirror to examine the bruise the moose left as a parting gift. It's round, the size of a small dinner plate, black in the center and blue around the edges. Horrifically ugly. Now that she's focusing on it, the pain grows. She sucks in her stomach then pushes it out, trying to feel for any broken rib bones, but she's still not sure how it should feel. Only that her stomach aches as if someone is continuously punching her.

Images of the gifts Dad used to bring her after business trips float through her mind. Usually, stupid little airport trinkets like bumper stickers that read, *"It's a beautiful day in Reno, NV!"* When she was a pre-teen, the gifts always made her giggle. When she got older, she took them for granted. She never knew exactly where he was going on those business trips, and he never said.

She steps into the shower for the first time since Tuesday morning. Despite the meek water pressure, the feeling of warm water rushing over her sends her into ecstasy. She watches the grime slip from her body and run into the drain, lines of gritty brown circling with the clear water.

When she exits the shower, it's as if she's molted away an extraneous layer of her body. Clean, warm, and her skin has become lighter and more alive.

Still red, but also better. A little calmer, approaching orange.

As she wraps a towel around her body and then another around her hair, she looks at the dirty hiking clothes on the bathroom floor. She sighs because she has no clean clothes to wear. But a fresh body in dirty clothes is still better off than a few minutes ago.

Lip balm. She wishes she had her lip balm, but it's probably in her purse, which is on the bed next to Spoon. Or it may be in the backpack with her phone, which is who-knows-where.

She reaches into her pocket, hoping that maybe she put the lip balm in there without remembering. Instead, she finds Dad's letter. She hasn't thought about the letter in hours.

Her eyes scan the water-ruined letter a few times. A line sticks out to her:

what the key in … farmer's market. You'll understand when you get there.

Farmer's market. The realization comes over her suddenly, like a wave that seems small and barely over knee-level yet hides a massive force that topples you onto your butt.

Naked, she runs out of the bathroom and yells, "I know where the money is. It's not in a safe deposit box."

She stops moving and closes her mouth when she sees Spoon. He's on one knee—or some approximation of it—with his bad leg pushed out in front of him, and he's holding something in his hand. It's a small, velvet box, opened, with a glistening diamond ring inside it.

"Oh my god," she says as the diamond sparkles under the lights of the motel room.

"Reagan Darby, I love you and I intend the spend the rest of my life with you. I know this is a terrible time and place to ask."

She's about to scream *yes* when she looks and sees what he's holding in his other hand. It's the baggie of medication, extended toward her.

Jim Heskett

Saturday

CHAPTER THIRTY-SEVEN

7:00 am

Dalton awoke with a start when a bird chirped outside his window. For a second, he thought he was still in the woods, hearing those never-ending alarm clocks trying to force him out of his sleep.

He'd dozed off in the passenger seat of Tyson's car. His father was leaning back in the driver's seat, head lolling back, mouth open and snoring like a chainsaw burning gasoline.

Dalton nudged the old man. "Dad, wake up."

Tyson snorted, blinked a few times, then pushed himself upright. "What?"

"We fell asleep."

Tyson sighed and pressed a button on the dashboard to make a digital clock light up. "Goddamn it. Go check if the car is still there across the street."

A flash of an idea walloped Dalton upside his head. "I got this."

He exited the car and peered over the fence at the gas station. The nose of the Honda was still poking out from behind the dumpster, quiet and untouched. The lovebirds were probably still sleeping off a good night of fucking.

230

He strolled across the parking lot toward the motel office and opened the door as an attached bell jingled. In front of him was a chest-high counter, with slits in the ceiling and walls where some kind of protection like safety glass would slide in. Didn't seem like a rough neighborhood, but with shady motels like this, who knew what kind of shit went down.

He whistled and started tapping a bell on the counter once every few seconds. After a minute, a young woman appeared from the back room. She was about his same age, but chubby and doe-eyed. Perfect. Fat girls loved him.

"Hi," he said.

She offered him a reserved smile. "How can I help you, sir?"

He struggled to get his elbow up over the counter. "I'm in a tight situation here. My cousin checked in last night, maybe with her boyfriend. Thing is, he's a not-nice kind of guy—if you know what I mean—and I'm worried about her."

The chubby girl stuck a finger in her mouth and chewed on the nail. "I'm not supposed to give out names or room numbers and things of that nature. I could get into trouble."

"I totally get that, sister. But you'd be doing me a huge favor and I would owe you until the end of time. I really need to find her."

"Can't you call her?"

Dalton almost laughed, because he had Reagan's cell phone in his pocket. "No, she didn't take her phone. We were hanging out last night, at my apartment, and her boyfriend came over, acting all like a big jerk. He started shouting about this and that, ordering her to leave."

The doe-eyes grew wide. "What did you do?"

"I told him to leave her alone, of course, but he's about ten times bigger than me, so there wasn't much I could do."

The chubby girl actually looked scared for Dalton's safety. He bit the inside of his cheek to keep himself from bursting out laughing at her.

"Anyway, he made her leave, and she didn't have time to grab her cell phone, but she'd told me before all this shit got crazy that if something bad happened—like he was going to hurt her—that she'd come here and I should meet up with her."

The girl studied him, her face twisted. Dalton held her gaze, and it seemed to go on forever.

Finally, she took in a deep breath. "I'm sorry, but I'm not supposed to. I could get into trouble."

Motherfucking bitch. Without meaning to, he pounded his fist on the counter, which echoed through the little office. The chubby girl jumped as if he'd stepped on her toes.

"Please. This is like an emergency situation here. I'm begging you."

She looked behind her shoulder, then huffed a few deep breaths in and out of her nose. "I understand. I'll get the book, but you can't tell anyone I did this, okay?"

"No problem."

She ducked down, shuffled through something for a few seconds, then came up with a ledger, which she flipped open halfway. "Name?"

"Reagan Darby."

She trailed a finger up and down, mouthing the words to herself as she did so. After several seconds of this, she shrugged and said, "I don't see it."

"She might not have checked in under her own name."

She frowned. "Do you know what it was?"

He struggled to think of what name she might use. Maybe the name of an old high school teacher or something? Movie star? There were too many possibilities.

"She's about medium height, thin, she would have been wearing hiking clothes. Stank real bad, probably, like she hadn't showered in days."

"I only came on my shift about an hour ago, I'm sorry."

He gripped the edge of the counter to stave off the urge to smack it again. "Can you at least tell me how many people checked in last night?"

She scanned again. "Just one."

He gritted his teeth. She could have saved a lot of time if she'd told him that first motherfucking thing. He tried to keep his voice calm. "And who was that?"

"Tori Amos. Checked into room 27. That's the fifth one from the—"

"I can find it, thanks," he said as he withdrew from the counter and headed for the door. He considered dropping a comment about her double-chin or her flabby triceps, but kept his mouth shut. No time to waste, and living her existence as that tub of lard was punishment enough.

As he walked outside, a car pulled up next to the blue Chevy. The door opened and a vision from the past stepped out.

Aunt Jules, Reagan's mom. He hadn't seen her for so long—at least five or six years—that it took him a few seconds to appreciate who he saw across the parking lot. Jules had disappeared not long before Reagan moved to Austin, and now, here she stood, only a couple hundred feet from him.

Seeing her stirred feelings in Dalton, but mostly, it made him think of Uncle Mitch. Going over to his house for holidays as a kid, watching Broncos games on random Sundays, sometimes even tossing a baseball with him in the backyard after school.

Mitch had always been kind to Dalton and treated him better than Tyson ever had. And that's why Dalton felt a surge of guilt when he remembered he was the last person to see his uncle alive.

CHAPTER THIRTY-EIGHT

On the day of his death, Mitchell Darby sat at a desk in his study, composing a letter to his daughter Reagan. Even with the door locked and the house empty, he still scribbled frantically. If Tyson or someone who worked for him came to collect what Mitch had stolen, a locked door wouldn't stop them.

He wrote:

Dearest Reagan,

I wish I had time to write everything I want to say, but I'm running out. There's a separate letter, it's attached to my will. I wrote that letter right after our last trip into Rocky Mountain. The letter asks you to take my ashes to Nanita, and spread them there. I had hoped that you would not have to see that letter until you were older, but I don't think I have much time left. I made some mistakes. I was selfish. And I'm sorry that you have to be the one to clean it up. Hopefully what I'm leaving you is going to help. What I'm leaving you isn't in the will.

You'll understand what the key in this envelope is for, but what the key goes to isn't in the same place as what this key opens. Think about the trips we used to take up to the farmer's market. You'll understand when you get there. Your grandfather can help, but he doesn't know anything. He has something of yours, and

234

you'll know that when you see it, too. I hate to be so vague, but I can't take the chance that someone else might see this.

When you find what you're looking for, leave Denver and don't come back here. You'll be safe if you just stay away. Use it to start the life you deserve.

I don't know how to say I'm sorry, other than to tell you that I'm proud of you and I love you. I know that's not good enough.

Dad

He wanted to write more about their backpacking trip together two years ago and how much it meant to him. How happy he was that she was steady on her medication and holding down a job. How he wished she would someday be able to go back to college and chase her dreams, whatever those were. Possibly, even tell her the truth about why her mother left six years ago. That conversation had been an object of dread haunting him ever since.

How could he explain to his daughter that he'd stolen over two hundred thousand dollars from his own brother, for no good reason other than a compulsive need to try to turn it into more money? How could she ever forgive him for that?

There was no time. He had to get to the post office and get this letter off in the mail.

He folded the letter and took an envelope from the desk drawer, wrote his daughter's Austin address on the front, and slipped the key inside. He held up the letter to his mouth and was about to lick it closed when the front door opened. Hadn't he locked it?

A voice came from downstairs. "Uncle Mitch? I know you're here."

Dalton. No, no, no, not now.

If Dalton found the key, he would never give it to Reagan. He and Tyson may never figure out what to do with it, but there'd be no way Reagan would ever get the money.

Mitchell jumped to his feet, whipping his head around to scan the room. There had to be a way to get the key to Reagan, but how?

Then his eyes landed on the urn on the bookcase. The urn he had purchased in that African shop in New York five years ago, which was supposed to hold his ashes. But he hadn't expected to need that for many more years, when he'd be ancient and withered and bed-ridden. He had hoped that Reagan would be old enough to take her own children with her to spread his remains into Nanita, the deepest, bluest lake he'd ever seen. But his time was up.

He raced through the prospective chain of events. It might work. She would get the letter with the will. The letter would instruct her to take the urn into Rocky Mountain National Park. She would find the key and the letter in the urn and know what to do. There were many variables, but he trusted his daughter. He had to; there wasn't another choice, if he wanted to keep the key out of Tyson's possession.

Footsteps came up the stairs. "Uncle Mitch? You know why I'm here. Anne's not here right now, it's just you and me, so why don't you come on out?"

Mitchell crossed the room and snatched the urn from the shelf. He opened the top and pressed the lid, making the secret compartment cover pop open. He'd designed and created the compartment himself, to hide certain valuables. No one would think to look in an urn. He took out a crumpled mass of emergency money and the little slip of paper he'd written his computer passwords on and tossed them aside. Pushing with his thumbs, he wedged the key and the note inside, then slid the cover back into place. He turned, and as he did, the urn moved and the key rattled inside. That was no good. Anyone might hear it and open the urn to investigate.

The idea that he was planning for events after his death sent slashing knives of panic up and down his spine, but he pushed himself forward. No time to second-guess.

The footsteps halted in front of the study door, and Mitchell saw the shadows of feet in the thin gap between the door and the floor.

"Open up."

Mitchell ran back to the desk and grabbed the duct tape from the bottom drawer. He reopened the urn, popped open the compartment and tore a strip of duct tape. Would the duct tape hold, or flake off? He had to trust it would stay in place.

"I can hear you in there. Open this motherfucking door."

Mitchell applied the duct tape and slid the cover into place. Would Reagan find the secret compartment? She was a smart girl. She would find it. Every bit of hope in his life attached itself to that one supposition.

The door rattled and splintered as Dalton threw himself against it.

Mitchell placed the urn on the desk. He stood tall, breathing deeply, and started to feel dizzy. Prickles of light edged his vision. His head and arms felt heavy, as if coated with layers upon layers of mud.

On the second try, the lock broke and Dalton stumbled inside, fire in his eyes. "Uncle Mitch."

"Dalton," Mitchell said, gasping for air. He felt only pity for this young man, barely an adult. Dalton looked like his father had at that age, with the same ambitious smirk always playing on his face. Dalton was a pawn in a game, and Mitchell felt no animosity toward him. "Yes, I know why you're here."

"Tyson says today you pay back what you stole. No excuses."

"I don't have the money."

Dalton took a paperweight from the desk and slammed it to the floor. "He told me you have it. I'm really not interested in going around and around with you, so I'm only going to ask you once. Where is the money you took?"

"Dalton, you don't have to do this. You can just let me leave. I'll go away and I'll never bother any of you again. We can forget any of this happened and I'll walk out that door right now, hop on a plane and it's over."

"What do you think he'll do to me if I let you go?"

Mitchell took a step toward his nephew as the spots in his vision multiplied and the world went blurry. "You don't have to work for him. Maybe you could come with me? We can work together. Vegas, maybe. You're a smart kid. We could make a lot of money."

"Whatever happens next, you caused all of this. All you had to do was return what you stole."

Mitchell shook his head. "You don't understand. He wouldn't have forgotten about it. Pay it back or not, I'm a dead man either way."

Dalton drew a pistol from his back belt loop. At the sight of the gun, Mitchell felt a tightening in his chest, as if a vice grip had squeezed his midsection. The room started to spin, and his lunch bubbled up from his stomach, threatening to eject onto the floor.

He toppled, grabbing the edge of his desk for support. Perspiration beaded on his forehead and his slippery hand couldn't hold on to the desk. He slid forward. When he collapsed, he found himself looking up at the ceiling of his study room, his life escaping. This was the last day he was going to be alive on this earth. The knowledge came to him swiftly and sent panic needling every inch of his body.

Dalton entered the corner of his vision, towering over him. "You stupid dipshit. We're going to find the money eventually, you know."

And Mitchell knew Dalton was right. They would hurt or kill Anne—and probably even Reagan too—if they thought it would lead to the money. In that instant, Mitchell knew he had likely doomed his wife and daughter, and he could do nothing about it.

All of this chaos was his fault.

"Help me," Mitchell said, wheezing. No matter how hard his lungs worked, he couldn't seem to draw a breath. "Please. Call someone. I think I'm having a heart attack."

Dalton shook his head. "Where's the money, Uncle Mitch? This is the last time I'm going to ask you."

Mitchell closed his eyes.

CHAPTER THIRTY-NINE

7:20 am

Reagan recognized the Seroquel hangover the instant she pried open her eyes and the sun touched her through a slit in the motel room curtains. Spoon had persuaded her to take a double dose so she could sleep, and it hadn't taken long. Give a guy the internet, suddenly he's a medical expert.

When she lifted her head from the pillow, she still felt the tingling of mania, but the sharpened edges of the last thirty-six hours had dulled into something less ferocious. The manic phase had only been in its baby stages, but enduring two days off meds after two years of taking them... being on meds was the right thing to do. The world made sense again, in the muddled and ambiguous way it had always made sense.

The day was pink and sexy. Her body felt good. Tired, but good.

The memory of her revelation reading Dad's letter the day before formed in her brain. They needed to leave soon, before Dalton caught up with them. Eventually, he would, and there was going to be a reckoning. He would not be too happy that she'd sliced his hand with a dull Swiss Army knife. Crazy to think that she'd actually cut him. The prospect of doing that seemed so odd now, yet so rational and necessary when she'd been manic and faced with no other option.

Spoon shifted in his sleep, and she remembered the rest of last night. Coupling the medication with the marriage proposal had been a clever trick. Overcome with joy, she'd downed her meds and showered kisses all over his bruised and battered face.

A yawning pang tore through her stomach as she pulled the sheets up to her neck. She hadn't eaten in two days, and Seroquel always gave her the munchies.

He turned over in bed and opened his eyes. "Hey, beautiful."

She smiled. "You can call me Mrs. Witherspoon."

"Not yet, I reckon. We have to let the judge do his bit first." He traced a finger in a circle around her stomach. "We should get you to a doc to look at that bruise."

"I'm okay. Doesn't hurt as much this morning as it did before."

"If you're sure," he said.

"Tell me again about the crabs and the little sand balls they make when they dig."

A knock on the door interrupted the stillness and isolation of the moment. They both went wide-eyed.

"Who is that?" he whispered. "Does someone know we're here?"

She shook her head.

From outside the door, muffled: "Reagan? Honey?"

That voice, unmistakable even after six years. Mom.

Reagan sat up. Spoon had told her yesterday about meeting her mom, but then it seemed just one more piece of information in the flood. That her mother was fifteen feet away after six years of absenteeism sent ice cubes all over Reagan's exposed skin. Mom. Here.

Spoon slid out of bed and put his clothes back on, and Reagan followed suit. The dirty shirt and hiking pants felt heavy sliding over her clean skin, but that hardly seemed important now. Jules Darby, here in Colorado. Or would her last name even still be Darby? Maybe she'd married and changed her name. Anything was possible. As Reagan crossed the motel room, she tried to breathe deeply to keep her heart rate at a reasonable level. A million options of what to say to her mother sprinted through her head.

But when she opened the door and saw her mom smiling back at her across the threshold, pure elation overcame her.

"Mom!"

Jules leaped forward and wrapped her arms around Reagan. "My sweet baby girl. I've missed you so much."

Those arms around her, like nothing she'd experienced in years. But Reagan pulled back, looking her mother square in the eyes. Part of her wanted to scream *then where the hell have you been the last six years?* Instead, she smiled as tears welled in her eyes.

Jules looked at Spoon. "Hello again."

Spoon tipped an imaginary cap toward her. "How are you going, Jules?"

"I'm well, thank you. If you don't mind, do you think you could give us a minute or two alone?"

"Sure," he said. "I'll hop in the shower if you're okay here."

Reagan nodded, so he left them alone. Reagan pointed at the bed and they sat together, joined by the hand.

The shock had passed. Reagan wanted some answers. "Where have you been, Mom?"

Jules' lip quivered. She rested a hand behind her to recline on the bed and fingered a cross hanging from a chain around her neck. "It's complicated. Your father, you see…"

Irritated orange started to blur the edges of Reagan's vision. "Why weren't you at his memorial service? You couldn't even come out of hiding for that?"

Jules dropped her hands into her lap, rubbing her thumbs against each other. Her breath hitched in little hiccups. "I have so much to tell you, and I don't know where to start. Things were difficult between your father and me for a long time, and there's a lot of reasons for that, and when you were leaving for college, everything came to a head. But it had nothing to do with you."

"I'm not a little kid, Mom. You don't have to convince me the divorce wasn't my fault. You and dad fought, you wanted out… I understand wanting to leave something that makes you unhappy. But six years with no contact at all? Do you know what I went through in the last six years, not being able to talk to you about everything?"

Jules took a tissue from her purse and dabbed the corner of her eyes, smearing her mascara. "I know. I'm so sorry."

"I was in the hospital because I tried to overdose on pills in a crappy little Austin apartment. I needed you and you weren't there. Dad visited me. Even Anne visited me. The state wanted to send me away forever to one of those dungeons, and I needed you to be there to fight for me."

Jules reached out and stroked Reagan's face. "My sister, your Aunt Sue... you used to ask questions about her and I never wanted to... she was bipolar too. I'm sorry that I never would admit it before, but I feel like I always knew it about you. I saw the signs and I used to worry and pray all the time, but what could I do?"

"Did you even know I was in the hospital?"

Jules nodded. "Tyson sent me updates. Anne, too."

Reagan's jaw clenched and her heart ached. This was something that she hadn't even considered, that Dad or her stepmom knew where her mom was, or at least how to get in touch with her. "Anne? You talked to her?"

"Sometimes, yes. When we needed to discuss important things. Your father would never tell me anything, and I think she felt sorry about that... I wanted to come back for you, Reagan, I truly did."

"Then why didn't you?"

Jules took a deep and unsteady breath. "Your father wouldn't let me. When he kicked me out..."

The blood drained from Reagan's face. Lightheadedness followed as the room started to sway back and forth, waving a few inches in each direction. "*He* kicked *you* out?" This went completely counter to everything Dad had told her. While he'd never badmouthed her mom, he hadn't stuck up for her either. He always maintained that she left for her own reasons.

"That's not what Dad told me," Reagan said.

Jules leaned across the divide between them and placed a hand on Reagan's knee. "Your dad probably told you a lot of things that weren't true."

Reagan was beginning to understand the depth of that statement. The water in the shower ceased and she heard Spoon step out onto the tiled floor.

Jules nodded toward the bathroom. "He's cute. Who did that to his face?"

Reagan looked down at her ring finger, then remembered she'd taken the diamond off before she passed out from the Seroquel. Part of her wanted to snatch the ring from the nightstand and show it to her mother. But part of her realized that she didn't know this woman sitting in front of her; she didn't feel comfortable sharing such an intimate part of her life with a virtual stranger. But was she? They'd spent eighteen years together.

So many conflicting thought patterns. So many choices and reasons and misunderstandings. The truth was a single grain of sand in a towering dune.

"What are you doing here, Mom?"

"I wanted to come home and see you."

Her mother's eyes were still wet with tears, and the left one spasmed, for a second. A jolt of fear shuddered Reagan. There was something disingenuous in her mother's glance.

"But why are you here, right now?" Reagan said, pointing a finger into the bedspread to enunciate. "And how did you know how to find me? How did you know Spoon and I were at this particular motel this morning?"

Jules pursed her lips. Her chest was heaving, and her words came out labored and slow. "Your dad stole a lot of money. Your uncle Tyson only wants what's his. That's all it is. Nothing more, just what's owed to him."

Reagan scooted across the bed, away from her mom. Her mouth fell open. "That's why you're here? For the money?"

"It's over two hundred thousand dollars. He wants it back. Listen to me: I'm the carrot. You don't want the stick. You have to understand how much this kills me inside to have to be the one to tell you all of this, and everything I had to go through to be able to see you again. They're right down the hall, waiting at the stairs. Let me go back to them and tell them what they want to hear and then all this can be over. We can be like a normal family again."

Reagan pressed her fingertips into her temples, trying to relieve some of the tension and make sense of the world. Maybe there was no sense to find, but she surely wasn't going to get it from the woman sitting across the bed from her. "Get out of here. I don't want to see you again."

"Be reasonable, honey. People should make amends for stealing, right? Tyson is family."

Reagan slipped off the edge of the bed. "*I'm* family."

Spoon walked out of the bathroom, half-dressed and running a towel through his hair. "What's going on out here?"

"Mom was leaving," Reagan said, lifting her finger to point at the door.

"He says you know where the money is," Jules said. "Please, if you tell me where to find it, I can protect you. It's best for everyone if this is settled."

Spoon stepped closer to Reagan. "She said she's keen for you to leave. The door's right over there."

Jules slid her purse over her shoulder. She peered into Reagan's eyes, searching for something, maybe the right phrase to justify all this betrayal. Whatever she intended to say, Reagan didn't want to hear it.

After a few seconds, Jules stood and left the room.

"What was that all about?" Spoon said as the door shut.

Reagan lunged across the room and grabbed her socks and the hiking boots. "Baby, we have to go, now. We have to go, go, go."

***

7:35 am

While standing next to Tyson at the edge of the stairs, Dalton watched his aunt Jules exit the motel room and dab her eyes with a little tissue. She walked to them, her head low.

"Damnit," Tyson muttered as they retreated a few steps down the stairs.

"I tried," she said through a mist of tears and snot. "I explained everything to her but she doesn't want to listen."

Jules grabbed Tyson's shirt, but he brushed her hands aside.

"Okay, woman, we tried this your way, and it didn't work," Tyson said. "I told you, your daughter doesn't listen to reason."

She stepped closer, now visibly shaking. "No, please, T. I appreciate everything you've done for me, but please don't do this."

What had he done for her? Dalton had no idea.

"He broke into my *store*, Jules. Broke in and took all the money I had to pay off a stupid sports bet. You think I'm swimming in so much cash I can write that off on my taxes? It's almost a quarter-million dollars."

"I know, but Reagan didn't take it. She had nothing to do with this."

"Not directly, but she knows where it is," Tyson said. "She knows and she's going to tell us."

"That's your niece. Please don't hurt her. Promise me you won't hurt her and you'll find a way to settle this without violence."

"I promise," Tyson said, but he flashed a sideways glance at Dalton. Dalton knew exactly what it meant. He'd made it clear in the car Dalton wasn't to kill Reagan, but that look had said he could mess up the bitch if he had to. Just nothing she wouldn't walk away from.

She pulled her hands back into her chest. "I shouldn't have come back. I made everything worse. Maybe give me another chance? I'll wait a few minutes and talk to her again."

"I don't think so. Go back to your hotel and wait for me," Tyson said. "I'll call you later."

A grimace contorted her face. Her mouth opened and closed several times as if she were trying to find the next right thing to say. Instead, she looked like a fish on the deck of a boat, slowly dying and trying to suck non-existent water through her gills.

Dalton felt her eyes boring into him, begging, and he tried to look anywhere but at her. He'd never seen Aunt Jules like this before, so weak and pathetic. He'd never known her well enough to say if he respected her before, but he sure didn't now. What a disappointment.

As she nodded her defeat and started to skulk down the stairs, the motel room door burst open. The limey and the bitch flew outside, with no idea of the surprise in store for them.

CHAPTER FORTY

7:38 am

Reagan threw open the motel room door as a blast of morning sunlight momentarily blinded her. Spoon joined soon after, clicking his crutches against the concrete of the outdoor hallway.

She looked left and right with no sign of Tyson or Dalton, only her mom descending one of the sets of stairs.

"There," she said, pointing to the opposite stairway.

She ran, bulky boots clomping against the concrete, making the outer railing shake.

Spoon grunted, trying to keep up with her. He bent his bad leg and hopped at a half-fast pace.

They reached the stairs and she looked back, catching two heads appearing where her mom had descended and disappeared. She wanted to sprint and take the stairs two at a time, an impossibility with Spoon struggling to keep up.

At the bottom of the first flight of stairs, the shouts echoed above her.

"We have to go, baby. I know it hurts, but we have to get to the car, right now."

246

"I'm trying," he said. A collection of sweat had pooled above his eyebrows.

When they reached the ground level, the sounds of shuffling footsteps materialized on their same staircase. They couldn't afford to lose any ground. She put a hand under Spoon's armpit to help him move faster.

They crossed the parking lot as Dalton and Tyson lumbered down the final set of stairs. Tyson's snake-skin boots tapped and clicked against the metal grating. She met his eyes, for an instant, and that split second of glancing drove fear into her heart. Not from any kind of menace in his eyes, rather the practiced look of disappointment. She detected it instantly.

But he and Dalton weren't running after them. They seemed to be taking their time. Why would they do that?

With no time to ponder motives, she helped Spoon hurry across the street as their pursuers finally reached the parking lot. She fumbled in her purse to grab the keys to the car. By the time they rounded the gas station, she had them out and ready to go.

Spoon huffed and puffed but skipped fast enough to keep up with her.

"Almost there." She unlocked the car, waited a few seconds for Spoon to catch up, and they both got in as Tyson and Dalton crossed the street.

She turned the key and slammed the gas, the poor aging Honda's tires squealing as it roared out from behind the dumpster.

Her cousin and uncle skidded in the street, turned around, and dashed to the blue truck.

"Are we seriously going to try to outrun them? On city streets? Reagan, where are we going?"

"We have to get to Boulder," she said. "I know where the money is. Not a safe deposit box. Not at a bank. We have to get downtown to the farmer's market. The whole time, right there in the note, telling me where I had to go, but I didn't see it until last night."

"Okay, let's not get straight onto the highway. They'll see us. We need to try to double-back and lose them before we get on the open road."

"What do I do?" she said as she buckled her seatbelt.

"Take a left up there," he said, pointing at a neighborhood street.

She slowed to turn, and as she did, the blue truck appeared in her rearview. "Crap. They're behind us."

"It's fine, we're going to have to make a few turns. We can ditch them if we do this right."

"Okay, okay, I got this." She twisted through the neighborhood, trying to make the turns as sharp and sudden as possible. The smell of burning tires drifted in through the vents.

She nearly ran over a man walking his dog when she clipped a curb. She tried to shout an apology, but was already four houses away by the time her hand found the button to roll down the window.

"Easy," Spoon said. "No good if we crash."

Houses whipped by in a blur of earth-toned colors. "I've never done anything like this before."

He let out a nervous titter. "Let's take it a little slower, please."

Up ahead, a street pointed back to the main road, and since the truck hadn't made an appearance for several turns, she decided they were now safe to rejoin the road and connect with the highway.

They slipped onto Highway 36 toward Boulder, and she checked the rearview every few seconds. Energy pulsed through her, making her heart thump and her vision feel laser-sharp. While the pills from last night had dulled her senses to some small degree, she was still racing. Ready set go. Possibilities, options, revelations all came to her faster than she could catalog them.

"Do you want to fill me in now?" Spoon said.

"There's a farmer's market in downtown Boulder, in a parking lot between a little park and some buildings. It's before you get to Pearl Street."

"Pearl Street. Why does that name sound familiar?"

She slammed the gas to pass a slow-moving delivery truck. "That's the outdoor mall. Just past that is a post office, and there's a row of outdoor lockers that have been there forever. In the letter, he mentioned the farmer's market, but it got blurred by some rain and I didn't understand what it meant."

"But you've sorted it now?"

"When I was in high school, sometimes we'd bike from Denver to Boulder, and we'd leave our bike gear in those lockers and walk through the farmer's market. It hit me last night. That's what he was talking about in the letter: the lockers. It's got to be there."

"Why did your grandad tell me that your dad had a safety deposit box?"

She shrugged. "Not sure. Maybe Dad told him that because he knew grandpa would blab to people. My grandpa also has memory problems, so who knows?"

She checked the rearview again and spotted the shiny chrome grill of the blue truck as they crested the hill descending into Boulder Valley. She licked her lips and started tapping her foot against the floor.

"Where is the farmer's market?" Spoon said.

"Downtown, which is a few miles off the highway. We'll have to lose them on the city streets."

After the hill, they entered the city proper within two minutes. She took the first exit in Boulder, onto Table Mesa Drive. Next came a right at the bottom and then an immediate left on a side street, cutting between a diner and a gas station. In the rearview, no sign of pursuers. Tension lifted from her neck, which had been aching all morning. The pain was a remnant of the trail.

She piloted the Honda through several turns in the Boulder neighborhoods as a precaution, but the blue truck didn't seem to be following anymore.

"We should call the police," Spoon said. "We're in heaps of danger here. At some stage, we have to admit that this is too much for us."

"No, not yet. Find the money, then we'll deal with that."

When they arrived at the edge of Boulder's tiny downtown, the farmer's market was in full-swing, hundreds of people milling about the small laneway between a tree-lined park on one side, and the Boulder Museum of Contemporary Art on the other. Booths stocked with organic produce lined the spaces usually reserved for parking along the slim street.

She searched Arapahoe Street past the farmer's market to find a place to park. Close to the edge of downtown, about four blocks away, a small burger joint sat at the next intersection. The restaurant faced the street corner at an angle, and behind that was a small lot, with enough room for four of five cars. Technically, she wasn't allowed to leave her car there, but they didn't have time to drive around downtown looking for a spot. Parking was usually impossible to find on a Saturday, anyway.

As she slid into the spot and took the keys out of the ignition, Spoon said, "I think I should stay here."

"No, I need you."

He frowned and raised his bad knee. "I'm just going to slow you down. I'll stay put and keep an eye out for Tyson."

"I don't have my phone."

He leaned back, sighing at the roof of the car. "Right. Just hurry, then. Do what you have to do and I'll stay ready."

Once again, she was going to have to go it alone. She couldn't argue with his logic, but she yearned for him to be there with her, to help find the truth.

He put a hand on her shoulder. "You can do this."

She pulled his face close and kissed him on the cheek. "Love you."

He offered a thin smile. "Go. You have to hurry."

She left the car and dashed back on Arapahoe toward the farmer's market, knees and hips and moose-hoof-shaped bruise on her stomach screaming at her to stop working her body so hard.

***

8:20 am

Not two minutes after Reagan had left Spoon, the blue Chevy Tahoe appeared in the side view mirror of the car.

"Bloody hell. Where do these wankers keep coming from?"

The big blue monstrosity turned into the same parking lot. Spoon tried to climb over to the driver's seat, but he was too slow. The truck parked at an angle, blocking his exit.

The passenger and driver doors opened, and Spoon stretched to grab his crutches from the backseat. He managed to collect both of them and stumble out into the parking lot, but Tyson and Dalton were standing on either side of him, smug grins on their faces.

"You are the most resilient goddamn person I think I've ever met," Tyson said.

Spoon said nothing. He puffed out his chest and stood tall, even though Tyson was preparing to knock the stuffing out of him for the second time in two straight days. But Spoon could take a beating if it bought Reagan some time.

"Where is she?"

"She's not here," Spoon said. "It's just me. I'm out for a Saturday drive."

"Bullshit," said Dalton. "We saw you two leave the motel. We put a GPS tracker on the Honda, you dipshit. She's around here somewhere, and you're going to tell me where she is, or I'm going to ram my fist down your motherfucking throat."

Spoon consciously tried not to look at the farmer's market, on the edge of his peripheral vision and a few blocks down the street. "What happened to your hand there, Dalton?"

Dalton hid his bandage-covered hand. "Don't worry about it."

Tyson turned in a circle, squinting at their surroundings. "There's a Chase bank at 13th and Canyon. That's where she is, isn't she? Or maybe it's the Wells Fargo up near Pearl. How did she figure out how to get into the safety deposit box? Does she have power of attorney?"

"I have no idea what you're running on about. If you're after an ATM, there's one at the servo across the street right there," Spoon said, pointing to a gas station on the opposite corner.

"Dalton," Tyson said, "why don't you stay here with him while I go find your cousin?"

"No problem," he said, flexing his fingers.

Spoon took a step back. "I told you already, she's not here."

Tyson sucked air through his teeth. "I like you, Australian. You got a big heart and bigger balls. Dalton, you take it easy on our friend here. He's had a rough couple of days."

With that, Tyson spun on his heels and walked toward downtown.

Spoon watched him go and had a think about his options. Cars whizzed by behind them on the street, but there was no one else in this parking lot behind the restaurant. The angles of the cars and the seclusion of the back parking lot meant that whatever was about to happen would be semi-private. Fight, instead of flight–since Spoon couldn't exactly escape–seemed the best option. He spread his legs into a boxing stance, then dropped his crutches to the ground.

"Just you and me," Dalton said, glancing at the deserted lot. "Why do you two keep causing so much trouble? We just want what's ours."

"Get fucked."

"If that's the way you want to do it," Dalton said as he narrowed the distance between them. "Looks like someone got a head start on me. Your face looks like shit."

"Still prettier than you," Spoon said, raising his fists, pretending he was ready and willing to do this.

Dalton threw the first punch, and Spoon dodged it easily. The bigger problem was keeping his balance with his legs spread so far apart.

He countered with a jab to Dalton's gut, which sent the little bastard into a coughing fit. So far, so good. Maybe this wouldn't be a beating as it had been with Gus and Tyson yesterday.

Dalton recovered and raised his fists, bouncing around on his heels, ready for more. He barked a laugh and beckoned Spoon to come closer.

As Spoon took a deep breath and raised his fists again, he saw Tyson out of the corner of his eye, turning into the farmer's market.

CHAPTER FORTY-ONE

8:25 am

Reagan sprinted through the farmer's market. Boulderites milled about in their Lycra and yoga pants, sampling locally sourced organic produce and homemade cruelty-free products as a crunchy jam band played frenetic bluegrass music at a gazebo in the park nearby.

She dodged several people and barreled straight into a teenager with dreadlocks in a dirty flower dress. "I'm so sorry," Reagan said as she tried to help the girl up off the ground.

"You should slow down," the hippie girl said.

Reagan didn't have time to respond, so she shrugged and kept on running. She spun to avoid crashing into a man carrying a bushel of corn above his head. A little kid fell in the middle of the laneway, and she hurdled him. The parents probably wouldn't be too happy about that, but she didn't bother to stop and explain herself.

At the end of the block, the farmer's market ended, and she sprinted across the intersection to Pearl Street. Her chest burned and her leg muscles felt as if they were about to snap, but she kept pushing herself beyond what her body told her was possible.

She dashed across Canyon street and then Walnut street. The lockers were only one more block away, and she didn't look left or right or behind her. Eyes on the destination only, breathing in and out and tuning out everything that was not her goal.

Ahead were the lockers, a row of them next to a big brick building. Painted mustard yellow, the same as they'd always been. The memory of Saturdays with Dad smacked her in the face. Lunch at Mountain Sun, afternoon coffee at Bookends, then racing home to beat the sunset. "Better get a move-on before your mom sends out the National Guard looking for us," Dad would always say.

She slowed her pace as she came within a few feet of the lockers. After pausing a second to catch her breath, she reached into a pocket. Empty. She checked the other front pocket, then her cargo pockets, back pockets.

She didn't have the key. Bolts of panic multiplied and stabbed her flesh.

She whirled around, patting all of her pockets again. Gone. Eyes on the ground, she started to backtrack, going over every inch of terrain she'd just covered. There wasn't time for this crap. She had to get in that locker now.

Ten feet up ahead, something shiny and silver glinted in the sun. Chest thumping, she raced to it, bent over, and as soon as she put a hand on the key, a pair of snakeskin cowboy boots stopped directly in front of her.

"What've you got there, Reagan?"

Tyson stood above her, blotting out the light. "I saw you at those lockers, and it feels like my eyes are open now. That's where it is, isn't it? It's not out in the woods, it's not in a random safety deposit box... that was all horseshit to keep me occupied, or the ramblings of a crazy old man, or some other kind of distraction. After all that nonsense, it's sitting out right here in a goddamn public locker in Hippietown, Colorado."

Reagan didn't know what to say. She was out of options.

"Go on then," Tyson said, digging his hands into his pockets and nodding at the lockers. "Let's get this over with."

She considered running. She still had the key. But it wouldn't do any good to escape, because he knew now. He could come back at night with a crowbar and bust open every one of those lockers until he found what he was looking for.

The key reflected the sun as she turned back to face the lockers. There were two rows of ten, with angled slits across them like her locker in high school. But which one was it? It's not as if they had a favorite locker.

She started at the bottom left and tried the key. Didn't work. She moved on to the next one, no good there either.

"Quit stalling," Tyson said.

"Screw you," she said as her eyes filled with tears. "I don't know which one it is."

The key opened none of the lockers on the bottom row. She moved to the top as Tyson grumbled behind her. Starting again on the left: first locker, no turn. Second locker, the key began to turn.

She jerked her hand away.

Tyson stepped behind her. His breath brushed the back of her neck. "Open it. Now."

Steadying her feet, she reached out and turned the key, and the mechanism made a solitary *clink* as the catch slipped. She grabbed the latch and lifted it, then swung the door open.

The locker was empty.

Tyson roared. "What in the holy hell fucking goddamn shit?" He pushed her out of the way, his face so red and engorged that he appeared to be on the verge of passing out.

She stared at the empty space in front of her, a cubic foot of nothingness in a metal shell. This didn't make any sense. "I don't... I don't know what's going on here."

"You've been here already, you devious little shit. You've already gotten it, stashed it somewhere else, and this is just some big show to trick me." Her uncle's meaty arms crossed in front of his body.

"No, I swear, I haven't done anything. I didn't even know about this place until last night."

He bent over, smacking a fist against his thigh and taking huge breaths. He winced and placed a hand over his heart. When he stood up again, he leaned close and looked into her eyes as if he could bore into her soul and find out the truth with intimidation.

Reagan wiped the tears that were dribbling down her cheeks. "I'm telling the truth, Uncle T. I don't know where it is."

His eyes darted back and forth over her face for a few seconds, then his expression softened. "Okay. Fine. You know what? Fuck this. Mitch probably blew it all in Vegas because that's what piece-of-shit gamblers like him do anyway. Steals from his own brother, doesn't take care of his family, doesn't give a shit about anyone but himself."

Reagan kept her eyes on the ground while her uncle berated her dad.

"I'm done with this whole mess of a family. You, Frank, your mom, and even Anne. All of you leave me alone."

With that, he strode away from her, turned at the next intersection, and disappeared into an alley.

Reagan's vision went muddy and unclear as she stared at the clean and modern brick buildings of downtown Boulder. A few people strolled by in each direction, barely stopping to notice the crying girl standing in front of a row of lockers. She turned back to them. How could it be empty? The key opened the locker, and the letter Dad wrote mentioned the farmer's market, so this had to be it. Why wasn't it here?

She took the letter from her pocket and read it again. Her eyes repeatedly dragged over the sentence fragment that had brought her here:

what the key in ... farmer's market. You'll understand when you get there.

You'll understand when you get there. What was she supposed to understand? That the locker was going to be empty? That didn't make any sense.

She put her hands on either side of the opening into the locker and leaned closer until her face poking inside. Then she saw something she hadn't noticed at first glance. On the back wall of the small metal space was an image that looked like it had been drawn with a black Sharpie. Five lines: the bottom three sides of a square, with two diagonal lines at the top, angled together. A house. A marker drawing of a house.

Another piece from the letter jumped out at her. Two words: *your grandfather.*

Reagan blinked as the world around her stopped spinning. She understood.

CHAPTER FORTY-TWO

8:40 am

Reagan jogged back through the farmer's market toward her fiancée, all these new realizations bouncing around in her head like a pogo stick in an inflatable castle. After all this struggle, the solution to where the money was actually hidden seemed so achingly simple that she hadn't seen Occam's razor staring at her in the face. Bend a stick, it breaks at the weakest point.

When she crossed Arapahoe, Spoon was sitting on the ground next to Dad's car. He was breathing heavily and wincing as he rubbed one side of his face. She broke into a run to him.

"What happened?" she yelled across the parking lot.

He waited to speak until she was within a few feet. "Your cousin found me and decided to have a bit of a go at me. Nothing major."

She knelt by him, caressing his cheek. A sweeping sense of guilt pounded across her brain. "I'm so sorry. You never asked for any of this and it's all my fault."

He shook his head. "Don't you even worry about it. I'm pretty sure you didn't ask for it either, love. Was a little hard to see him with only one good eye, but I held my own."

258

Reagan looked around the lot. No sign of Dalton or Tyson. "Where did they go?"

"No idea. Tyson came by here a minute before you did, yelled at Dalton, and they hit the road together. I'm guessing you didn't find what you were after?"

"Oh no, baby, I found what I was looking for. Now we just have to go get it." She helped him up and put him in the car, then rounded the driver's side and they held each other's gaze for a few seconds in silence. Her sweet, battered boy. Soon, she would settle everything and they could do whatever they wanted. She would have to find a way to make it up to Spoon, if that were even possible.

The drive was short, across town to the Assisted Living center where her grandfather stayed. "Your grandpa has the money," Spoon said, wide-eyed and grinning.

She bypassed the office and drove straight to his apartment. "Kind of. Would you mind waiting in the car? I need a few minutes alone with him and I think it might be easier this way."

"Sure, sure. Do whatever you need to do. I'll rest my knuckles. They're pretty sore from pummeling that miscreant's face."

She smiled and kissed his cheek. "My brave little prize fighter. Thank you for being supportive. I know the last few days haven't been easy for you."

"All I care about is that you're safe."

She kissed him again, tasting the rusty blood on his bruised lips. "I am. And we are. I have to do a couple more things to make sure, but this will all be over soon. You stay here and I'll be right back."

She left him there and knocked on the door. No answer, so she tried the door and it opened. Then she eased into the apartment, closing the door behind her.

A rhythmic beep came from the bedroom, and she walked toward the sound, navigating stacks of newspapers and piles of trinkets. Frank Darby's Hoarder Palace hadn't changed one bit since her last visit.

He was sleeping, and the beeping sound was some kind of monitoring machine on a stand next to his bed. A green line jumped with each beep, painting scratchy trails across the screen. His eyes were closed, and although Reagan had seen him not too long ago, he seemed to have aged at least a decade. His cheeks looked sunken, his skin dry, and as red as an apple.

"Grandpa?" she said as she took a seat in a chair across from the bed.

He stirred, mumbling, then opened his eyes. He looked at her, but his expression didn't change. "Hey there, pumpkin," he said, and the words sounded like the guttural utterance of a talking bear. "I heard you were camping."

"I was, grandpa."

"Did you have a good time?"

"I got into a fight with a moose. At least, I think I did."

He cackled, a wet grumble that sent him into a coughing fit. "Did you, now? I hope you won. Darbys don't back down, even from moose."

She grinned. "You could say I won, yeah. I'm here, aren't I?"

He tried to sit up in bed, but only managed to raise a few inches, then he sank back into his pillow. "And why are you here? I thought you moved to Texas."

"I did. I came back early this week for Dad's service."

"Who?"

The awkward look on her grandpa's face squeezed her, made her want to cry. "Mitchell, your son. He passed away last week."

He turned his head to the side, concentrating on the shiny sextant hanging on the wall. She couldn't tell if he was confused, or contemplating, or what else might be going through his head. "Good riddance," he finally said. "That kid was nothing but a pain in my ass, for a long time now."

She sniffled, trying to keep the stinging at the corners of her eyes from turning into tears.

"At least his brother—your Uncle Tyson—still comes and visits me. Mitch only turned up when he needed something. He was always like that, though. If I knew how those brats were going to turn out, I might never have had kids.

"Your dad was a gambler. Did you know that? Spent up all his 401K and retirement accounts. What kind of a man does that? What kind of man gambles away all his family's money? Did you know about this?"

Reagan leaned forward until she had his attention. "Yes. I know about him now, and I understand. Whatever he did, though, he was still my dad."

He shifted in bed, sighing. "It's your life, kiddo. All that matters to me is that you're healthy and happy. Now, tell me why you're visiting your poor old grandad."

"I used to have this dollhouse," she said.

He pointed across the living room to the dollhouse sitting on the stand. "That old thing?"

"Yes. Dad used to keep it at our house, when I was a little girl. You maybe don't remember. He gave it back to you when I was in high school."

Frank opened his mouth and pushed out his dentures, clacking them together. After a few seconds, he pulled them back in. "That old ratty thing was my mother's, a long time ago. Don't exactly know how your dad ended up with it, but he said you didn't need it anymore. He still comes by sometimes to look at it, even though it's just another piece of crap in my collection."

"Do you think I could have it? I think there's some money inside that Dad left for me."

He chewed on his lower lip, his jaw bouncing back and forth. "Money, you say? You're welcome to whatever you find, I suppose. I don't have much use for it. All of this is going to have to go sooner or later."

She walked to his bedside and kissed him on the forehead. "Thank you."

"I'd like to visit with you, pumpkin, but I'm very tired. Can you come back some other time?"

She brushed a hand against his shoulder. "Sure, grandpa. I'll come see you again soon."

He smiled and closed his eyes, and Reagan walked to the dollhouse. As a kid, she remembered it towering over her, feeling almost as big as a real house. It still seemed big, at least three feet tall and a few feet around the base. She picked it up, and the girth of the thing challenged her more than its weight.

She carried it into the hall, then sat it on the carpet. With an ear pointed to the bedroom, she listened to the beeping machine and the warble of her grandpa snoring.

On the outside of the house, she found no switches or buttons to push. The base was thick, at least six inches deep, so she started poking around, and found a tiny lip near the bottom of it. She placed one hand on the side of the dollhouse and one hand on the lip, then pulled apart, and the dollhouse moved but the lip stayed put.

As the two halves separated, crisp wrapped bills started to spill out of the opening. Stacks of hundred dollar bills bound with adhesive paper slips, the number *10K* printed on each one. She counted bills and stuffed them into her purse, then pushed the top part of the dollhouse back into place.

She slipped the now-heavy purse over her shoulder, put her hands underneath the base, and stood up, groaning from the weight and the general collective weariness of her muscles. Opening the front door was a struggle. She had to set it down, open the door, move it outside, shut the door, pick it up. Spoon tried to get out of the car to help her, but she waved him off.

"Picking up some family heirlooms?" he said as she lifted the dollhouse into the trunk.

"No," she said. "The money was in here, hidden in the base. All of it. Grandpa had no idea."

Spoon's face lit up. "You found it? You really found it?"

"I did."

"I had no idea my future wife was such a great detective."

She wrapped her arms around his neck. "Baby, there's a lot of things you're going to learn about me."

"So, we're rich, yeah? What's next on the agenda? Rome? Paris? Singapore?"

She frowned. "We have one more stop to make."

CHAPTER FORTY-THREE

9:45 am

Halfway between Boulder and Denver, Reagan exited Highway 36 in Broomfield as Spoon pivoted his head around to survey the surroundings.

The sense of comprehension on his face appeared in an instant as his jaw tensed. "What are we doing here?"

She reached across the seat and ran her fingers up and down his arm. "I said we have one more stop to make. This is it."

"And we're going to the lawnmower shop? We're going to see *Tyson?* Did you forget that an hour ago, these blokes were chasing us across Boulder?"

She lifted her hand from his arm to the side of his face, caressing the bruises there. "Trust me, baby."

"I'm not comfortable with this," he said. "This guy was just trying to hurt us, and you want to walk right up to his door?"

"This is going to be okay. I know what I'm doing."

He didn't seem convinced but held his tongue anyway. The lawnmower store was close to the highway, but Reagan parked across the street at the Slinky Grape coffee shop.

"Why are we parking here?" he said.

"I know this all doesn't make sense, but it will. It's better if you don't know right now. Because after we go in there, I have something else to show you."

He reclined in his car seat and dragged a finger along the fabric covering the roof of the car. "Today is a day for mysteries, apparently. Alright Spoon, keep your head down and don't ask questions."

She kissed him, then reached for the door handle, but she paused. With everything he had been through in the last few days, he deserved to know the truth. "First, I need to tell you something."

"Alright then."

His expression was calm and even, no hint of apprehension. She loved his poker face.

"I know I've told you before that I sometimes struggle with taking my meds, but I don't think I've ever told you how hard it's been. How I've had little lapses like this before. Maybe you've seen it in me, but I've tried to shield you from it."

"I knew, but I also didn't know, if that makes sense," he said.

A tear dribbled down her cheek and ran into her mouth, salty and warm. "It does. The truth is, though, that it's probably always going to be like this. You have to ask yourself if you want to be with someone as unstable as me."

He held her gaze, not blinking or looking away to find his answer. "We're getting married, remember?"

She cried, but tears of relief instead of pain for the first time in more days than she could recall. She kissed him, careful not to press against his bruises.

They emerged from the car together. Reagan slung her bulky purse over her shoulder as they crossed the street. "Just follow my lead. I've got this under control."

Spoon turned his palms to face the sky. "Don't see as I have much other choice, but carry on, Captain."

As they crossed into the parking lot, Spoon raised a finger. "There she is."

"There's what?"

He pointed at a black car. "The Lexus Anne let me borrow. Long story. I have to get it back to her next door neighbor. Thank God it's here though, I had no idea how to explain that one."

She shrugged it off and stopped in front of the door, taking one last deep breath to ready herself. They walked inside together, Reagan leading. She hadn't been here in five years, maybe more, but the scent of oil and grease and metal spilled over her as it had in high school, visiting uncle Tyson after class. Asking him for money to buy sodas from the gas station across the street, before it became the Slinky Grape.

Tyson was sitting behind the counter, a stack of receipts in one hand and his other hand typing on a noisy adding machine. *Tick tick kah-cherg kah-cherg.* A pair of glasses sat on the edge of his nose.

Dalton was on a stool nearby, rubbing a bandaged hand over a bruise on the side of his face. Whatever dust-up he'd engaged in with Spoon, looked as if her man got the better of it.

Another man was leaning next to the counter, a guy almost as big as Tyson. Tattoos poked out of every opening of his dark leather jacket.

"Alright, Gus," Spoon said as he raised a hand toward the tattooed stranger. "Looks like you're well."

Dalton jumped off his stool, his eyes bloodshot but wide open. "What the fuck are you two doing here?"

Gus snatched a stray lawnmower blade from a nearby shelf.

Tyson stopped clacking at the adding machine, took off his reading glasses, and tossed them onto the counter. "I thought I told you I didn't want to see you anymore. Maybe I stuttered, but I distinctly remember saying I was done with you."

"You will be, after today," Reagan said. She let her purse fall from her shoulder into her hand.

Dalton took a step forward, and Spoon raised his fists.

"No," she said. "No fighting. I'm here to settle this, and then it's over."

Tyson chuckled. "This ought to be good. Alright, Miss Reagan, what can we do for you?"

"First, I have two questions."

Tyson crossed his arms in front of his barrel chest. "Go ahead."

"Where's Charlie?"

Tyson and Dalton exchanged a look.

"He's at home," Dalton said. "At his apartment in Westy. His leg got scratched up a little bit when he fell down that hill, but he's fine. No stitches or any shit like that."

"What's your other question?" Tyson said.

"Not yet," she said. "I want you to cut him out of whatever it is you guys do here. Whatever gangster crap you're doing now, or whatever illegal stuff you're going to do in the future, Charlie doesn't get to be a part of it. Deal?"

Tyson laughed, looking equally amused and annoyed. "And why should I make a deal with you?"

Reagan reached into her purse. Gus lifted the lawnmower blade. Tyson stood up. Spoon took a step closer to Reagan.

She lifted her hand out of the purse, now holding three stacks of bills, wrapped together in cucumber-colored bands. "I have twenty-one more of these in my purse. Two hundred and forty thousand, right, Uncle T?"

Spoon gasped. "Reagan, what are you doing?"

She met Spoon's eyes and winked.

"That's right," Tyson said. "Two-forty large."

"Do we have a deal?"

He squinted at her and started chewing the inside of his cheek. "You said you had two questions. What's the other one?"

She nodded at Dalton. "What happens to him?"

Tyson placed his hands on the counter, then lifted one to stroke his goatee. "I've been wondering that myself. He did screw up the one job I gave him and I can't just let that go."

Dalton took a step toward his father. "Dad, what are you saying? This wasn't my fault. I went into the park like you said. I followed this bitch around for four days. It's not my fault the money wasn't there."

Reagan closed her eyes and took an unsteady breath. She put all of her energy into ignoring the betrayal, the conspiracy, the unbelievable truth that every single member of her family wore masks to hide their true selves.

The only thing that existed for her was this moment, getting through it, and leaving unharmed.

Tyson pursed his lips and tugged on his facial hair. "You're out too. If Charlie's out, then you're out. I can't have liabilities like you working for me."

Dalton grabbed a coil of wire from a nearby shelf and twisted it in his hands. His chest heaved. "No! You can't do this. It's all her fault!" He glared at Reagan, fire in his eyes. "You motherfucking bitch."

Tyson nodded at Gus, who dropped the lawnmower blade on the counter, then placed himself between Dalton and Reagan.

"Easy, kid," Gus said. "If he says you're out, then you're out. Don't make a scene."

Dalton glared at Reagan over Gus' shoulder, then stormed toward the back of the store. A shelf screeched as he moved it out the way of the back door. "This isn't over," he yelped as the door slammed shut behind him.

Reagan took the rest of the stacks from her purse and set them all on a metal shelf in between two lawnmower engines. She scooped them together, and then set them down on the counter in front of Tyson.

He picked up a stack and dragged his thumb across the top. The bills made a *fwip* sound as he fanned them. "You remind me of your dad, you know? That slippery bastard could be pretty shrewd, too. But I like the way you do business; real upfront and no horseshit. It's a shame how all this went down, but we can't do anything about that now."

"No, we can't," she said.

"Do you know how your dad came by this money?"

"I think so," she said. "He stole it?"

Tyson nodded. "I didn't want to hurt you, kid. I'm sorry about what Dalton did to you and your boyfriend here. All I ever wanted was to get back what he took from me."

Reagan eased backward, toward Spoon. "And now you have it, and we're done here."

Tyson bowed his head to her and raised a hand at the door. "We're all squared away. You'll get no trouble from me."

***

9:55 am

Dalton slammed the back door and stomped across the concrete porch toward the fence. He laced his fingers between the chain links and squeezed until his digits turned blue and started throbbing. Didn't care. He hardly felt any physical sensations at this moment, only rage welling up inside him like nothing he'd ever experienced before.

Motherfucking bitch. All that bitch's fault.

He sucked in a lungful of air and roared until his voice cracked and his throat went numb. How could she walk in there, flash some money, and cut him off from everything that was important in his life? How could Tyson value that over family?

All her fault.

If Charlie was out, that was fine. Dalton knew his brother would eventually get pushed out, one way or another. The whiny punk was never suited to this kind of life. Going on money collection runs, leaving persuasive messages for the guys who couldn't pay, destroying private property… Charlie complained about all of it. Plus his class schedule always interfered with important work.

But Dalton, this was his *future*. Going into the lawnmower business with his dad was all he'd ever wanted to do with his life. Two minutes inside the store was all the bitch needed to steal it all away from him. And Tyson hadn't even spent five seconds considering it. The dollar signs flashed in his eyes and the greedy bastard took a big shit all over his favorite son.

Dalton couldn't even decide where to point his anger. Reagan? Tyson? Both of them?

No, only her.

Definitely her. If she had handed over the key in the park, none of the rest of it would have happened. She was the root of all the trouble and she had to pay for what she'd done. Right now.

He checked his pockets. Didn't have his knife. His gun was at his apartment. He looked around the back of the store and rifled through the collection of parts and assorted shit strewn about. Needed a weapon, and quick. Plenty of lawnmower parts sat in a tall pile next to him, but nothing like a blade or something long enough to use as a club.

Then he saw it. A pile of lumber, and a piece about as long as his arm with a nail poking out of the top. Not exactly a ninja sword, but he could swing it and cut up that bitch's face pretty good.

268

No more playing. No more holding back. Reagan would get what she deserved.

CHAPTER FORTY-FOUR

10:00 am

Reagan opened the front door and she and Spoon stepped out into the hot summer day as a wave of relief blanketed her. After keeping her nerves level during the exchange inside, the adrenaline finally surged. Her knees wobbled, but she struggled to walk to the car as quickly as possible. She'd done it. She'd actually pulled it off.

Spoon opened his mouth, but she cut him off. "Just a minute more. I'll explain everything."

He raised his hands in surrender, his eyes gleaming. "Okay, Captain, whatever you say."

As soon as they started to cross the parking lot, a blur of fabric appeared out of her peripheral vision.

Dalton.

He was running, screaming, holding a piece of wood about the size of a baseball bat in one hand. During the time it took her to understand, he'd narrowed the distance between them and was raising the piece of wood with two hands to swing it at her.

Spoon jumped in front of her, then nearly fell when his bad knee connected with the ground. He raised a crutch and jabbed it into

270

Dalton's chest, but that only knocked her cousin off balance for a second.

Dalton spun, then kicked his foot out and swept Spoon's leg, which sent him sprawling.

No one between Dalton and Reagan now.

She thrust her hand into her pocket.

Dalton lifted the wood above his head, screaming, "you motherfucking bitch. All your fault!"

As he started to bring down the weapon, air rushed toward her. She lifted her hand from her pocket and flicked open the blade of her Swiss Army knife in one motion. She whipped one hand upward to block the weapon while thrusting her other hand forward, connecting with Dalton's cheek. A rush of wetness met her hand as she pulled it back.

He dropped the wood, staggered, putting a hand on his face. Blood dribbled between his fingers. He lurched forward, then teetered on weak knees.

"You cut me," he said, seeming dazed. His eyes drooped.

The front door opened, and Gus rushed out, followed by Tyson.

Dalton dropped to his knees, swaying back and forth. "Bitch cut my face. I'll kill her for this."

Gus reached behind him and pulled a gun from his waistband. He pointed it at Dalton, then glanced at Tyson for approval.

The world slowed. Reagan watched this scene play out in front of her as if on television, a grainy layer on top of real life.

Dalton's head lolled on his shoulders, blood dripping down his chin.

Spoon struggled to collect his crutches.

Gus put a hand on top of the pistol and drew back the slide.

Reagan could practically hear the bullet entering the chamber. "No!" she shouted.

Everyone stopped and looked at her. All was quiet except for the sound of the cars on the street, which seemed distant and muted.

"No more fighting," she said. She looked at Tyson. "This isn't what I wanted. You said this was over."

For a few endless seconds, no one moved or said anything.

Tyson tilted his head. "Gus, put that away. Take the kid here to the hospital. When he gets out, don't bring him back here. I don't want to see him again."

The burly man did as he was told, seizing Dalton by the shoulder. Gus dragged him toward the blue truck, and Dalton barely had a chance to look back at her. His eyes were frantic, confused, and she felt pity for him, for a brief moment.

Tyson cleared his throat. "I'm sorry about all that, but it doesn't change our deal. We're done here. Go on you two, clear out."

Reagan helped Spoon to his feet, then helped him cross the street as Tyson strutted back into the store. Spoon grimaced with every step, labored breaths turning his face crimson. He could barely move his knee.

There seemed to be no one on the street at that moment, no one around to gawk at the insane scenario Reagan had experienced.

When they reached the car, she stopped to catch her breath. The lawnmower store had gone quiet and still, as if nothing had happened there. Just a regular American store, open for business on a Saturday to serve the lawnmower repair and parts needs of Broomfield and the greater Denver area.

"Are you okay?" she said.

"Fell on my knee," he said. "Hurts like hell."

"Maybe we should take you to the hospital."

"I'd like to lie down and take some Ibuprofen. First, though, perhaps you could explain to me what in the world happened inside that shop."

"I wanted it to be over, and that wasn't going to happen until they got paid. My dad stole, and Tyson just wanted what was his."

He nodded. "I understand. Anne told me your dad cashed in their life insurance policies."

This notion no longer surprised her.

Spoon grunted as he tried to flex his knee. "I have to say, though, two hundred forty grand would have been nice to have."

"You're absolutely right."

"But maybe now you can tell me why we couldn't call the cops before?"

"Let me show you something," she said as she fished the car keys from her pocket. She unlocked the trunk and pulled the dollhouse to the edge. Put pressure on the lip around the base and wrenched it free of the top section. Piles of money stacks tumbled out of the crack, flooding the trunk of the car in a sea of green.

"Oh my God," he said as the color drained from his face. "How much is that?"

"No idea," she said. "At least two or three times what I gave Tyson. I need to give some to Anne, of course. She deserves to be able to start over somewhere else after what my dad put her through. And some for my mom, maybe. I haven't decided about her yet."

"Alright, now is it time to call the police?" he said.

Reagan brushed the hair back from his forehead and caressed the bruise that had nearly sealed one of his eyes shut. "I don't care about any of that anymore."

He put his arms around her waist. He kissed her, and she folded into him. The world disappeared for a few seconds, and she held tight to this moment with her fair-haired Australian boy. She needed nothing else.

Reagan closed the trunk lid.

A NOTE TO READERS

Thank you for reading my book. Seriously, thank you. I hope you loved it and it helped you escape for a little while.

Next, please consider leaving a review on Amazon and Goodreads. I know it's a pain, but you have no idea how much it will help the success of this book and my ability to write future books. That, and telling other people to read it. Don't you love it when your friends recommend good books?

I have a website where you can learn more about me and my other projects. Check me out at www.jimheskett.com and sign up for my mailing list so you can stay informed on the latest news. You'll even get some freebies for signing up. You like free stuff, right?

ABOUT THE AUTHOR

Jim Heskett was born in the wilds of Oklahoma, raised by a pack of wolves with a station wagon and a membership card to the local public swimming pool. Just like the man in the John Denver song, he moved to Colorado in the summer of his 27th year, and never looked back. Aside from an extended break traveling the world, he hasn't let the Flatirons Mountains out of his sight.

He fell in love with writing at the age of fourteen with a copy of Stephen King's The Shining. Poetry became his first outlet for teen angst, then later some terrible screenplays, and eventually short and long fiction. In between, he worked a few careers that never quite tickled his creative toes successfully, and hasn't ever forgotten about Stephen King. You can find him currently huddled over a laptop in an undisclosed location in Colorado, dreaming up ways to kill beloved characters.

Details at www.jimheskett.com

Made in the USA
Lexington, KY
07 June 2015